CONFESSIONS OF A HOLLYWOOD AGENT
A novel by William Louis Gardner
230 pp.
Bald Eagle Publishing Co.

By Ellen Singer

Only an industry insider could write a story filled with such nuance about the glam and grim of Hollywood in the 1950's and 60's. William Gardner takes you on a (manicured and bejeweled) hand-held tour of Beverly Hills and its crusty and upper-crust inhabitants.

You'll be privy to the name-dropping and bed-hopping among a large cast of loveable and loathsome characters, including a minister's daughter who poses for Playboy but tithes ten percent of her earnings to the church and an internationally famous comedian who wastes his money on gambling and drugs.

And enjoy the odd, but enduring alliance between the story's leading man and lady: Clint Nation, a Montana cowboy, and Dorothy Winters, a small-time thief, who will re-invent themselves and traverse the Hollywood Hills together as agent and movie star, occasional lovers and loyal friends.

There's plenty of sinning in "Confessions", but is there redemption? You'll stay awake trying to find out. But don't rush – or fast-forward – to the closing credits. They come much too soon.

Ellen Singer's most recent book is *"Quicksand"*
[HarperCollins, 2001]

Published by Bald Eagle Publishing Co.
P.O. Box 848
Bemidji, MN
56619-0848

e-mail bldeagle@paulbunyan.net

ISBN: 0-9722312-0-X

William Louis Gardner

To Celeste

Confessions of a Hollywood Agent

A novel
by
William Louis Gardner

Bald Eagle

Cast of Characters

CLINT NATION	Young Hollywood agent
GALE LAWRENCE	Hollywood extra. Changes name to Dorothy Winters
DOROTHY WINTERS	Movie star
GEORGIA EVANS	Hollywood starlet
LUIS VERANO	Cuban movie director
MARTY FALLON	Famous Hollywood comedian
NATHAN WISE	Hollywood godfather
MEYER LANSKY	Mafia kingpin
GEOFFREY LANDSDOWN	Race car driver
THORTON NORTH	Race car owner
MARGE NORTH	Thorton's wife
TANA WILLIAMS	African/American film actress
JIMMY	Thorton's male nurse
MARSHALL	Thorton's business manager
ERROLL FLYNN	Himself
FIDEL CASTRO	Himself
JFK	Himself
PORFIRO RUBIROSA	Himself
JOHANNES DIEDRICH	German industrialist

ONE

Clint gawked at the glamorous young blond as she swung her long, hose-less legs out of the driver's seat of a new 1957 Thunderbird. Noticing Clint staring at her, she opened her legs. He could see she wore no underwear. She stood, adjusting a blond mink stole around her bare shoulders. As she passed him on her way to the front door, the smell of her perfume knocked him out. She gave him a slight smile and a bump with her body, looking straight ahead. Clint felt her hand caress his crotch. Astonished, he stared at the woman and then at Everett, who was standing at his side, slicking back a shock of thin gray hair.

"Didja see that? She grabbed my balls," he yelled.

Everett put his finger to his lips. "Keep your voice down, this is a chic party," he whispered.

They were met at the entrance of the pink Beverly Hills mansion by a midget wearing a medieval court jester costume who ushered them into a silk ornate room that resembled a reception room in an old European palace. There stood a throne, with a plump middle-aged blonde sitting on it. If that old gal's my date, I hope I can get it up, Clint thought. "Who is she?" he whispered to Everett.

"She bought a grand duchess title. She thinks she's a queen."

The lady hadn't seen them. She leaned forward on the arm of the high back chair, enthralled with a young Latin in Argentine gaucho attire, strumming a tango on his guitar. The man moved to her side finishing the last words of the ballad.

"Manuel, how wonderful. Do come back and play again before you leave." She extended her jeweled hand and slipped him a fifty-dollar bill.

"*Gracias*, your Highness," he said as he kissed her hand and backed away, bowing.

Everett stepped onto the throne platform as Billie Rodgers shifted and saw him. "Everett, you finally got here." She turned her cheek for him to kiss. "Where's the medal I presented you? You are my minister of culture. You should wear it to all my official gatherings."

"I'm sorry, your Highness. I wasn't told the party was to be so formal," he said in a clipped English accent.

"My parties are always formal. And tonight especially. We're unveiling my official portrait." Billie glanced past Everett. "And, who is the handsome young man?" She looked Clint over.

"May I present Mr. Clint Nation. Her Highness, Billie Rogers." The jester pushed Clint onto the platform.

Clint's tall lanky body moved self-consciously forward in the rented tuxedo. His straight blonde hair fell in his eyes as he fidgeted with his too-small shirt collar. Billie extended her hand that Clint took and shook clumsily. "Pleased to meet ya, ma'am. Your worship... I mean ya... Highness," said Clint, in a western drawl.

"You may call me Billie, if I may call you Clint. Clint, I like that name...it sounds so western."

"I'm from Montana, ma'am, I mean, Miss Billie," said Clint nervously.

Billie pushed herself up from the throne. As she did her diamond tiara slid to the side of her head and dropped onto the throne platform near Clint's feet. He rushed to pick it up. And handed it to her. She gave him a pleasing smile as she put the crown into place, mussing her thin blonde hair.

"Thank you, young man," she said, patting his hand. "What a pleasure to have such a strong man to help a lady when she needs someone." She turns her head towards the jester. He handed her a gold-headed cane. She stepped off the platform adjusting a blue silk gown that was a size too small.

"Come, I'll introduce you to my guests." Billie took Clint's arm as they exited the throne room with Everett and the jester following behind. "You have a strong arm, Clint. Walking with you is a joy. As you see I need help. I fell off a horse a few years back and my hip never healed properly. I love to dance, but that's over now. I'm so excited about my official portrait. You have no idea what I had to endure with the artist, Mr. Reinholt. He wanted me to pose in the morning light. I never get up before three. It's inhuman of him to think I could. We had so many quarrels. I wanted to sit on a horse to look regal, like they do in Europe, but with my hip it was impossible."

They approached an aging dowager covered with jewels, who stood with two effeminate-looking men. They gave Clint a look that made him nervous.

"Cynthia, darling, when did you arrive? Meet Mr. Nation."

Cynthia extended her thin hand, enhanced with large jewels. "Oh, darling. He's divine. You must bring him to Honolulu. "Do you surf, Mr. Nation?"

"Yeah, sure, I surf," lied Clint "Nice meetin' ya, ma'am."

"See you at the unveiling," said Billie as she and Clint walked off.

"I wish I had her money. Millions!" said Billie.

Clint glanced back at Cynthia for another look.

Everett and the jester observed Clint's actions from behind.

The Jester in his high nasal voice said, "Her Highness seems to be happy with this young man."

"That's why he's here. replied Everett, assured.

"I hope he sticks around. It's been miserable since the last one left. She's been on me constantly. I'll get a rest again if she picks up with him."

Billie turned around. "Everett, Clint tells me he's a Scorpio. I've always loved Scorpios. They're so much fun. And sexy. Find me a chair. I want to sit. It's time," she said to the jester. "Have the servants bring in my official portrait, and tell the orchestra to be ready."

The Jester rushed to the orchestra leader and then left the room. The orchestra started a musical fanfare.

"They'll play my official waltz. I wrote it. I love my music when I hear it. I feel so royal," she said as she made herself comfortable in the chair. Two male servants dressed in footman costumes rolled the portrait in on a dolly. It was covered with a purple cloth. Billie searched the ballroom.

"Where is Mr. Reinholt? He must be here with me."

"I'm sorry, your Highness, he sends his regrets. He's ill," said the Jester.

"Ill? The paint-slapping fairy! He goes to the top of my unwanted list. He's barred from the house. I hope I haven't paid him. Find out if I made payment," she said scowling at the jester.

"Yes, Your Highness."

"Send the painting away. I'll see it later." She said to Clint. "I'm getting bored with this party. Come along to the honeymoon suite with me, Mr. Nation," she said pushing herself up from her chair and extending one arm to Clint.

The Jester ran after them. "Your Highness?"

She turned and said. "Have a few of my select guests come up for some fun." They started up the long grand staircase.

"Anyone in particular, Madam?" called the jester.

"You know who I like. And have the waiters bring champagne." Billie turned to Clint. "Come along Mr. Nation. Do you play the horses?" she asked, as they moved slowly up the curved stairs.

"I spend most of my days at the track, ma'am."

"You do? I adore the horses, but my information is so poor these days. You can help me pick some winners."

"I do real good, ma'am. I got a couple of sure winners for tomorra."

"Wonderful, you can go with me. Come along, angel. I've arranged for some marvelous entertainment."

At the top of the staircase, Billie led Clint down the hallway into a large pink satin bedroom that resembled a theater. On the far end of the room stood a circular bed covered in pink silk, a canopy positioned above. A cluster of cupids hung from the ceiling on strings. Heavy pink silk drapes covered the tall windows and numerous chaise lounges were scattered around the bed and other areas of the room. A small stage stood opposite the bed, a soft pink curtain concealing it. Billie, with Clint's help, moved toward the canopied bed and sat on the end.

"Come sit next to me, angel. Tell me about yourself."
Clint sat down cautiously, smoothing the bed cover as he did.

"There ain't much to tell, ma'am. I just got out of the army. I want to be an actor like Gary Cooper. He's from Montana. Could ya know a agent who could git me a part?"

"I do have a friend who's an important agent. He just might be interested in a handsome young man like you. You'll have a chance to show what you can do shortly. We're going to do improvisations. Where did Everett find you? He brings the most handsome young men for me to meet, he's so sweet."

"I lives in the same apartment house, ma'am. We all met at the swimming pool," said Clint nervously.

"You must look magnificent in a bathing suit! Don't be so nervous, angel. I won't bite you."

"Well, ma'am I ain't never met no one like ya before."

"I hope that's a compliment. My dear boy, do you realize you're sitting in the presence of the future Queen of America? My whole life is dedicated to achieving it. The trouble today is there's no hope for this country. All this tax business. I paid more tax last year than the President's salary. It's horrible. Look how wonderfully the Queen of France, Marie Antoinette, lived. A marvelous time."

"Didn't she get her head cut off, ma'am?"

"That's not funny. That remark does not gain my favor, you're here to gain my favor. Everyone is." Clint glanced at his wristwatch.

"I better get goin, ma'am, it's kinda late," he said starting to get up. Billie gripped his hand.

"Don't go, angel, I like you. Stay to see my surprises." A waiter entered the room with a tray full of glasses of champagne.

"Here comes the party. Sit down, angel." Billie took two glasses of champagne and handed one to Clint, who sat back down on her bed. She lifted her glass. "How old are you, angel?"

"Thirty, ma'am." Clint was twenty-three. Billie lifted her glass to him and said. "To my new prince of the realm, or would you rather be a duke? I can give you any title you want in my monarchy. I'm the Queen!"

"Being a prince is OK, ma'am," said Clint, as he smiled at Billie drinking the champagne.

A group of merry guests came into the room talking and laughing among themselves. They sat on the lounges as the waiter passed champagne to them. The jester approached Billie and whispered in her ear.

"Should this be a costume night, Your Highness?"

"Of course," she replied, also whispering. "Get them into outfits, and hide the young man's pants when he takes them off. I'm going to have some fun with him."

The jester smiled and got up on the stage. As he did the room quieted. He said, "Voyeurs and voyeurettes. Her Highness, the future Queen of America, has requested your presence at this soiree. For the benefit of the few who have not been here before, go to the room behind the stage. There you'll find costumes for everyone. Pick out whatever you choose to be for this night of fantasy. There's an assortment of delusions from the past as well as the present to choose from. Put on whatever appeals to you and let the games begin. Take your drinks and on to the costumes." The jester came off the stage and grabbed Clint's hand, pulling him off Billie's bed. Clint didn't want to go, but Billie waved him on, laughing.

Clint followed the jester through a small door behind the stage. He felt shy and self-conscious. But, what the hell, I ain't got nothing to lose, he thought.

The smell of mothballs hit him as he saw rows and rows of costumes of every description. He walked over to a wolf's head and put it on, looking into the mirror. He saw the blonde with the nineteen fifty-seven Thunderbird who grabbed his balls come up behind him. She carried a slave girl costume in one hand and a Roman centurion costume in the other.

She checked Clint out in the mirror and said. "Take that ridiculous thing off, and put this on." She handed Clint the Roman costume. "This is how I see you. A handsome Praetorian guard." Clint was taken by her directness.

"Take your pants off."

"What?"

"Don't just stand there looking dumb, sweetheart. Let's see those legs."

Clint laughed. "Gal, what's your name? I'm Clint."

"I'm Gale, cowboy. You're sort of cute. I think our hostess, that old bag, thinks so too. Are you reserved for the evening?"

"Huh? Do it look that way?"

"Mighty suspicious."

"Can I see ya later? Give me ya phone number."

Gale reached into her bra, pulled out a card, and handed it to him. "I don't give my number to strangers, but you and I should get better acquainted. What do you do besides hustle?"

"I ain't no hustler," he said acting indignant. Gale glanced into his scowling face and said, "Sure you're not," smiling.

The room started to clear out. The other guests had gotten into costumes and had gone back into the bedroom.

"We'd better get dressed. Where do I get into this?" he asked, holding up the costume.

"Come, we can change together." Clint gave her a look. "Don't look so startled, cowboy. Haven't you ever taken your clothes off with a girl before?" Gale pulled Clint into the small dressing room and closed the door. She moved into him unbuckling his belt. Clint gripped her and tried to kiss her.

"Not now. You'll ruin my makeup. God, you're a hot thing. Get dressed, I got plans for you."

Clint could feel the heat. He pushed Gale against the wall, holding onto her large breasts. "No. Not so fast, cowboy."

"You started it, gal," he said, panting.

Gale broke out of the dressing room and entered another next to Clint, locking the door. Clint pushed down his erection to get into the Roman costume. He came out of the room and walked over and checked himself in the mirror as the jester came in.

"Her Highness is asking for you. Have you finished dressing?" he asked.

"Yep, I'm ready," replied Clint as he exited.

After Clint had gone, the jester glanced around and went into the dressing room and picked up Clint's trousers. He put them into a clothes hamper by the door as he left.

The bedroom had taken on a carnival atmosphere. Everyone except Billie was in costume. The guests stood around laughing and checking each other's outfits. The waiters moved through the room handing champagne to everyone.

When Billie saw Clint in costume coming towards her she said.

"You look so handsome! You almost take my breath away." Clint felt uncomfortable, but managed to smile. He eyeballed the room and spotted Gale. She reminded him of a showgirl he had met in Las Vegas. He liked the way her boobs swelled over her strapless brassiere. She smiled and winked at him, not letting Billie see. The jester gave a sign to Billie.

"Shhhhh...my dear subjects. Our entertainment is about to begin."

Two

The lights dimmed as the sound of Ravel's "*Bolero*" filled the room. Everyone quieted down as the curtains on the stage parted. At center stage stood a frame of white canvas. Into the spotlights danced four shapely young girls, their naked bodies covered in wet paint. One girl fuchsia, another yellow green, one Chinese red, and the other sky blue. They danced gracefully in front of the canvas, touching it as their bodies swayed. Hans Hoffman-style colored shapes began to appear on the white background. As the music grew more intense, the color disappeared from the nude figures with every contact against the canvas. The music stopped, the girls took a deep bow, the curtain came down. Everyone clapped and whistled as the jester went to the stage.

"That painting is called "Inspiration". Each of you will now do your own living painting. Dream up whatever perverse ideas you might have and bring them up here for us see," he said, leaving the stage. Two girls dressed in tutus rushed up, taking a pose of Degas dancers. One pushed the other. She fell down. The Degas girl fell on top of her. They laughed, uproariously. The jester ran up and helped the girls to their feet and off the stage, feeling slightly ridiculous as everyone laughed at them.

"Very good, girls," encouraged the jester. "Who's next?" Gale got up from the lounge and grabbed Clint's arm, pulling him off the bed next to Billie. Billie laughed as Gale dragged him on stage.

"Wait, we need music," said the jester as he rushed in back of the curtain. "Mr. Wonderful" sung by Peggy Lee came over the speakers.

Clint stood erect, his arms folded in front of him, chin up. His jaw stretched out rather like an old photo of Mussolini. Gale flung herself down on the stage floor and wrapped her body around Clint's feet and legs, her breasts totally exposed. Clint reached to bring her to her feet, but she held herself at his crotch. He could feel her warm breath there. He tried not to become aroused. The last thing he wanted to do was to perform for these strangers. How in the hell did I get into this? He forced Gale to her feet. She pushed away from him, arching her back, holding her body against his. Now, Clint was getting into it. This was starting to be fun. He took a look at Gale's large breasts, then stared at the audience for a their reaction. Everyone was laughing.

Gale, not to be undone, pulled Clint's feet from under him and sent him to the floor. She jumped aboard, straddling his hips and rode him like a horse beating him on the chest with her fists.

Everyone enjoyed the pair's performance except Billie, who yelled at the jester in her hoarse whiskey voice. "Enough! Stop the show! Get that horrible stripper off the stage. Everyone leave." The laughter stopped.

"Why, Your Highness? It was just starting to get interesting," said one of the male guests.

Gale and Clint got up and started to leave for the dressing room. The jester held Clint back.

"Her Highness does not want you to leave. Just the girl."

Clint glanced at Gale who gave him that knowing smile again and left his side. "Call me," she said and walked off.

Clint went to Billie on the bed. "It's late, ma'am. I have to go too, ma'am."

"No, Springtime. Stay. Please, I have so many wonderful plans for you. It will take days to explain them. Please stay with me. We'll go to the track tomorrow and bet your winners and if you're a good boy, I'll introduce you to my agent friend. Come, sit down. Have some more champagne and let us get better acquainted."

The party was still going on downstairs. An overweight middle-aged Irish tenor stood in front of a piano singing "Danny Boy" with an accompanist. The singer wore an obvious toupee that sat on the top of his head. He hit a high note and stayed until his breath ran out. The remaining guests clapped as he finished the song. As he took a bow, he saw Everett leaving the party. The singer ran and caught him at the front door.

"Where's Queen Billie? I have a song I wrote for her. I want to sing it to her."

16

"She's upset, old boy, some young twit has set her off. She told us to leave. If I were you I'd slip out like the rest of us old sports."

"I want her to hear the song. It's called "The Queen of Beverly Hills".

"Appropriate. But I would stay away tonight. She's got romance on her mind. Fare well, old chap," said Everett as he left for his car.

The singer climbed the staircase to the second floor. He went on to Billie's suite and opened the door. Clint and Billie were on the bed, talking.

"May I come in?" asked the tenor.

Billie, seeing him, smiled and said, "Jack, you old drunk. Who brought you? I heard you lost your driver's license. Meet my prince, Clint." Clint tried to rise, but sat back down on the bed.

"Pleazzse to mee-eet you."

"I wrote you a song, Billie, love. Listen to this." Jack started to sing.

"MY QUEEN, MY LOVE, MY DESIRE,
THE HEAVENS HAVE BROUGHT ME TO YOU
I'M YOUR PRINCE, YOUR SERVANT,
YOUR SLAVE, I'M YOUR LOVE FOREVER
IF YOU TRIED YOU COULD NOT RELEASE
ME FROM YOUR REGAL SPELL, MY QUEEN OF BEVERLY HILLS."

"Do you like it?"

"Jack, it's beautiful. I'm about to cry. Sit with me. I want to hear it again."

Clint felt a wave of dizziness. He wanted to leave, but he felt he couldn't move. They must've put something in my drink.

"Where is the bathroom?" he asked.

"Outside, down the hall. Don't be gone too long, Springtime." Clint left the bedroom to find his clothes. He went to the dressing room, his evening jacket lay there, but his pants were missing. He checked out the other rooms. No pants. Did Gale take them? She'd do something like that, he thought. He checked his coat pocket and found her telephone number and put it back. His head swam. He had to get out of the house, but he had no pants. How could he leave without his pants? He stumbled down the upstairs hallway and opened a door into a large bedroom. He saw a bed and dropped on it. His head felt dizzy, like he was riding on the "tilt-a-whirl" at the county fair. His stomach started turning and he ran for the bathroom.

Clint awoke to a scream coming from Billie's bedroom. He raised his head and glanced out the window and saw daylight. He got up. He was still wearing a Roman costume. He felt dizzy as he opened the door and ran down the hallway into Billie's room. She sat up in her bed; dressed in a gown she had worn at last night's party. The singer he had left in her company was stretched across her bed, his toupee in his eyes. His false teeth were lying next to his chin. The zipper on his pants was open to reveal a protruding stomach bulging out beneath a tight girdle. Billie laughed.

"Look at him. I thought I went to bed with a handsome lover man. He tricked me. He was illusion. Get this old drunk out of my bed, for Christ's sake. He's making me sick."

Clint, amused, pulled Jack off Billie's bed. Jack grumbled. Billie picked up the Racing Form as she watched Clint drag Jack out of the room.

"After you've thrown Jack out of the house, come back, Springtime, and help me pick some winners. I have a feeling you're going to change my luck. Breakfast will be here when you return." Billie pulled her hair up and got up from the bed. She splashed some Jean Nate fragrance from a large bottle on her body and between her breasts.

"I ain't got no clothes. My pants ain't around. Miss Billie, I can't go anywhere."

"Nonsense. I have a closet full of clothes you can wear. Get the jester to show you. And hurry, we don't want to miss the first race."

Jack had come to. He mumbled as Clint escorted him from the bedroom and down the stairs to the front door.

"Who are you?" asked Jack.

"The undertaker," said Clint as he pushed Jack out the front door and locked it.

The jester, called him from the staircase. "Her Highness has asked me to get you into some clothes. I will be in the last room down the hallway."

Clint climbed the staircase and followed the jester as he went into a bedroom and on to a closet full of men's clothes.

Clint said, "Whose duds are these?" He examined the rows of garments.

"They belonged to her last gentleman friend. She bought them for him."

"How come he didn't take' em?"

"He left in a hurry under strained circumstances."

"What's that mean?"

"Let her Highness tell you," said the jester.

When Clint had gotten shaved and dressed he came back into Billie's room. Billie had changed and was waiting for him. He had gotten into a camelhair sport coat, gray gabardine slacks and a tie. The clothes fit as if they were made for him. The maid had brought in the breakfast tray, which included a glass of champagne, prunes and spaghetti for Billie and bacon and eggs for Clint. Clint sat down and started to eat. Billie stared at him and smiled. "Those clothes look wonderful on you, angel. But do you have to eat so fast?" She picked at her spaghetti and prunes.

"Everyone says that, ma'am. It's a bad habit I picked up in the army. Tell me, ma'am, do you like what you-all eat?"

"I never eat anything else, angel. Don't you like spaghetti?"

"I do, ma'am but not for breakfast."

Billie picked up and studied the Racing Form. "What's the name of the horse you liked today?"

"Morning Glory in the fourth and Sledge Hammer in the sixth."

The maid and the jester were outside in the driveway loading the Rolls Royce with champagne, a portable television set, two-way radios, a chest of ice and other racing paraphernalia.

They arrived at Santa Anita racecourse in Arcadia. The driver turned the limousine into the parking lot and stopped under a public address system attached to a long pole. Clint opened the door to get out. He tried to assist Billie from the limo, but she remained seated.

"How come we parked here? Ain't we goin' to the Turf Club?"

"No, angel. The maid will make the bets for us. It's more comfortable in the car. You can hear the race from the PA above and I can see it on my little television." Clint was disappointed. He'd never known anyone before who could get him into the Turf Club, and now that wasn't going to happen. He remained quiet, sulking.

"Who do you like in the first race? I'm going to bet on One More Chance across the board." She handed three, one hundred dollar bills to Alma, her half-African American, half-Cherokee maid, who sat in the front of the car with the chauffeur. "Hurry angel, it's almost post time." Clint sat and said nothing. "Aren't you going to make a bet? Alma has to go or she'll be shut out."

"I ain't got no money. It was in my pants," he lied.

"Here, Springtime." Billie handed Clint a hundred-dollar bill. "I'll stake you," she said smiling.

Clint took the bill and pushed it toward Alma. "Put fifty to win on Too Far to the Right.

Alma rushed off to the betting window in the Club House. Over the PA they could hear, "The horses are lining up at the starting gate. They're off."

At the end of the day, Clint had a thousand dollars in his pocket. Billie had lost all but the sixth race (for which Clint said he had inside information). Clint had relieved Alma from making the bets. He made them and his luck remained. He had pocketed some of Billie's bets. He knew the horses were long shots and wouldn't come in, and they didn't. He kept her money. Clint was pleased with himself. It's like taking money from a moron.

That night at the house they had dinner in Billie's bedroom. They sat in front of the television set, their dinners served on trays. Billie was in an up mood. She was getting drunk. "I gotta to go, Miss Billie. I got things to take care of tomorrow. Gotta take back that old monkey suit I rented for your shindig."

"Nonsense, I'll have the chauffeur return it for you. I'm planning on a trip to Europe. I want you to escort me. Have you ever been there, angel?"

"I flew over when I was on a troop plane, ma'am. I guess that wouldn't count, huh?"

Billie smiled. "Let just say you haven't been. I was getting bored with the United States. My efforts for a monarchy seem futile. In Europe I can find a deposed king. If he likes my money I will marry him and then I'll be a real queen. I want you to come with me, Springtime, as my private secretary. The position will pay well."

Clint thought, I like the idea of going to Europe in style. I'm sure I can handle this old gal, but do I want to be one of them gigolo guys? "When am I goin to meet ya agent friend?"

"Who?"

"The agent, you know. Remember, ma'am? Ya mention him last night."

"Oh, him! Why is he so important to you?"

"I want to be an actor, ma'am. I guess I wanted that most of my life. I come from a small town in central Montana. Hell, there be six-grain elevators and a post-office. There's more tumbleweeds than people. I worked with my pappy and ma farming grain. There's no TV yet, so I went to the movies. That weren't easy. I had to hitchhike because the movie house was thirty miles away. In the winter, I'd go for matinee and stay all day and into the night watchin' double features. I could remember every part word for word and I could do them parts, even the women. My older brothers thought I was daft. They'd hear me doing my movie stuff and they would laugh and tease me. I dreamed of going to Hollywood. I'd see my name in lights on that little old movie house. When the Korean War broke out I enlisted. Instead of going to Hollywood I ended up in Korea. That is sure funny, ain't it, but I learned a lot in that army. How to get along with people, even the stupid ones."

Billie smiled at him softly. "You're a sweet young man. I'll get you that introduction."

Billie kept putting her hand to her neck. "I slept badly last night. That awful Jack in my bed. He gave me a crimp in my neck. Angel, come and massage it for me. You have such big hands. Make me feel better." She turned on her back and dropped her nightgown.

Clint thought, here it comes. I'm trapped. All the talk about being with a rich woman was in his mind, he discovered. He wasn't suited when he saw what it entailed. He kept thinking about Gale. I got to get out of this place. This old gal would keep me a prisoner if she could.

"I have to make a phone call, ma'am."

"To whom?"

Why would she ask me that? She wants to know everything. "About a job, ma'am."

"Stop that ma'am business, Angel, you have a job. You're my secretary."

"I am, ma'am?"

"Don't you remember? We're going to Europe."

"I'd like to get some things at my apartment and pick up my jalopy."

"I'll have the chauffeur get your things, and we'll pick up your car tomorrow or I'll get Everett to bring it over. He lives in your apartment house, doesn't he, Angel?"

"Yeah." Clint felt trapped. The house had become a prison. He had to get out. He saw a button by Billie's bed that said "Silent Alarm", a burglar alarm, he thought. He got up from his chair and walked over to Billie who lay on her stomach. He sat down on her bed and, when Billy wasn't looking, he pushed the alarm button. "Where do it hurt, Miss Billie?" She took his hand and brought it to her neck. Clint squeezed the muscles and tendons around her upper spine. "Oh, I'm in heaven, Angel. I love the feel of those big hands. Now, do my back."

Soon, they heard a knock at the bedroom door. It was Alma, the maid.

"Wait," said Billie. Clint left the bed and Billie pulled up her night-gown. "What is it?" asked Billie, annoyed.

Alma said, through the door, "Your Highness, the police are down-stairs. They say the house alarm had gone off at their office, and they would like to speak to you."

"The police! I'm not going to talk to the police. Angel, would you see what it's all about?"

"Ya, sure, I'll right back." Clint left the bedroom with Alma. He walked downstairs to the hallway entrance where two uniformed Bel Air patrolmen waited for him.

"Howdy. I'm Clint Nation. What's the trouble, officers?"

"The alarm went off in our office. Could we look around and check the grounds?"

"We ain't heard nothing. Go out through them doors," said Clint as he pointed to French doors at the end of the hall. Clint watched until the two patrolmen went outside to the verandah, and then he went to the telephone and brought a card from his pocket and dialed a phone number.

"Gale? Howdy, Clint Nation. The guy ya met at Billie Rodgers's house. Would ya do me a big favor? Pick me up at her house? ...You will?... I'll meet ya by the gate." The police returned from the garden. "Can't talk, bye." Clint hung up the phone.

THREE

Car headlights appeared, coming up the driveway and shone into Clint's eyes, blinding him for a second as he stood in front of Billie's ornate iron gates. The car was a two-door 1957 Ford Thunderbird, the same car she'd been driving when they'd met. Gale moved across the front seat to open the passenger door.

"You're driving my favorite car, gal," said Clint as he checked its white interior. "What color is she? I can't tell in the dark."

"Turquoise. That old bag had you as a prisoner, huh?"

"I never seen no bars, but I sorta felt I was. It's a crazy place." Gale handed him a bottle. "Here, have a drink."

"What is it?"

"Tequila."

"Tequila. I heard about this stuff, but I ain't never touched it before," he said as he swigged a gulp from the open bottle. "Hot damn! This stuff got a kick to it."

"It's supposed to. Where are we off to?"

"My place on Franklin."

They moved onto Sunset Boulevard toward Hollywood. Lights from the oncoming cars allowed Clint to check out Gale. Her long blonde hair fell down around her shoulders in a pageboy cut. Her mouth was wide with full lips and even, white teeth. He liked when she smiled; two deep dimples appeared on her cheeks.

"Whatcha do for money?"

"I'm an actress. I work as an extra, but I have big plans for myself."

"An actress! I was right. I knew ya was. I'm an actor. Can you give me some pointers?"

"Have you done anything?" Clint was puzzled.

"Have you ever acted before?"

"Nah. Just in my imagination. I ain't got no parts yet. I see myself doing a lot of good parts, though."

Gale smiled. "Don't count on it. First you've got to stop saying "I ain't got no." That's no class, sweetheart. You got to learn how to talk if you want to act. I'll turn you on to a voice elocution coach. She's got a girlfriend of mine from Mississippi talking like she's Katherine Hepburn."

"You think I talk bad? Hell, gal, I talk ordinary-like where I come from. Can you get me to be an extra, like you?"

"It's a shitty way to start. You never get out of it. I don't recommend it. I like being around the set to see what goes on and get some experience, but it doesn't count when it comes to getting a speaking part. You get no respect, and every producer thinks you're his for a bed partner."

"Hey, gal, you got the looks to be a star."

"That's a sweet thing to say. You're not so bad yourself, cowboy." Gale pulled off of Sunset Boulevard and drove up a winding road into the Hollywood Hills.

"Where we goin? This ain't the way to my apartment."

"I have to stop to see a girlfriend and pick up a dress." They continued to wind around the narrow road toward the top of the mountain. At the top of the hill Gale stopped and parked next to an empty car. They sat in the Thunderbird for a minute and stared out onto the flickering lights of Los Angeles below. A large house sat on the cliff above them. Clint figured Gale came up to neck but, when he put his arm around her, she jumped from the car and ran to the cliff's edge.

"Come! Check out at this view!" she yelled. Clint got out of the car. The wind blew toward him as he walked up next to her on the edge of the cliff. He stared out at the bright flickering colored lights of the expansive view and then down at a black drop-off below.

"Steep, isn't it?"   asked Gale.

"Yeah."

"Let's push that car next to mine off the cliff." She left Clint's side.

Clint watched her as she opened the car door of a nineteen fifty-two Chevy and got in. He saw her release the hand brake and then get out and move to the back of the car. Clint stood in wonder, not believing what she was doing.

"Hey, are you nuts?"

"Sure, help me give it a shove." Gale started to push the car forward.

"Come on, sweetheart, push. Don't just stand there looking like a dummy, help me."

Clint walked to the car. He stood for a minute watching her shove the car forward. The car went nowhere. He shook his head. He couldn't believe what he was about to do. He put his hands on the trunk of the car and pushed. The car started to roll forward to the edge of the cliff and over it went, down with a loud crash into the ravine below.

"Come on! Let's get out of here," said Gale as she grabbed Clint's arm and pulled him toward her car. She jumped into her seat and Clint slid in next to her. Off they went down the hill.

They sat silent until Clint said, "'Why'? I asked myself. I could have stopped you."

Gale kept glancing at him as she drove. "I know why, because you dig it. Got you excited didn't it?"

"Hell, lady, you're crazy. You took me from the frying pan into the fire. What else do you do for kicks?"

"I work for the Los Angeles Police Department."

"Yah don't say."

"I got a thing about cops. I guess it goes back to my childhood. Someone told me once my father kept beating up my mother, and the cops would come. I felt the cops were protecting me."

"What you said about being an actress is a doggone lie?"

"No. I'm a part-time actress, and you wait, I'm going to be a star."

They were back on Sunset Boulevard and the traffic had stalled. Up ahead Clint could see a half a block of backed-up cars.

"It must be an accident," said Clint.

Gale pulled out around the stalled cars and drove up the street in the wrong lane.

"Hey, what the...you're nuts, lady," yelled Clint. "Look, it's a cop. He'll throw our stupid ass in jail, you fruitcake."

Gale pulled the car up to a policeman who, signaled her to pull into the curb. Gale stopped and swiftly got out and ran to the policeman and started talking to him. Clint slid down in the seat, hoping he wouldn't be seen. He watched as Gale kept talking to the policeman. He was smiling at her. What the hell, should I run? He started to open the door to get out, but Gale was back and slid in next to him. She waved to the policeman who smiled back and said, "I'll see ya around." Gale started the car and they sped off.

"How did you? Whatdya say to the cop?" asked Clint with amazement.

"I threw around a few captain and lieutenant names on the force in Hollywood. No problem, sweetheart, what time is it?" Clint checked his wristwatch. "Ten-thirty."

"I have to stop at my place. A couple of friends are coming over. I couldn't get in touch with them after you called."

"I'll get a cab."

"Sweetheart, I thought you liked me."

"I do, but you scare me. I can't take it".

"Sure you can. I know a hustler when I see one. Staying in that old bag's house... cowboy... you can take anything."

Gale turned her car off Fountain Avenue and drove into an underground garage of a Spanish Colonial apartment house and parked. Clint followed her onto a patio and up a small staircase. Gale opened the apartment door with her key and Clint followed her inside. The room was two stories with a staircase that came down from the second floor.

The place reminded him of a second-hand furniture store, thought Clint. Paintings, appliances, television sets, pieces of antique furniture were scattered and stacked around the living room. "You got a lot of stuff in this place. It wouldn't be hot, would it?" asked Clint with a straight face.

"You mean stolen? Does it look stolen? Really! I like going to rummage sales. I can't resist a good buy. Sit down, sweetheart. Can I fix you a drink?"

"Naaah."

"Make yourself comfortable. My friends should be here any minute. Excuse me." Gale went up the staircase to the second floor.

Clint examined the objects closely. She's a liar, this stuff is hot, he thought, as he put down a small French antique painting. This chick is dangerous.

He heard a knock at the door. He looked up to the second floor and yelled nervously to Gale, "Someone's at the door."

"Well, let them in," Gale yelled back from above.

"Me?"

28

"Who else, sweetheart?" Gale yelled back.

Clint went to the front door and pulled it ajar. He peered out. A young pretty blonde, wearing a tight black dress and a lot of make-up stood in the doorway with a long haired young man dressed in a black turtle-neck sweater and black pants.

"Is Gale in?" asked the girl.

"Yeah, come in."

"I'm Candy and this is Norm."

"Hi," said Norm as he walked by Clint and sat on the sofa. "Where's Gale?"

"Upstairs."

Candy walked past Clint and up to Gale's room. Gale had changed into a pair of black slacks and black sweater.

"Who's your friend?" asked Candy.

"He's the one I told you about. I met him at Billie Rodgers's house. I sorta dig him. He's square, but that's what interests me. Besides he's strong, we'll take him with us tonight and break him in. He can carry the heavy stuff."

"You haven't told him anything?"

"No, but he's been asking questions about the loot in the living room. He's suspicious, but cool." Gale picked up her purse.

"Let's go, it's getting late."

They drove up the alley in a residential neighborhood in West Los Angeles. Clint was having second thoughts. Why? He had joined a ring of burglars. Gale had turned him out. He followed her as if she were leading him to a jail cell. She was right. He did like the danger. The rush. He was feeling a rush and it excited him. He knew she was trouble and dangerous, but he still stayed with her. She could be right about me. I might be like her.

Gale pulled the car in front of a garage. She reached under the front seat and pulled out a pair of black leather gloves and put them on. She reached back down under the seat and pulled out a crowbar and got out of the car; she glanced around the property and then used the crowbar to pry off the lock and open the garage door. She got back into her car and drove it in and parked. Clint sat in the car and watched her.

"Come on. Let's go." Clint hesitated. "Get out! There's nobody here. We cased the place. They're out of town."

She waited to close the garage door until Clint exited the car. Candy and Norm parked their car in the back alley and came around to the back door as Gale ripped the lock off and the door opened with her crowbar.

"Check the hall closet for furs," she said to Candy.

"Norm, see if there's silver. Remember if it says sterling on the back, take it." Norm nodded and went on the dining room.

"Clint, you come with me." They walked down the hallway to the bedroom.

"Look in the closet, see if there's furs." Clint moved to the closet and Gale went to the dresser and pulled open the drawers. She picked up a sparkling necklace in her gloved hand and examined it.

"Bunch of junk. I was told these people have good stuff." She looked at Clint, who had the closet door open.

"What's in the closet? Is there a suitcase?. If you find one, bring it here." Clint spotted a suitcase and pulled it out. He grabbed three full-length fur coats and a stole and brought them over to Gale. She opened the case and threw the jewelry inside. She grabbed the furs from Clint and examined them.

"I might get a few bucks out of these in Las Vegas." She glanced at Clint, who was nervous.

"Relax, sweetheart," she said as she got into an Autumn Haze full-length mink coat and walked to the mirror. She posed. Clint watched Gale as she admired her long reflection, turning around to look at herself from the back and then again from the front.

"It matches my hair, doesn't it? I think I'll keep it. Do you like it on me?"

"The coat gives yah class," said Clint.

"Aren't you sweet, dearheart. I thought I already had class. Come here. I want to feel that strong body of yours." Gale moved to Clint and put her arms around his neck, and stared into his gray-green eyes giving him a long kiss. She pulled him over to the bed and fell backward on the mattress, her mouth still on his, his body on top of her. She whispered in his ear. "When I steal I get so excited and horny. I hope you're as good a fuck as you look."

Clint felt his hardness and the excitement as he moved to give this chick a fuck she'd never forget. He smiled as he gazed down at her. A strange thought came to him. It was like Eve had given Adam the apple.

FOUR

Gale stood on the set of a Bob Hope picture, when Bob's agent, Mel, a little man with a pear-shaped body, small sloping shoulders, and a large waist, walked on wearing elevator shoes. "Look what's left over from the "House of Wax," Bob cracked when he saw Mel. Everyone laughed, but the remark didn't seem to bother Mel. A few jokes were exchanged, then Mel spotted Gale. She wore a long gown that gave her the vision of a New York society girl. The set was decorated like the New York nightclub, El Morocco, complete with zebra-skin covered-booths.

Mel walked over to Gale, who kept adjusting the front of her dress, showing her large breasts, while giving him a flirtatious smile. As Mel approached he tipped his small brimmed fedora, which he never removed from his baldhead. "Hello, I'm Mel Cantor."

"Pleased to meet you Mr. Cantor, I'm Gale Lawrence."

"Have you considered getting out of extra work and going for speaking parts?"

"All the time, Mr. Cantor, but as an agent you know it's not easy. I studied acting and have tried to find work as an actress, but it takes a good agent to get you in the right doors," she said, giving him a sexy smile.

"I have a script in my office. It's a new feature that starts in a month. Come by tonight after you finish here and we can discuss a part for you. Here's my card."

Gale took Mel's card and put in down the front of her dress. Mel's eyes followed the card lustfully as it disappeared into depths of her bosom. He cleared his throat.

"I'll see you about seven," said Gale as Mel again tipped his hat and walked off the set.

Gale was excited about the fortunate encounter. This could be the break I've been waiting for, she thought. Mel Cantor can get me in any studio in town. He knows everybody.

"I'm thrilled," said Gale into the phone. "I'm going to see Mel Cantor tonight. You know who he is? The big Hollywood agent. I've been thinking all afternoon how to get you to meet him. Call Candy, and have her call Jean. She's a showgirl at the Sands, in Las Vegas. She's been a customer for my hot furs and is in town looking to get in the movies. I'm going to get Mel to take me to the Brown Derby. You be there with the girls and I'll introduce you."

"I don't get it," said Clint. "What does you seeing Mel have to do with me?"

"Mel Cantor is an notorious lady's man. I'll tell him you have a string of gorgeous girls that would do almost anything for you. I won't come right out and tell him you're a pimp. He'll know that when he sees you with the girls. This is a perfect way of getting into his confidence. If I read him right, and I know I do, he'd do almost anything for some new nooky. You can book it for him, and if I'm right he'll be booking you and me."

"So now I'm a pimp?"

"Darling. You want to be in the movies, don't you?"

"Yeah."

"Well?"

"What time do you want me there?"

"Between eight and eight-thirty. Make sure you wear a suit. Leave everything to me, and sweetheart, be nice to me. I love you." Gale hung up the phone.

At eight o' clock, Clint, dressed in a suit and tie, sat in a booth at the Hollywood Brown Derby with Candy, who was heavily made up and dressed in a tight body-clinging black sheath dress with spaghetti straps. The low neckline revealed her ample breasts. Her eyes darted around the room as she fidgeted with a cigarette holder.

"Don't you get any ideas about me going to bed with this agent we're meeting. I'm a lot of things, but I'm no whore. I'm here only as a favor to you and Gale," said Candy.

Clint placed Candy's hand in his and said. "Just tease, let him think you could be available. I'll handle everything."

They sat up as a tall striking brunette who looked like a showgirl arrived at their table. Clint checked her out. Her lips were painted scarlet over a non-existent lip line. Dark eye shadow applied over her gray eyes made them look enormous, and her skin was made up to look whiter than it actually was. She wore a long black diamond mink coat that she dropped off her shoulders when she sat down, revealing a low cut strapless red dress. All eyes in the restaurant were on her as she adjusted herself, getting comfortable. Clint was sure she hadn't seen the sunlight in months.

Jean pushed her long hair back from her eyes and said to Clint.

"Hi, I'm Jean."

"The name's Clint. Pleased to meetcha. I'm not the agent."

"Honey, I wish you were," said Jean, giving Clint a full smile that show off her capped teeth.

"Mel's this little guy that looks like a turtle, and he keeps a mink coat in his office he lends out to the starlets he takes out."

"You can see I don't need a mink coat," said Jean as she adjusted the coat around her shoulders. i

The maitre d' escorted Gale, wearing a blonde mink coat down below her calves, to a booth near them, with Mel following her, looking a foot shorter. Clint, Candy and Jean gave each other knowing smiles and laughed. Gale spotted them, walked over to their booth and waved to Mel to join her. "Mel, let's sit with my friends. This is Jean, Candy and Clint. Can we join you?" asked Gale.

Clint got up and said, "Please do."

Mel was impressed and nodded his head. Jean pulled Mel down next to her as Gale sat on his other side. Mel tipped his fedora, but didn't remove it.

"Mel, darling," said Gale, "My girl friends are actresses. Aren't they gorgeous?" looking at Mel, then to Clint, smiling. "What brings you to the Brown Derby?" asked Gale.

It's Jean's birthday, we're having a party," said Clint.

"Let's get the waiter. I want to buy champagne," said Mel.

Jean grabbed Mel's hand under the table and eased it up to her crotch and held it there.

Mel said to Clint, "What do you do?"

"I'm trying to get into the movie business, and it ain't easy."

"Doing what?" asked Mel.

"I want to be a actor."

"Well, you got style, and you seem to know the right people," Mel said, smiling at the girls. "If you want a job, I need a new trainee in my office. You'll have to start in the mail-room," said Mel matter-of-factly. "Everyone does; that's how you find out what's going on in the business. It pays a hundred a week and the hours are long. But in time, if you show promise, I'll make you assistant agent with an increase in salary."

Gale gave Clint a fast look and gave him a kick under the table anticipating he'd say yes. When she saw him hesitate she said, "Mel, you're a darling." She stared at Clint. "What a great opportunity for you, Clint. It's an honor that Mel wants you in his office. You'll say yes, won't you?"

"I've always wanted to be an actor," replied Clint.

Gale gave Clint a "don't be stupid" look.

"When do you want him to start, Mel?" asked Gale.

"Be in my office at seven-thirty Monday morning."

"Okay, that's settled. Where's the champagne? We have to celebrate Jean's birthday and Clint's new job," said Gale, looking for the waiter. The waiter poured their glasses full.

Clint was dubious about being an agent, but deep down he knew he didn't have the temperament or even the talent to pull it off as an actor. "A toast to Mel, who's the most, and to us girls who should be his clients." Everyone laughed. "Who knows, Mel, one of us could be a big star," said Gale, holding up her glass as they joined in the toast.

"I'll drink to that," said Jean as she turned to Mel and tossed in a kiss.

"To Mel." said Jean.

Clint liked the agency business in a way that surprised him. He put in his time going through the mail, delivering scripts, going for coffee for the other agents and clients, driving clients around to casting calls.

Before long the clients got to know him and trust him. A few confided about their lives and careers.

"I'm taking some of the loot to New York," Gale told Clint on the phone.

"Like what?"

"A few fur coats and some jewelry. New York's a better place to get rid of it. The market is better. It's harder to trace and I can get a better price for the stuff."

"What about your fence in Las Vegas?"

"I don't trust him. Couple of the working girls I know who are wearing my furs said they thought he'd been busted, and is now turning everyone in to get a lighter sentence."

"I'm not doing any more burglaries. I never wanted to get involved. Besides, what have I got out of it? A few hundred. It's not worth it to me to go to jail for a lousy hundred bucks. I like this new job. It's my career now. I'm not going to jeopardize myself anymore."

"Sweetheart, remember how you got it. I sucked that ugly little man's cock to get you that job. Remember?"

"Yes, and I told you more than once how much I appreciated what you did for me. But I have the strangest feeling that you want to be caught, and take me down with you."

After a moment of silence, "I'm sorry you feel that way," she said and hung up.

The phone rang in Clint's apartment. He woke and checked the time. One o'clock in the morning.

"Hello."

"Thank God, I got you. The most awful thing has happen. They arrested Gale in New York," said Candy hysterically

"I knew it would happen. I'm not a bit surprised. Who told you?"

"Her mother called me. She told me to get rid of anything I might have," said Candy. "You don't suppose that she'll rat on us?"

"Nah, that's not her. She's got a lot of psychological problems from

35

her youth. She's been looking for a way to punish herself, and she found it."

"Aren't you smart, or did she tell you that?"

"We talked about it."

"You did?"

"What about your boyfriend, Norm? Does he know?"

"He's skipped town and left me with a ton of bills."

"Let me know if you hear anything. Bye."

The Hollywood police department brought Gale back to Los Angeles. She confessed to the charges of burglary, and they gave her two years at Terminal Island, in Long Beach, with parole. Neither Clint nor any of Gale's associates in crime were brought into the case. Clint relaxed, putting his past with Gale out of his mind. He hoped he would never see Candy, Norm, or anyone else who would remind him of that part of his past.

Meanwhile, Clint was moving up rapidly in the agency. He left his Franklin apartment and took an option on a small Spanish house with big windows overlooking a wooded canyon. The house was, in Realtors' jargon, on the outskirts of the Beverly Hills Post Office. This meant he didn't really live in Beverly Hills but had the address.

Just as in Beverly Hills neighborhoods, there was name value in Clint's area. Tyrone Power's widow lived on the same street; Hedy Lamarr had a house just up from him and, on the hill directly across the canyon, lived Doris Duke, the tobacco heiress, who owned Rudolf Valentino's old house "Falcon Lair". Sunday afternoons he could hear jazz music filtering down the hillside from a jam session taking place at Duke's.

Clint had made himself over. No more cowboys. The voice coach Gale had found for him had completely changed his speech patterns. He'd lost the western twang, the 'ain't got no' had disappeared. He'd fall back on western speech when he felt he needed it to charm someone.

Mel liked his agents to wear dark suits, which gave Clint the look of a clean-cut young executive. He started giving parties at his new home. He could fill the place within an hour with young beautiful starlets to amuse the producers he wanted to impress. Everyone came to his parties because the word was out that Clint knew who and how to entertain. His boss, Mel, and the other Hollywood bigwigs always showed up. They knew he'd produce new beauties to play with. They even liked his food and booze. Clint had learned how to do it right.

FIVE

Georgia Evans couldn't imagine how her life was to change when she walked out on the stage Sunday morning to compete for the Miss Muscle Beach contest in Santa Monica.

Georgia was a blonde version of Elizabeth Taylor, but with a pouting mouth. She had competed for the title before, winning it first at seventeen and again at eighteen. And once more she had the crowd going for her. Time and experience had given her the confidence it took to win. She was miles ahead of the other girls on the stage when she walked in front of the judges to pose. A handsome blonde body builder, wearing a leopard bathing suit, lifted her above his head with one arm as she extended her lean, perfectly-proportioned body into the air. Georgia worked the appreciative crowd with her poses and stances.

"Go for it, Georgia, you're the best," they yelled as they applauded her beauty and athletic ability.

Clint Nation appeared on stage as the Master of Ceremonies and also as one of the judges. Clint found himself impressed with Georgia, and he and the other judges voted her the winner.

He went to the microphone and announced, "Ladies and gentlemen, it's unanimous. The winner is Georgia Evans."

The crowd cheered. Georgia ran to Clint as he handed her the shiny silver trophy.

"Georgia, on the behalf of the city of Santa Monica and the Muscle Beach talent association you have been voted Miss Muscle Beach of nineteen hundred and fifty-eight."

Clint handed the silver trophy to Georgia and she walked around the stage showing it to the audience who whistled and applauded her.

A slight, intense young Latin male sitting in the front row of the outdoor arena had a camera, and clicked pictures of Georgia as she toured the stage. His hands trembled as he tried to hold the camera steady, focusing the lens on her. When Georgia left the stage, he left too and followed her to the back. Clint Nation had stopped Georgia and had her in conversation. The Latin man walked behind them to be within hearing distance.

"Georgia, have you ever thought about working as an actress?"

"It did cross my mind. I've done some acting in high school, but I never though about it that seriously."

"There's a movie starting production next week. I can get you a part."

"I live with my parents. I'd have to talk it over with them. It would sure help if you met with them. Would you?"

"When?"

"Now, if you have time."

"Where do you live?"

"It's south of here, Westchester."

"I'll follow you. Where's your car?" Georgia pointed to the parking lot. The Latin man stepped up.

"Hello, my name is Luis Verano. I'm from Cuba. I'm here to cast a film I'm making in Cuba. I have a part for you," he said to Georgia in a heavy Spanish accent.

"This girl is my client. You'll have to talk to me. Here's my card. I'll be in my office in the morning," said Clint, as he handed Luis his card and ushered Georgia off to the parking lot, Luis looking after them.

"Why are you making me leave? I wanted to talk to that man."

"Those kind of guys are a dime a dozen around beauty contests. If he calls, I'll find out if he's legit. You saw how you need an agent. From now on I handle those kind of inquiries."

"You certainly move fast, don't you, Clint?"

"It's a fast town and a fast business and there are a lot phonies you learn to duck," said Clint.

Georgia got into a blue MG TD and drove off, with Clint following in his red 140 Jaguar roadster.

Clint stayed behind Georgia on the drive to Westchester, a new tract-home community south of Los Angeles. Georgia pulled in front of a residence and parked. To Clint all the houses were the same. It was one of those tract homes built almost overnight over southern Los Angeles county. Clint followed Georgia inside into the living room. Silver trophies filled the room. They stood everywhere, all for beauty contests. On the wall hung a haunting oil painting of Georgia. A tear dropped on her cheek.

A middle-aged man and woman who Clint figured to be Georgia's parents sat in the living room. They rose as Georgia and Clint entered.

"Mommy and Dad, this is Clint Nation. He's a Hollywood agent and wants to put me in the movies. Clint, this is Reverend Evans and my mother." Clint put out his hand and the Reverend took it.

"Sit down, sir," he said. "What is this about putting my daughter in the movies. The movies are full of sin. No God-fearing folks we know go to the movies. That is, not since Bing Crosby made "Going My Way" and that was to me to be Catholic propaganda."

What have I gotten into? Clint thought. "I understand, Reverend. Myself, I'm a Baptist. My pappy brought me up by the book, and our preacher would come ever' week to our house to have some of my mama's cooking. So I know about religion." Clint could tell they saw him differently. "Hollywood can be Sodom and Gomorra, but that don't mean you have to live that way. Your lovely daughter has great potential. She could be a movie star with an agent who knows about Jesus to guide her. You shouldn't have to worry about her doing an injustice to her Maker." Clint saw how the Reverend looked at his wife, whose expression had softened.

"Elmer, I feel we can trust this man. He's God-fearing. After all, we let Georgia do the beauty contests, and it hasn't changed her. What harm can come from it? We've raised her to trust in the Lord," said Mrs. Evans.

"Let me give it some thought, sir. We'll pray to the Lord tonight for his guidance," said Reverend Evans.

Clint got up to leave. "Thank you for letting me come into your home. I await your decision," he said and turned to leave.

Georgia followed him. "You're a great salesman, Clint. I'll call you tomorrow."

They smiled together as Clint got into his car and drove off.

Clint thought, Pappy always said I could sell snow to the Eskimos.

Georgia called Clint the next day. "My parents and I had a long conversation about my future, and we prayed to the Lord. It wasn't easy, but they said I could sign your contract. Tell me, are you really a Baptist?"

"Yes."

"You won't be mad at me, but I thought you made that up."

"I didn't sound convincing?"

"Oh, you did a good job in convincing my parents, but it's me who's not convinced."

"You and I will talk about it sometime. I have great plans for you. Tell me, how do you do what you do when your parents are so wrapped up in religion? It seems to me that beauty contests somehow don't go with that lifestyle."

"It's difficult. They know that I've always been different. I had problems when I started, but I stood up to them and they gave in. I'll let you in on a secret. To convince them, I told them I would give twenty percent of what I make to the church. I think that made it happen."

Clint laughed. "I'm sure. I never heard of a religion that didn't need money. Be in my office tomorrow at two. I'll have the contracts ready to sign. And be ready to go out on an interview. I'm sending you to a photographer to have some photos taken. He's good. Shoots big stars. Here's his number, Crestview 27555. His name is Nick Ferre."

"I'll call him now. I'll see you tomorrow," said Georgia as she put down the phone.

The girl's got a lot going for her, Clint thought. I hope she can act, but with her looks who's gonna care?

Georgia called Nick after she and Clint hung up. He told her to come by his studio on Robertson Boulevard that day at five and to bring some outfits she would like to wear for the shoot. She arrived at the scheduled time. In a window on the street stood a large color portrait of Ava Gardner. A sign said to ring the bell. Georgia rang, and a voice came over an intercom and asked who was there. She gave her name and the door opened to a staircase leading to the second floor. Georgia walked up into a large studio. Giant windows opened to the north framing the Hollywood foothills. She smelled the scent of incense burning in the room. She felt nervous. She had never been with a photographer of distinction or fame.

A small Italian man of about forty-five greeted her. He wore a long brown silk oriental robe. He smiled at her with a mouth too full of big fake-looking white teeth. He took her hands and then stood back and looked her over.

"My darling, how beautiful you are," he said in a raspy cigarette voice as he breathed laboriously. She tried to relax with him, but it was difficult. He took a cigarette from his pack of Camels and lit it. His fingers were stained yellow from smoking. She hated the smell of smoke but tried not to let him know.

"Have you ever had your portrait taken before?" he asked.

"An artist painted me, but the only portrait was for my high school year book," she answered.

"You're almost a virgin then, aren't you?" he said and smiled. "Come over and sit down on the divan so I can see you through the lens."

He grabbed Georgia's hand and walked her in front of a view camera. "Sit down, my pet." Georgia felt self-conscious but tried to disguise it by smiling at him.

"You're an angel in the lens, my darling. Now let's see what you brought with you for wardrobe. Georgia got up from the divan and took her tote bag and pulled out a blue sheath dress with spaghetti straps and showed it to him.

"I like that. We'll use it. What else do you have in there?" he asked.

Georgia showed him a red sweater and a pair of white short shorts, and a blonde mink stole she had borrowed from her aunt.

"Here, put this on," he said handing her a leopard two-piece bathing suit. Georgia looked at it.

"The dressing room is over there," he said pointing to a door. As she walked from the studio for the dressing room, she noticed wetness under her arms and on the dress she wore. This man bothered her. She put on the bathing suit and came out into the studio.

"It looks marvelous on you. You could star in a jungle epic. Come! Get in front of the camera." Georgia sat on the divan.

"Now do some poses for me," he said.

Georgia started to pose. She stretched out the divan. She flirted with the camera. She smiled at it. She mocked it. Nick kept clicking away.

"Wonderful, lovely, I like that. Lift your head up. Some more. I like that. Hold it!" he said. Georgia started to enjoy herself. She felt good. She was having fun and felt the camera loved her. Nick breathed harder now. A clatter of air came from his lungs as he worked.

"You're a natural, my pet. Playboy asked me to submit some photos to them for an issue. You could make three thousand dollars if they used them. With me as the photographer, it's money in the bank. Would you be interested?"

"Isn't Playboy a nude magazine? My father is a minister. I couldn't do that to him. He wouldn't understand."

"I only do class photos. Let me tell you how I'll shoot you. I'll build a long box like a coffin and line it with mirrors." He animated the story with his hands. "Holes will be made at the top for the lights and a hole in the center for my camera. You will be nude in the box. I will shoot you as if you were a jewel in a mirrored sitting. It will give the illusion of three dimensions," he gasped. "It'll be sensational, and so will you. It could do wonders for your career. How about it?"

"The three thousand dollars sounds interesting," said Georgia.

"Well then. Let's do it."

"I don't know if I should. I'll embarrass my family."

"Clint told me you've been doing beauty contests for years."

"Yes, they're with a bathing suit. I've never taken my clothes off for anyone."

"Times are changing. It's getting to be accepted. Believe me. If the right photo was taken of the right girl, that girl would be a star overnight. Look at the past, at some of the great nudes in history. Goya painted the Duchess of Alba nude. It made her immortal. The nude calendar picture of Marilyn Monroe. Look what that did for her. You're in the same category. Believe me. I know. It's my business," said Nick.

"And I could approve of the photos?" asked Georgia.

"You'd have complete approval."

"Okay, I'll let you, but under another name. Will you agree to that?"

"Of course. Now let me see your body. Take off the bathing suit."

"Now?"

"Why not? You're here. I can measure you for the box."

Georgia was skeptical. She got up from the divan and removed her bra. She stepped out of the bottom part of the bathing suit and was naked. She felt strange and wanted to get back in her clothes. Nick observed her nakedness. "I like it, but there's too much hair around your crotch," he said as he stared down.

Georgia blushed, but said nothing. She started to feel dirty and uneasy. She reached for a cloth drape that covered the divan. "Can I get back into my clothes? It's cold in here," she said.

"I want to take a picture of your pussy so I can show you what I mean when it's developed. Stay there for a minute." Nick picked up his Nikon and clicked away. Georgia started to get up from the divan. "Wait a minute. I want to measure you." He ran to a desk a pulled out a tape measure.

"Hold this," he said. He pulled the tape down across her body getting a feel as his hand moved to her toes. Georgia gave him a look. "I'll make the box six feet," he said rolling up the tape. "You can get into the blue dress you brought. I'll take your portrait now," he said.

Clint sent Georgia out on interviews. She drove her blue MG around Hollywood with the top down. The wind blew her long blonde hair and the sun kissed her golden skin. She knew she looked good and got attention everywhere she went.

She landed her first part in a horror film at Del Mar Studios on Bronson Avenue. She played a vampire. They dressed her up in a long black dress that plunged in the front. She wore a black wig and her make-up was almost stark white. Her lips were painted scarlet and when she smiled her two eyeteeth resembled fangs. She thought she looked hideous. The director knew that it was her first part so he tried to make her comfortable by telling her she was beautiful and that he would gladly change places with the actor in the scene so he could bite her neck. That made her laugh and it gave her confidence as she continued with the scene.

Clint's big client, Marty Fallon, an actor-entertainer, had been in the movies most of his life. His parents had appeared on the vaudeville stage and he carried on the name. Marty could make you laugh or make you cry in seconds by moving his mobile face. Marty had been married a few times, and his present wife had just moved out of his house. He couldn't figure out why. He attached a great importance to marriage, but it never was to work for him. Marty was a born romantic. So he kept romancing some pretty girl or looking for one to romance. He had a problem. He didn't want to grow up. In his heart he remained a kid. That gave him tons of charm, but also lots of heartaches and trouble. Marty had offices at Del Mar Studios where he ran his movie company.

When Clint arrived at the studio he went directly to Marty's office. Marty sat at his desk with some charts, going over the Racing Form figuring today's winners at Hollywood Park track. He glanced up from the Form as Clint entered.

"Hi, kid, do you wanna go to the track today?" He always asked Clint when he saw him and Clint answered, as always, "Love to, but I can't today."

Since Clint became an agent he had given up the track. He said he didn't have time for the horses, but they had burnt him out.

"MGM liked the idea of yours of remaking "The Kid." said Clint. Marty jumped up from his desk. "They're goin for it. I knew they would," he yelled.

"Wait a minute, not so fast. They haven't said that yet. They got to find a "kid" to play your son, and kid actors with star potential are scarce."

"I'll play both parts," said Marty. He pulled his hat down over his eyes and put his finger in his mouth. "Gee, dad you gotta knock him out in the first round for me," said Marty in a little boy's voice, looking innocently at Clint.

Clint was amused. "They'll get back to me in a week."

"That's great. You're sure you won't go to the track?" asked Marty as he sat down at his desk, looking pleased.

"No, but come to Stage Two with me. I've got one of my new actresses working on a picture. She's a looker and I want you to meet her."

Marty smiled a smile that lit up his famous face. "No kidding. Let's go." He and Clint left his office and crossed the street to the front of a large building. A sign on the door said STAGE 2 as a red light flashed. They waited outside a few minutes until the light stopped. Then they opened the door and entered. The set was a dungeon with the backdrop painted to look like large fitted stones. Sconces with burning candles created flickering shadows on the walls. Cobwebs hung all over the set. A large black coffin sat in the middle of the stage in front of the camera. The crew ran around repositioning the lights for the next setup.

When Marty came on the set, work stopped. Some of the crew recognized him and said hello. Marty had known and worked with a few of the crew for years. He cracked a couple of bad jokes, then followed Clint to a dressing room door that read "GEORGIA EVANS." Clint rapped.

"Georgia, can you come out? I have someone who wants to meet you." The door opened and Georgia stood stooped over, because the door was small and the trailer sat on blocks forcing her to step down to exit. Georgia was shocked to see who stood in front of her. Her bosom stuck in Marty's face. Marty took one of his famous takes. Clint laughed.

"Oh, Mr. Fallon, what a pleasure to meet you. I've been a fan of yours most of my life," she gushed.

"Well, thank you, but you make me feel old, darling, with the `all my life' bit. I've been at it a long time, but you have to remember I started young."

Georgia felt embarrassed at what she had said. He must be sensitive about his age, she thought, and she started to blush. She hoped it didn't show through her make-up.

"Do you like horse racing?" asked Marty.

"I've never been," she said.

"I'll take you. It's a great place to relax. Would you like to go one day?"

"I'd love to, Mr. Fallon," she said.

"Marty to you. Clint can give me your number. I got to go; are you coming, Clint?"

"No, I want to talk to Georgia about an interview I'm sending her out on next week. I'll call you at home tonight."

Marty walked off the set waving goodbye to the crew.

"How does he know me?" she asked.

"Oh, ah, he saw you coming into the studio in your car. He figured I might know you. Should I give him your phone number?"

"He's married, isn't he?"

"He is, but separated."

"Oh," she said changing the subject. "What about the interview you just mentioned?"

"I just got the script. There's a good part for you. I'm getting more details on the money and when it starts," said Clint.

"Did that Cuban man, Luis, call you about the film in Cuba?"

"He did. And I told him you weren't interested."

"Why did you tell him that?"

"I used my better judgment. The location is too dangerous. They're shooting in the jungles of Cuba with a band of revolutionaries led by a guerrilla leader called Fidel Castro. Luis has Erroll Flynn set for the film, but it's hardly a place for you to go to get killed."

"Thank you, Clint, for protecting me."

"It's part of the service."

They heard a rap at her dressing room door.

"Georgia, we're ready for you on the set."

SIX

Clint's office in Beverly Hills had a spacious feeling, high ceilings, walnut paneling that matched his desk. His window faced on Rodeo Drive. Mel had promoted him to full agent, and he'd gained a list of successful working actors and actress. He also had taken over two of Mel's big stars that were part of old Hollywood. Mel felt he wanted to cut back on his work schedule. It was late in the afternoon and his secretary had left for the day when the phone rang.

"Hello, Clint. Do you answer your own phones? I thought you'd be out of the mail room by now."

"Who's this?"

"Has my voice changed so much? It's Gale, sweetheart. You remember fast Gale."

Cautious and worried, Clint asked, "Where are you?"

"I'm having a drink at the Luau. Can you join me? I want to discuss something with you."

"Give me ten minutes. Bye." He hung up. She's out. I knew this day would come.

Clint walked over to the Luau on Rodeo Drive a block from his office. Steve Crane, the owner, was at the door when he walked in. Steve would always show up at Clint's parties with a beautiful girl. He was once married to Lana Turner.

"Getting much?"

"You know, Steve, agents get laid a lot. I've got no complaints."

"There's a young lady waiting over at the corner table."

Clint glanced in the direction of the bar adjusting his eyes to the darkness. The room was decorated in a tropical atmosphere of the South Sea Islands. Fake tall palm trees looked almost real. Bamboo chairs were placed around polished monkey pod tables. Soft burning candles glowed in the hurricane lamps on tables. The drinks were made of rum. You never knew you if you were getting drunk until it was too late. The patrons at the Luau did and said things they wished they hadn't because of the influence of those powerful, wonderful-tasting experiences that arrived with flowering floating gardenias and miniature parasols. Clint spotted Gale and joined her at a table near a dark pool with a waterfall. He sat down and they stared at each other. A Filipino waiter came to take their order.

"Bring me a Gold Cup and an order of ribs. How's your drink?" he asked.

"I'll have another."

"It could be yesterday. You look the same," said Clint.

"I put on a little weight, but I'll get if off. You can't do much about prison food. Lots of potatoes. You're handsome as ever. I hear you're getting on well. I'm happy for you."

"You did the introductions. You knew better than me I was made for the agency business. I never did thank you for keeping me out of the trouble you were in."

"Those were my demons. A lady shrink I saw in prison helped me. One of my problems was I kept hiding the fact from myself that I'm a bastard. It gave me an inferiority complex. That gave me a drive to be somebody. My neuroses are still there, but I recognize them for what they are. You'd be relieved to know I got over chasing after cops. Hooray!"

Clint laughed. "What are you going to do?"

"I'm hoping you'll advance me some money so I can change my appearance. I want to get back into the business. I found this wonderful doctor. I saw him yesterday. He's going to take this hump out of my nose. It's a new operation he learned in Germany. He does the surgery inside the nose, so there's no scars. I'll knock off a few pounds. Change my name and hair color and you can invent me as new actress you've discovered. What's the matter? You look skeptical. You're not interested?"

"I didn't say that. What about Mel? He'll remember you. He told me you were the best blowjob he ever had. He calls you "The Greatest".

"Oh, sweetheart, that's funny. I'll have that engraved on my tombstone."

"I'm glad you haven't lost your sense of humor. How much do you need?"

"Five hundred would help."

"I'll give you a check. Is this going to be the start of something?"

"What do you mean?"

"Will I be paying for not going to jail?"

"Clint, you can be a real asshole. You don't know a thing about loyalty."

"I'm sorry. I shouldn't have said that. Let me give your proposition some thought. It could work. I know you can act. You're a good actress."

"Thank you, sweetheart." Tears appeared in Gale's eyes. She opened her handbag and found a handkerchief and blew her nose. "I'm sorry. It's that I haven't received many compliments lately. I'm just happy that's all." She pulled herself together and stared Clint straight in the eye. "Now, you're sitting with a women who's had no sex with a man in over a year. Why are we sitting here?"

Clint called in sick the next morning. He and Gale stayed in bed most of the day catching up on sex and each other's lives.

"I wasn't completely unproductive shut-in. I spent my time in the prison library working as a librarian. I got interested in writing. I wrote this story about this woman who was to die in the gas chamber for killing her husband who abused her. It's a sensitive and dramatic story from a tortured woman's perspective. Would you read it? I think it would make a great movie. I can do the lead. I wrote it for myself."

"You're an unknown. The part sounds like it has be a dramatic actress that has name value."

"Gregory Peck, James Stewart or that new actor Paul Newman could play the lead, the lawyer. You won't need a actress with a name. Just a good actress. Any one of those stars could carry the picture."

"Get it to me."

"You wouldn't believe what I learned from the girls in prison. I got a real education in sex."

"Oh yeah? You're already good in that department."

"Sweetheart, you can always learn more about sex. Remember the Arabian Nights? Didn't they do something like a hundred and one positions? I know I've tried many of them, but if you want to get kinky, I've got some new tricks for you. There was this pretty Chinese girl. We got to be good friends. She's an actress also."

"What was she in for?"

"Attempted murder. She tried to kill her boyfriend."

"Oh."

"Anyway, she worked in a whorehouse in Hong Kong when she was twelve years old. She told me how she had learned the ancient sexual practices in China. Now I can take care of any problem that might come up in love making, no matter what it could be. She said that's how the Duchess of Windsor got the Duke."

"You don't say. Do you want to practice on me?"

"Why, sweetheart, how could you have guessed? I'll need some props, though. What do you have around the house that I can tie you up with? And I also need a feather."

"You're getting me hot again."

"That's the idea, sweetheart. I'm going to get you so hot that you'll think you're going to explode, but I won't let you. You'll beg me. You'll plead with me. You'll promise me anything. And if I think you have suffered enough, I'll let you come."

"What else?"

"I'm not going to let you in on all my tricks at once. If, you're a good boy and nice to me, I'll let you have one at a time. I don't want to spoil you, sweetheart." Clint jumped out of bed.

"Where are you going?"

"To find some rope. And if I can't find a feather, we'll open up one of the pillows on the bed," he replied as he ran naked from the bedroom.

Gale laughed as she heard him stumble down the hall.

Gale had been hiding in her small apartment for a month, recuperating from plastic surgery and dieting. She was down to a size eight. Dr. Gordon had straightened and shortened her nose by taking out a small bone on the bridge; he had also given her a slight cleft in her chin. She was ecstatic with the results. The surgery had refined her face, giving her a younger look and a leading lady image. She made an appointment with Jerry James, the famous Beverly Hills hairdresser to change the color and give her a new style. Jerry was a wizard.

When Gale came out of his salon after her makeover, she walked over to Clint's office. She stepped up to the young girl at reception and said, "I would like to see Clint Nation. Tell him it's an old friend."

"Can I have your name?"

"I'd rather not give it. I want to surprise him."

"I'll see if he's in." The girl got up from her desk and left the room.

Gale sat down and picked up a magazine and paged through it. The receptionist came back with Clint behind her. He walked over to where Gale sat, and peered at her closely. She smiled up at him.

"I'm sorry. I meet so many people. I can't place you," said Clint. Gale got up and stood next to him and whispered in his ear.

"My God! It can't be," he said in amazement.

"How do you like the new look, sweetheart?"

"It's the red hair that threw me." He stared at her again. "There's something else. Come to my office." He turned to the receptionist. "No calls."

Gale sat in a comfortable armchair in front of Clint who stared back at her. The outside light shone in on her face.

"Have you thought of a new name to go with the image?"

"Yes. Dorothy Winters. Do you like it?"

"It's dull, but it doesn't turn me off. I'll have to get used it. I have some good news for you. I took your story, "The Battered Spouse" to a producer friend of mine, Axle Flood, at Columbia. He likes the story and wants to develop it into a screenplay. He told me your theme has the same kind of feeling that won Susan Hayward the Oscar in "I Want to Live" and it did great box-office."

"Clint. I'm in shock. Will I get any money?"

"No. Don't look so shocked. How does fifteen thousand sound?" he said smiling.

"Wonderful, but I want to play the lead."

"That's what I like about you, Gale... I mean Dorothy. You're never satisfied. You always want more."

"But, Clint. The part's me. I grew up with that tragedy. My father was always beating my mother and me too. There's no one in Hollywood who could play that part as well as me. Try to get me a screen test. If your friend sees me on the screen, I know he'll cast me."

"This is a character part. It doesn't go with your new glamorous face."

"I'm an actress, darling. I can play that down. Please Clint. Help me. You know I can do it. I was meant to do the part."

"Okay, you sold me. What are you doing later? I'd like to get back into that bag of tricks of yours."

Clint arranged for Dorothy Winters to test for the part of Bonnie in "The Battered Spouse". It was a big day for Dorothy. She arrived at Columbia at six o'clock for make-up and wardrobe. The make-up man had to put bruises and a create a swelling and a cut over her right eye for the scene. When he finished, Dorothy examined her face in the brightly lit mirror. What she saw looking back was a dumpy, nervous-looking women with a face that had been almost deformed from a supposed beating. The image put her into the character she was playing. The wardrobe lady helped her slip into a plain-looking housedress, and she walked on the set. The scene took place inside a house trailer on the sound stage. They had taken out a wall to open the trailer up so they could move the camera around for the action that was to take place.

Dorothy walked over to Hal, the director, a middle-aged, old-time Hollywood master-maker of woman's pictures. He said to Dorothy. "I like it. Stay with the feeling you have."

Dorothy nodded and went to her position on the set. Campbell, who played her husband in the scene, came on the set dressed in a tee shirt and jeans. His hair was uncombed, and he wore a four-day beard. A cigarette hung from his crooked mouth. The prop man handed him a fifth of whiskey, which was half empty.

Clint had gotten up early that day to come to the studio to watch his new client Dorothy Winters in her test and to give her moral support.

He walked on the set and stayed in the background as he heard the assistant director call out. "Lights! Quiet on the set!" the sound man yelled, "Rolling". Hal said, "Action."

The sound of a radio blared. Dorothy stood at the small sink washing up some dishes. She was crying and picked up a cloth and applied it to the cut on her face.

The door to the trailer opened and Campbell walked in; he picked up some kids clothes off the floor and said. "This place looks like a pigsty. What the hell did ya mother ever teach you about keeping a place clean?" he yelled.

"I'm sorry Kip, I didn't feel like doing much and I couldn't go to work today. It's my eye. I can't see out of it. Does it look bad?" She held her face for him to see.

"Nothing wrong with ya that another good beating wouldn't cure. Ya know you are the laziest old woman I ever had the privilege to meet. My ol' daddy told me when I married ya you'd be trouble, cause you ain't educated... yer stupid. Dinner ready yet?"

"It's in the oven."

"Where're the kids?" he asked.

"I sent them to ma's for the evening."

"You're always sending them to your ma's. Who in the hell's kids are they anyway, mine or your ma's?"

"I'm sorry Kip. I didn't think you cared," she said as she opened up the oven and took out a casserole of macaroni and cheese, put it on a plate and set it in front of him.

"What! This crap-a-do again. Can't ya feed me anything else? Why are ya always giving me this shit?"

"It's all I can afford on what you give me for household."

Kip got up from the table and hit her with his fist. She fell back against the stove. The teakettle turned over and hot water spilled on her. She let out a scream. Kip punched her in the stomach. She collapsed on the floor groaning with pain. Kip went back to the table and sat down. He poured whiskey into a glass and gulped it down. He continued eating his dinner.

Dorothy crawled to the back of the trailer. The camera followed her on the dolly. She reached under the bed and pulled out a paper bag. She reached in and pulled out a .38 caliber handgun. She stared at it and turned her head toward Kip. She got to her feet and walked back into the small room. Kip sat with his back to her. She pointed the gun at the back of his head. With no expression on her face, she pulled the trigger three times. Kip's head fell onto the table, and Dorothy stood over him in a daze.

Hal, the director yelled. "Cut." He went on the set to Dorothy and said:

"Perfect for me. How was it for you?" Dorothy nodded.

"How about you, Campbell?"

"I'm happy."

"Good," said Hal. To the cameraman. "Set up for close-ups."

Clint walked up to Hal.

"What do you think of my new star?" he asked.

"She's got a lot going on behind that sweet face."

"You mean she has talent."

"There's no question about that. She is a very talented young lady, but there is something else. That girl is capable of almost anything." Clint quizzed him further. "Could she murder someone?"

Hal peered at him. "What an odd question. Are you worried she might kill you? I heard a few actresses tell me they like to kill their agents but I haven't heard anyone who has. Don't push it," and walked away. Clint laughed to himself as he did.

Clint found Dorothy in her dressing room.

"Great scene. Where did you learn to act like that?"

"I'm so glad you got to see it. I studied with Michael Chekhov. He taught me the Stanislavski method. Marlon Brando uses it. It's called method acting."

"It's strong. You're constantly full of surprises. If you don't get the part, it'll have nothing to do with your acting. It will be politics."

Dorothy smiled at him and said. "Maybe I can do something about that too."

"What does that mean?"

"You'll see."

"They're ready for your close-up, Miss Winters," said the assistant director.

Dorothy gave Clint a strange smile and walked onto the set.

SEVEN

Dorothy had caught the attention of Nathan Wise, a Hollywood power broker or, as some said, the Hollywood God-father with a huge appetite for sex. He'd been married thirty-eight years to the same woman, who had learned long ago not to ask questions of her husband. A few of Hollywood's female stars could claim Nathan had put them in the movies, and their rise to the top would not have been possible if it hadn't been for Nathan's help. Nathan had taken an interest in Dorothy's career and was pushing her with the studios he did business with. He had giant pension plans at his disposal. He directed their movements and controlled their activities. He invested the funds in the movie business and, most of the time; they gave him a big return. His ruthless ways and cunning mind had helped him survive the old mob days in Chicago. His power came from deep within organized crime. It was said he had a direct line to the White House and the union bosses. Nathan kept an apartment on Wilshire Boulevard in Westwood, where he used to entertain his mistresses.

Dorothy hurried over to the apartment after she had finished her screen test. Nathan had not arrived. She had a key and let herself in. She went to the bedroom and took off her clothes. She had removed the make-up at the studio. In the bathroom she turned on the hot water and let it run. Out of her bag she took a packet of strawberry Jell-O and poured the contents into the hot full tub. The water turned cranberry red. Out of the closet she grabbed some expensive Jewel Park handmade lingerie. She had it made for Nathan.

She stepped out of her panties and submerged herself in the soft feel of the solution, letting it come up to her neck. The faint smell of strawberries filled her nostrils. She lay in the hot water letting the tensions of the day leave her body. She knew her performance should get the job, and so did everyone on the set. She had to get the part. Everything she had ever dreamed about was riding on it. Clint was right when he said it would be politics that would keep her from it. No one ever heard of Dorothy Winters, but she knew they would if she were to play "Bonnie."

Nathan is my ace. He's powerful enough to tell those studio heads that I should have the part. Oh, Nathan, you love. What I'm going to do to you today? she asked herself. It's got to be something real special, she thought. It came to her. Nathan, have I got a trick for you. She got out of the tub. The Jell-O left her skin feeling soft and smooth. She put her tongue on her arm to taste her skin. She smiled to herself. The smell and the taste of her body would make Nathan delirious with passion. She continued drying herself with the large towel.

She checked herself in the long mirror. She had to admit she had the body of a goddess. Her long shapely legs, her high-sitting pink-nippled breasts, all in perfect proportion to her height and weight. Her skin was white and creamy. And she loved the new hair color. It changed every-thing about her look, she thought.

She finished drying herself and went into the bedroom and got into a black silk and lace garter belt. Out of a drawer she pulled a pair of long black sheer stockings and put them on, fastening them to her garters. Next came a pair of patent leather spiked high-heeled shoes. The final touch was a sheer black chiffon negligee, edged in black French lace. She checked herself in the mirror. Perfect! Now for some red lipstick and eye shadow. She loved how she looked when she dressed this way. It made her feel powerful and secure. Nathan would be a little lamb in her hands. She'd punish him today. She knew he'd been a bad boy. And for her reward, Nathan would talk to Columbia and make sure that she would play "Bonnie". As she reached in a drawer to pull out a long black velvet whip, she heard the key in the door turn.

She called out. "Nathan, your Venus is waiting for her Apollo in the bedroom."

Nathan came through. He put the pressure on Columbia. He threat-ened them with a strike, and Dorothy got to play "Bonnie" in "The

Battered Spouse". The great reviews of the picture matched its box-office receipts. The movie changed Dorothy's life. Clint took credit for her success. He told everyone he had discovered her. A few people in town recognized her as being Gale Lawrence, a screen extra, who went to jail. But Hollywood had a way of inventing and reinventing its cast of characters, and Dorothy was accepted as a major new star on the Hollywood horizon.

EIGHT

Clint liked sports car racing and found himself a big fan and went to all the races. He knew most of the drivers and racecar owners personally. A big race was to take place in Palm Springs at the airport, and the cars and drivers came from around the world to participate in the event. Clint had his client Georgia Evans to be race queen for the weekend. It gave her publicity, and Clint a certain amount of prestige, to be able to bring Hollywood personalities to the colorful events.

The night before in Beverly Hills a party had been given at the home of a young producer, Matt Shapiro. He had gone to school with a car driver from England who was an English viscount, Geoffrey Landsdown. His mother was an American heiress. Clint took Dorothy Winters as his date. Matt had a group of young and attractive friends there to meet Geoffrey. When Dorothy and Geoffrey met it was an instant attraction. Dorothy led him to the pool house to be alone. He hadn't much experience with women, and Dorothy overwhelmed him with her beauty and wit. It didn't take much for her to end up in his arms. He pushed her down on the sofa and tried to remove her dress. Dorothy pushed his hand back and said. "Let's save it for another time, when we can be by ourselves."

"Would you come to Palm Springs for the weekend to see me race? I've built a new racecar, and I'm going to compete with Ferraris and Maseratis. Racing is exciting, and I'm sure you'll enjoy it, and beside I really like you, and I want you to be with me. I'll get you a suite of rooms."

"I'd like that. My agent is going to the race. I'll drive down with him," she said.

The door to the guesthouse opened and Clint walked in. "I've been looking for you."

"Geoffrey has been telling me about racing. He's invited me to Palm Springs to watch him race. Can I ride with you?" Clint nodded. He could tell something had happened between them.

Clint and Dorothy arrived in Palm Springs and checked in at the Howard Manor.

"I'm going to find Geoffrey," said Dorothy. "Call me later."

"Don't forget the party at the El Mirador hotel. Be there at seven," said Clint. Dorothy went on to her suite and Clint picked up the house phone.

"Georgia, I need you at the El Mirador for photos. Wear a bathing suit."

While everyone was at the Concours de Elegance on the El Mirador Hotel lawn Geoffrey invited Dorothy out to the racecourse. His mechanics were still working on his racecar.

The hood was up on the low sleek car when they arrived. His head mechanic had finished putting the last screws into place.

Geoffrey was worried. He said to Dorothy. "I have to win tomorrow. So much is riding on this race. I'll prove to the Europeans that Americans can build sports cars too, and I spent a lot of money to prove it".

"You'll win," said Dorothy, smiling at him.

"I'm so glad I met you and have you on my team."

The head mechanic put down the hood of the car. "We got it fixed. Take it around again," he said as he gave Geoffrey his helmet.

Geoffrey slid into the racecar and started it up. The twelve cylinders purred, and he took off down the track.

As Dorothy watched, she found herself thinking how she liked her new friend. This could be a great guy to marry, she thought.

Geoffrey had the track to himself as it started to get dark. He turned on the car headlights. The light beams focused on the airport runway as the wind whistled past his face and ears. He sped down the fast track. The car ran perfectly. A big smile came to his face as he brought the car into the pit. Dorothy and the crew gathered around as he got out.

"I'm going to win the race tomorrow, guys," he said as he took off his helmet. The crew smiled between themselves and helped him out of the car. "See you guys in the morning. Get some sleep." He and Dorothy got into his car and left for the hotel.

"Let's have dinner in your room. I don't want to go to the party. I want to be with you tonight. Just us," said Geoffrey. Dorothy peered into his handsome face, his hair still wet with perspiration from the heat in the racecar.

"A lovely idea. I couldn't bear those people tonight. I'll give you a relaxing massage. Looking at you tells me you're in dire need. Take off your shirt and lay on the bed," she said.

Geoffrey immediately took off his shirt and went to the bed and lay on his stomach.

"Let me get comfortable." Dorothy left the bedroom and came back in a few minutes in a shortie see-through nightgown. She put on her favorite perfume, "Jungle Gardenia"; she knew it always worked for her. She got on the bed and on top of Geoffrey's back. She straddled his waist as she moved her fingers up his strong back and kneaded the muscles around the back of his neck.

"Geoffrey, you're so tense," she said gripping his tendons. "Is that better?" She could tell he was pleased. She felt the muscles loosen as he relaxed.

"Hey, you're real good. Where did you learn your technique?"

"A Chinese girl taught me. I'm glad you like my hands."
Dorothy sensed Geoffrey's naivetè about sex.

"Take off the rest of your clothes so I can give you a complete massage."

Geoffrey turned over on his back and she unbuckled his belt and slipped him out of his trousers. She went to remove his underwear (she could see he had an erection), but he grabbed her hand to stop her.

"I said all your clothes, darling," She patted his erection. His face turned a slight shade of red as he pulled down his jockey shorts.

"Would you like me to?" she asked. Geoffrey nodded his head. She went down on him. He acted as if it had never happened to him before, and he ejaculated immediately. She brought herself up beside him and held and kissed his body with tenderness. In a matter of minutes she felt him erect again. She pulled him on top of her as his body quivered with excitement. He had difficulty entering her, not that he was big, but she was tight. He almost ejaculated. She calmed him down by holding him still. She had made up cute names for her vagina; she liked to refer to it as "the mouse's ear." He tried entering her again. Dorothy let out a sigh and he ejaculated at the same time.

"I'm sorry, I feel terrible."

"Has this happened to you before?" He nodded.

"Tell me about it."

"I'm too embarrassed to tell you. It was the first time with a girl at school. I felt guilty, but tried to put the experience out of my mind. I excused it for the excitement of the occasion."

Dorothy recognized his problem, "premature ejaculation", but she also knew how to solve it. Qu Ling had told her how to handle this situation.

"Relax, darling," she whispered into his ear.

Dorothy got up and went to a refrigerator and pulled out a few ice-cubes and wrapped them in a napkin and brought them over to the bed. She lay next to Geoffrey and put the ice cubes down between his legs onto his scrotum.

"What are doing?" he asked in alarm.

"Helping our situation, darling face," she said slowly into his ear. Geoffrey could feel the coldness around his testicles. He didn't like the feeling, but the anticipation and the rush he had experienced left him.

"Now, isn't that better?" she asked as she moved over on the top of him. She helped him to penetrate her by guiding him. She reached down behind her and with her hand she pushed her fingers against his urethra muscles holding them tight. It worked. He started moving. In and out, slowly moving his body as she moved hers with a rhythm against him until he could no longer hold it back, he climaxed.

When he got back his composure he said. "Oh, God, that was wonderful. I felt something heavenly happened to me... You gave me an experience I never knew existed."

Dorothy felt pleased with her accomplishment. She liked that he had a problem and that she knew how to remedy it. Most girls, she thought, wouldn't have the faintest idea of what to do in this predicament. She thanked Qu Ling again for what she had taught her. She felt Geoffrey getting aroused again. By the time morning arrived he'll be cured, she thought, but he won't be worth damn in his racecar. She turned over and started to kiss him again.

At the El Mirador, the Mount Kenya room was packed with racing notables. Thorton and Marge North, rich car owners, whose race car, a 4.9 Ferrari, was entered in the race, arrived with Rally Jones, Thorton's driver, and a pretty blonde girl who resembled Kim Novak; Jimmy, Thorton's male nurse, and Tana, a beautiful black actress, who was also Thorton's mistress. Marge never knew of Thorton's dalliance with Tana; she was passed off as Jimmy's girl. Following behind was Marshall Owens, Thorton's business manager. Marge, in her fifties, could pass for Joan Crawford. She had Joan's hairstyle and wore similar large diamonds and glamorous clothes. They had been drinking in their rooms, even Rally, which was unusual for him before a race.

The waiter approached the table for an order.

"Make mine another double," said Thorton as he gulped down the remainder in his glass and handed it to the waiter.

Georgia and Clint walked into the party. Georgia was every bit the starlet. Heads turned. Jennifer, the Kim Novak look-alike, jumped up from the table screaming her name. "Georgia, Georgia, over here," she yelled and motioned her to come to their table.

They approached Jennifer as she found a chair for Georgia. She pulled it up and the waiter brought another for Clint.

Georgia and Jennifer knew each other from work in Hollywood. Jennifer worked as an extra. She emulated Kim Novak, the same style hair, make-up and clothes. Everyone who knew her thought she was a joke, except Jennifer, who took herself seriously.

"I heard you were in town. I hoped I'd run into you." Jennifer said to Georgia. "I met Rally here last year. Isn't he cute? He's going to race tomorrow," she said looking at Rally and kissing him.

"Do you know my agent, Clint Nation?" Georgia asked Jennifer.

"Hi, Georgia is my best friend," said Jennifer slurring her words.

"I've never seen such good-looking poon tang," said Thorton as he broke into the conversation.

"Oh, shut up," said Marge in her whiskey voice. She was disgusted with Thorton. "Try to behave yourself tonight," she said, annoyed. Thorton grabbed Tana's crotch under the table.

After an expensive dinner at Romonoff's on the Rocks, where Thorton's new tie dropped into the soup and he threw the escargot at the waiter because he couldn't get the snails out of their shells, they drove back to the "Howard Manor" for a nightcap. Almost everyone except Georgia was drunk.

Georgia and Clint walked into the bar-lounge. The Guadalajara Boys were performing with their upbeat Latin rhythms. Clint and Georgia went on the dance floor. Georgia wore a sexy dress with her back completely exposed. Her skirt fitted tight across her butt. She threw her rear and hair to the beat of the music. As Clint watched her dance she reminded him of Abby Lane, Xavier Cugat's wife, who danced the same.

Rally, seated at the table, watched Georgia dance with great interest. Jennifer became jealous of the attention he gave her.

"If you ask me, she's got a fat ass," said Jennifer.

"No one asked you," he said.

"You're being rude," she answered, pinching him in the leg.

"Hey! That hurt," he said and took Jennifer's hand away.

She got up and pulled Rally from the table. "Come on, we're gonna dance. I can dance circles around that bitch." Jennifer staggered toward the dance floor pulling Rally behind her. She danced the bumps and the grinds, and was ridiculous. Rally was drunk enough to imitate her. Jennifer glanced at Georgia, letting her know she could dance too.

Georgia knew better and kept her distance.

Jennifer and Rally flew around the floor making fools of themselves.

Rally took Jennifer's hand and swung her into a tall Latin girl who fell to the floor. When the girl got up she picked a glass off a table and came at Jennifer throwing the drink in her face.

Jennifer came back at her grabbing the girl's hair and pulling her down on the floor. "You bitch! What did you do that for?" she yelled beating the girl with her fists.

The Latin girl took a bite of Jennifer's arm and Jennifer screamed. The girl's boyfriend came to break up the fight. Rally hit him in the face, and the boyfriend took a swing at Rally's jaw. Rally fell to the floor, out cold. Clint pulled Rally from the dance floor as the girls continued their brawl.

"You Kim Novak phony!" yelled the Latin girl. "I'm goin' get you, you bitch," she spat out as she limped off with her boyfriend.

Clint and Marshall came to help take a drunken Rally to his room. He was unconscious when they laid him on his bed. Jimmy came in. He examined a large swelling on Rally's chin. Marshall stood over him, watching closely.

"Will he be able to drive tomorrow?" asked Clint.

"He has no choice. He won't feel so good," said Marshall.

Jennifer staggered into the room and rushed to Rally. She pushed Marshall aside and grabbed Rally around his head and pulled him to her bosom and started to cry. "My sweetie, thank you for sticking up for me. I love you for it. Talk to me, please talk to me," she said in a drunken slur.

"Get away from him, you stupid broad. Can't you see he's out of it?" said Marshall as he pulled Jennifer off. Marshall took Jimmy aside.

"Get her out of here. Give her a shot and put her in with Tana."

"Thorton is in with her," said Jimmy.

"You take her then." Jimmy helped Jennifer out of the room.

"What's going to happen with Rally?" asked Clint.

"He'll be all right. I'll give him a shot in the morning, and he'll be like new." Marshall threw a blanket over Rally and turned out the lights as they left the room.

Clint went to Georgia's room and knocked. She opened it.

"Can I come in?"

She was reluctant. "How's Rally?"

"He'll be all right. I came to see him drive the 4.9 Ferrari. He'd better be."

"I'm mad at Jennifer. She always makes trouble, especially when she's drinking."

"I think she's funny. Some performance she gave."

"She might be funny to you, but her routine gets old."

"Can I sleep here tonight?"

"I have a terrible headache. I'm going to take an aspirin and go to bed." Georgia took Clint's hand and moved him toward the door.

"You owe me a few favors for what I've done for you," he said as he stared at her.

"I can't believe you said that. I'll say goodnight now," she said, opening the door.

"Not so fast. I haven't had a kiss yet".

Georgia turned her cheek. Clint rushed her and kissed her putting his tongue down her throat.

She used all her strength to push him away. "Clint, please, let's not screw up a good relationship. I like you, but I'm not your girl. You're drunk. Please, I need sleep if you want me to look good tomorrow. Good night." Georgia pushed Clint through the door.

Georgia closed the door and went into the bathroom and removed her clothes and put some cream on her face. I bet Clint will act like he won't remember about tonight. I hope I don't have to be around Jennifer tomorrow. She's nuts. I'd rather be home. In fact I think I will leave in the morning. I've had enough of this place, she thought as she got into bed and turned off the lights.

The next morning at the track, the crews were busy with the race-cars. This time of year the desert was perfect. The hot summer had left, and the evenings were cool. The air felt clear and crisp. The snowbirds had not yet arrived, so the community had a calmness about it. A desert sand storm blew in the night, covering the cars with a thin coat of fine dust. Some of the crew worked at polishing the exterior of the racecars, bringing back the gleam and luster of their paint.

Gossip traveled around the pits about Rally, the trouble he caused at the "Howard Manor". Rally had not arrived. His pit crew were concerned; the speed trials for starting position were taking place.

Over breakfast, Geoffrey asked Dorothy to marry him. He wanted to fly to Las Vegas after the race and get married. Dorothy was rattled by this sudden change of events in her life and couldn't think straight, which bothered her. Geoffrey had showed her how to use the stopwatch. She stood in front of the pits with the timepiece in her hand, clocking Geoffrey as he raced around the track qualifying for starting position.

He finished the course and came into the pit. He motioned for one of the crew to bring his oxygen tank and mask as he stood up in the cockpit. The mechanic ran to him giving him the mask. He took some deep breaths as the gray color left his face.

Dorothy was alarmed when she saw him. "Darling, are you all right?"

"My asthma, I'm fine. Just a blast to bring me around. You're going have to get used to my condition. How's my time?"

"You're in front row pole position. Aren't you thrilled, darling?" He got out the car and his crew came up to congratulate him. He gave Dorothy a big hug. Some newspaper photographers took their picture. "You brought me good luck. I'm going to win today."

Dorothy kissed him, and more pictures were taken.

Cary Grant, the actor, and a friend of Geoffrey's mother, came to Geoffrey's pit to say hello and wish him luck. The press had a field day shooting photos of the three of them.

The overall picture was colorful. Bright flags waved in the wind. Women wore multi-colored, scanty outfits. The sweet smell of Castrol oil traveled in the wind. Hay bales had been positioned at the corners of the course to protect the drivers from injury. Most of the spectators arrived driving sports cars. They were big fans of the sport and waited anxiously for the event to start.

The cars lined up at the starting line. Carroll Shelby's car, a Ferrari, stood in number one position; John von Nuemann was number two in a Ferrari; and Geoffrey Landsdown in number three in his own special car. The other cars and drivers followed in order of their qualifying time.

The race starter called out "Gentlemen start your engines".

The sound of the cars engines thrilled the racing fans.

The squealing of tires of a Jaguar could be heard as it stopped in front of Thorton's pits. Rally, Jennifer, Jimmy and Tana got out of the car. Rally was in a daze.

Marshall said to Jimmy. "He looks like a corpse. Did you give him anything?" he asked.

"The "feel-good" injection. He vomited when I did." said Jimmy. Marshall handed Rally his helmet.

"Get out there. The race is going to start. You're in last position."

"Shit, I'll be in first at the first corner in this car. You'll see." Rally put on his helmet and climbed into the Ferrari and fired it up. The gas from the Webber carburetors flowed into the powerful twelve cylinders. The pit crew pushed him on to the starting grid. The drivers waited nervously at their positions. The pit crews left the starting grid. All eyes were on Lester, the race starter, dressed in a black and white striped shirt, holding the checkered flag. Lester dropped the flag.

"They're off!" The roar of the engines was deafening. The cars and drivers dived for the first turn. As the cars jammed together going into the turn, three cars rammed each other and crashed. Geoffrey's car was pushed to the side of the track.

Rally, in the powerful V12 Ferrari, came roaring down the track with full throttle into the first turn and hit a Maserati, driven by Masten Gregory pushing into some hay-bales. Rally's car flew into the air and came down on the top of Geoffrey's car with a horrific sound, exploding into a ball of fire.

The crowd let out a scream as the fire shot into the air. Fire engines and ambulances tore down the track to the scene of the accident. The black flag went up as some of the spectators ran onto the racecourse toward the crash.

Dorothy was horrified. She screamed and ran toward the accident calling out Geoffrey's name. One of his mechanics ran after her and caught her to hold her back, but she broke away sobbing and ran toward Geoffrey.

It was complete pandemonium. The fire trucks pumped liquid onto the fire. Rally jumped out of the cockpit of his car, his clothes smoldering from the crash as he watched the scene before him; his Ferrari on top of Geoffrey's car burning and shooting smoke into the air.

As Dorothy got nearer she could see Geoffrey's arm extended from the car; only the bone was visible.

NINE

Georgia knew she made the right decision to go home early. Clint wasn't happy. He got rude with her because she wouldn't stay to pose with the racecars. I hope I haven't screwed up with him. He might not send me out on interviews. Oh well. I'll make it up to him somehow but I'll be damned if I will go to bed with him. You can't screw everybody, but these guys in Hollywood think it goes with the job.

She hadn't told him yet, but she and Marty had been dating. She liked Marty, and found him intelligent and fun to be with. He was considerate and helped her with her acting. She believed he was in love with her; at least he acted that way. If I'm going to be an actress I should make the best of it, and Marty could help with my career. There had to be a twenty-year difference in tour ages, but Marty acts younger than me. In fact he's like a big kid, she thought. He asked her to move in with him, but he's still married, that I could never explain to my parents. They'd be convinced I had gone to hell.

She turned on the car radio and tuned the dial to a station that played Latin music. The music filled the car with the mambo sounds of Perez Prado. She moved her body to the music as it played. The news came on and she heard the announcer say, "Viscount Geoffrey Landsdown, the son of American heiress Lorraine Gilbert and an Englishman, the Earl of Landsdown, was killed today at a sports car race at the Palm Springs airport. The young viscount had been racing his own car that he had built for competition." Georgia turned off the radio. Dorothy must be devastated. To see Geoffrey killed before her eyes. Was I lucky I left, she thought.

Georgia drove into her underground garage on Havenhurst off Sunset Boulevard. Marty called it "Hookers Row" because of all the kept women who lived along the street. She didn't care. Her parents didn't know. That was her only concern.

She parked her car and carried her bag up to the courtyard of the building. The apartment house was Spanish in design, built in the twenties. It had two stories, with a wide open stairway decorated with antique tile going to the second floor. In the center courtyard stood a tall fountain where water cascaded into a large tile pool. Brazilian pepper trees grew within the enclosure. Their berries dropped staining the stone walks. Tall French windows opened out onto the serene setting. Georgia's apartment was on the second floor. She felt secure there.

As she approached her door, she heard her phone ringing. She opened the door and rushed to pick it up.

"Georgia! It's Erroll Flynn. I've been calling you all weekend", he said.

"Hello Erroll, I've been away."

"Listen gorgeous, I'm having Luis Jose Verano, the Cuban director, here tonight for dinner. There's a part for you. I want you to come up and meet him."

"I've met him. My agent has also. I'll be there in an hour. Bye." As she hung up the phone, she thought, Clint is not going to like this.

Georgia drove to the top of Mulholland Drive above Hollywood. The vista of colored lights down below sparkled like jewels, sending off red, green, yellow and diamond-like beams flickering in the early evening sky.

Erroll's house stood perched on its own hill with a private driveway off Mulholland. He had lived there for years. He kept the house through all of his divorces, which you could credit either to luck or a good attorney. Georgia stopped in front of the gates and rang the bell.

Georgia had been there before and knew the house. It was long and rambling and had views of both Los Angeles and the San Fernando Valley. She had heard the stories about Erroll. Especially about the two-way mirrors in the bedroom where he supposedly watched other people get it on. When she had last visited, Erroll had chased her around the house, drunk. He couldn't have done anything if he had caught her, but they remained friendly.

Erroll let her in. He had put on weight since she had seen him. His face was bloated and his eyes were like hound dogs. When he smiled at her, she could see the old magic, that famous grin that had made women swoon in the past.

"Georgia, darling," he said and gave her a kiss on the cheek. He escorted her into the living room where the other guests had gathered and introduced her. He stopped by the bar and made himself straight vodka on the rocks.

A young straight-haired blonde came into the room. Errol brought Georgia to meet her.

"This is Beverly. She's my baby."

Georgia, thought, you can say that again. I hear she's fifteen, but Beverly didn't look fifteen, more like twenty-five.

"Luis, this is the little actress you wanted to get acquainted with. I think she's perfect for "Norma". Give her the script."

Luis took her hand and brought it up to his lips and kissed it. "Good to see you again. I have been in contact with your agent, but he keeps putting me off," he said in a soft Spanish accent gazing into her eyes. Georgia felt taken back by his directness. Georgia knew she had a weakness for Latin men. She'd had an affair with a Mexican boxer, and she hadn't forgotten him. She hadn't met any-one who reminded her of him until now. She went weak in the knees. It is the way they look at you, she thought, like I have no clothes on. She hoped he didn't pick up on the way she felt, as a flush came to her face.

"I have a script here," he said as he handed her a copy of "Cuban Rebels". Come and sit with me. I will tell you about it," he said, as steered Georgia to the sofa.

"Let me tell her, old boy," said Erroll. "The story is about a band of revolutionaries. These chaps are trying to throw out President Batista and his cronies from power in Cuba. It's documentary, but isn't. We'll be filming in the mountains at Castro's headquarters. Luis and Fidel Castro are school chums. Fidel is supplying his army. We will be shoot-ing the picture at the same time he's trying to take the country. Doesn't it sound exciting, Georgia?" asked Erroll.

"It sounds dangerous. Who's going to protect us?" she asked.

"Why Castro, of course, with his army. The corruption of the

Batista regime is appalling. Meyer Lansky and his boys run Havana," said Erroll matter-of-factly.

Georgia had met George Raft with Marty. George was involved with a hotel and casino in Havana. George wanted Marty to bring his act down to perform at the Havana Riviera. Marty had been considering the club date. Georgia's mind started to race. That might work. I could be in Cuba at the same time Marty is there. We would be together, she thought.

"Luis, when is your picture going to start?"

"When the rain stops, December."

"Will you be filming near Havana?" she asked.

"No. Santiago de Cuba, in eastern Cuba. Castro's guerrilla headquarters," said Erroll.

"My agent thinks the location is too adventurous for me. He hasn't been enthusiastic about your film."

"Agents are all alike. If they don't see some big money, they're never interested," said Erroll.

Georgia could smell a delicious aroma coming from the dining room. She hadn't eaten since last night.

Beverly, with the help of the Mexican maid, called everyone to the dinner table in the dining room. A huge platter of spaghetti, surrounded by grilled Italian sausages, a large tray of antipasto, baskets of Italian bread and bottles of Chianti wine awaited them.

Erroll escorted Georgia to the table and the others followed. Georgia sat down and Luis sat next to her. Luis acted attentive.

"Luis, you live in Havana?" she asked.

"No, in Madrid," he answered.

"I hear they're shooting big pictures in Madrid," she said.

"Yes, Samuel Bronson has the Spanish army under contract for his epics. You see Ava Gardner, Charleton Heston, Steven Boyd around town as if it were Hollywood," he said.

"Why would you want to make a picture in Cuba, when picture-making seems easier to do in Madrid?"

"See, I told you she's smart," said Erroll, slurring his words.

"I believe in Fidel Castro and his cause," he answered.

"Viva Castro!" said Erroll lifting his glass in a toast. Everyone lifted their glasses with him.

"VIVA CASTRO!" they clinked their glasses and drank the toast.

The phone rang in the early morning. Georgia lay in bed asleep. She'd been dreaming about Luis. They were dancing in a nightclub on a tropical beach. Los Tres Aces played their Mexican love songs as they swayed to the music, gazing into each other's eyes. Luis kept kissing her neck, her lips, her hair. She was in a trance, not wanting to separate her body from his as the music played on. The phone kept ringing and it finally brought her out of the dream.

"Hello."

"Georgia, it's Luis."

"Luis."

"You got away last night without taking my script. Can I bring it by?" His accented voice thrilled her with its sound.

"Um, sure. My address is 1027 North Havenhurst, Apartment C upstairs."

"I take you to breakfast. I tell you more about the picture."

"I'll be ready by ten. Bye."

Georgia jumped out of bed. She went to the mirror. She flushed with excitement at the thought of seeing him. What's going on here? You're acting like one of your romance-crazy girl friends. Go easy girl, first you got to see what this man's about.

She showered, and dressed in a sweater and matching skirt. She pulled her blond hair back and picked out a small black velvet bow and tied it to her hair in the back. She checked her appearance in the long bedroom mirror. She'd make a smart housewife and mother, she thought, laughing at her thoughts. "Sure", she said out loud, not quite believing what had been going through her mind.

The phone rang. She went to the bedroom and picked it up. She heard Marty's voice. "What are you doing? Can I come by?"

"Not today. Clint has me out on an interview at Metro."

"How about tonight? I'll come by and we can go to dinner."

"I'd like that... but, my parents called and they want me to go to their house tonight for dinner... My aunt from Denver is going to be there. I haven't seen her in ages... You understand. Family."

"It seems that I never see you anymore. You were in Palm Springs over the weekend. I couldn't find you last night. Where were you?"

"Oh, I went to see Dorothy. You heard about Geoffery being killed. A terrible tragedy. She's taking it hard."

"When am I going to see you?"

"Tomorrow. Come tomorrow, I'll cook for you. I've got to go. Goodbye, you sweet man, you." She hung up the phone. Complications, always complications. The zing is not there with Marty, but the ZING is there with Luis. The doorbell rang. She took a deep breath. Get hold of yourself, Georgia, he's just a man.

She moved toward the door and opened it. Luis stood with a bunch of red roses.

He's smaller than I remember, she thought.

Luis brought her hand to his mouth to kiss, gazing into her eyes. He handed her the roses.

"They're beautiful. Please, come in. We can walk up to Schwab's drug store. It's on the corner. They have great breakfasts. I'll get my jacket." She went into the bedroom. Luis carefully surveyed the room.

They walked up the street Georgia pointed out places of interest as they walked. "That's the "Garden of Allah", over there."

"I am staying there."

"You are! I love that place. I like to go there and dance. They have a great Latin band. Do you dance?"

"I'm Cuban, we all dance in Cuba. We invented the mambo, the rumba, and the new dance, the cha cha cha. Will you come tonight? You can dance with a real Cuban."

"I'd like that. That tall building across the street. That's the Chateau Marmount. Lots of European movie stars and New York stage stars stay there while they're here making movies. I heard that Greta Garbo... do you know who she is? "I vant to be alone," lives there."

They stood in front of Schwab's. Luis opened the door and they walked in. Everybody goes to Schwab's. Lana Turner supposedly was discovered sitting at the soda fountain. They sat down in a vacant booth, across from the counter. Steve McQueen sat next to them with a couple of girls that were actresses. Georgia recognized Sidney Skolsky, the Hollywood columnist, and waved to him.

He came over to their booth. "Hello, Georgia," he glanced at Luis.

"Hello, Sidney, nice to see you. This is Luis Verano." Luis got up to meet Sidney and then sat down again.

"Luis is a producer-director from Cuba. He wants me to do a picture for him. Enroll Flynn's the star."

"Can I put that in my column?" he asked.

"I'm not set yet. If you don't mind."

"How's Marty? Have you two got any wedding plans?"

"No, Marty is still married," she said, uneasily.

"Good seeing you. Let me know if you do the picture," he said as he left the drug store.

"You are seeing someone?"

"Yes."

"Is it serious?"

"Well, let's say it's sorta steady, but you heard, he's married."

Luis smiled.

"What's so amusing?"

"Then you'll marry me. I have decided."

"Oh, you have, but I just met you."

"You see, you marry me," said Luis.

Georgia felt rattled. She glanced at the menu as her hands shook. What's with these Latin men? They're so direct, so positive. She remembered that her old lover, the Mexican fighter, was that way.

"What are you going to have?" she asked."

"You."

"Luis, please."

Luis kept looking at her, staring. The waitress wrote their order. They both ordered ham and eggs with coffee. Luis started to explain the script to Georgia and what her part would be. When he had gotten halfway into the story, she thought it sounded awful, mediocre. The story was about revolutionary girls, camp followers, following Castro's army. Her part was nothing. When Clint reads the script, he won't let me do it. I'm sure of it, she thought.

The food came. Luis ate his quickly. Georgia picked at hers.

"Well, what do you think, you like it?"

"I know I sound like an actress, but my part is small."

"I can fix. I make it bigger for you. I even pay you twenty-five percent more money than you got for your last picture."

"You really want me to do this picture, don't you?"

"Yes, I want you with me... I have fallen in love with you." Luis took Georgia's hand. Georgia's face flushed. "I want you to be my wife."

"Luis, you know nothing about me."

"Love can be this way. It's fate. You believe in fate?"

"Luis, you're too fast, you really are. You got me thinking crazy." She glanced at her watch. "I've got to go." She got up from the booth. "I have to meet my agent at Metro Golden Mayor. I'm up for an Elvis Presley movie."

"Can I go with you?" he said as he followed her out of Schwab's on to the street.

"I don't think that would be a good idea. My agent might object to you being there. He'll want to know what I'm doing with you. As you know, he doesn't want me to go to Cuba."

They stood and stared at each other on the street.

"You don't have to walk me home."

"We're going to dance tonight?" he asked.

"I'll meet you at nine o' clock, in the bar." She reached up and kissed him on the mouth and left.

Luis stood there staring after her as she walked away down the street.

Georgia arrived at MGM in Culver City. She drove to the main gate in her MG with the top down.

The guard had her name and directed her to Stage Fifteen where Elvis was shooting his new musical.

Georgia had changed her clothes. She wore a bright blue tight sheath dress, cut low in the front. The color matched her blue eyes. Her hair fell around her shoulders. Clint stood waiting outside the stage door when she arrived. Georgia parked her car, and joined him.

"You're absolutely gorgeous, baby. Elvis is going to flip when he sees you."

"Thanks, she said, as Clint opened the stage door for her. They walked into the brightly lit stage. Elvis stood in the center rehearsing a dance number with a big group of dancers and singers in the background. His costume was powder-blue western in style, with white fringes hanging down from the sleeves. The other dancers and singers dressed the same, but Elvis's costume had more glitz.

The part Georgia came to read for was small, but the chance to be in an Elvis Presley picture mattered more than the part. Elvis had to be the biggest star in Hollywood. His pictures made big money. Elvis's entourage of guys made all the work seem like a party.

Georgia and Clint watched the rehearsal from behind the large camera boom, as it moved in on Elvis for the final close up.

A couple of Elvis's boys spotted Georgia and approached her.

"Hi, there pretty girl. You in the picture?" One of them asked.

"Oh, hi, I'm Georgia Evans. I don't know yet. I'm here for an interview," she said.

"You got the part, honey. I'll take a bet on it."

"Oh, are you the producer?"

"Naw, I work for Elvis, and if I know Elvis and I do, he's my country cousin, you got the part."

Elvis had finished the production number. His attention had taken him where Georgia stood on the set talking to one of his guys and walked over to them.

"Elvis, this pretty little girl is Georgia Evans," said the cousin.

"Pleased to meetya." Elvis took Georgia's hand up to his mouth and flicked the tip of his tongue between Georgia's fingers, which raised goose bumps all over her body.

Georgia was taken back by him; she could hardly get words out of her mouth. "It's a... pleasure to meet you, Mr. Presley."

The assistant director came up to Elvis. "Mr. Presley, they're ready to shoot the dance number."

"Thanks, Charlie. Well, pretty girl, don't you go away," he said as he left for the set. He stopped by a man wearing a fedora hat and smoking a cigar and spoke to him as they looked toward Georgia.

Clint recognized the man as the producer, Sam Katzman. Clint said. "You got the part."

"How do you know?" she asked.

"Let's say I'm chalking it up to experience," he said with confidence.

Sam Katzman came over and shook Clint's hand. Clint introduced him to Georgia.

"Elvis told me he wants your little girl here for the part of "Traci, says he knows her work. I'll get back to you tomorrow about the money and billing. It's a nice part for her. Should get her some recognition." He tipped his hat to Georgia and went back to his position on the stage.

"Quiet on the set. Ready to roll." yelled the assistant director. The bright klieg lights switch on. Everyone quieted down. Elvis and the dancers stood in their places. Someone yelled "speed". The director yelled "action" from up on the camera boom. The music started; the dancers went into their routine. It was to be the usual Elvis number with lots of pretty girls dancing around him. Elvis, playing his guitar, sang a country western song in a barnyard set.

"That's a take." said the director.

The crew set up for the next shoot.

Elvis's cousin came over to Georgia after the shot. "Isn't Elvis great? I love my old cousin. He told me to tell you that he's havin' a party tonight at his house. Wants you to all come. Here's his address. He says about nine o' clock," said the cousin as he handed Georgia a small piece of paper.

Georgia stiffened.

"What's the matter? You act like someone said a dirty word. Don't tell me you didn't like what happened here?"

"Of course I did, but I can't go to his party."

"The hell you can't, girl. His party is the most important engagement you have ever had to attend. Do you realize how many girls in this town would trade places with you? What ever you have planned, you're going to cancel. I insist on it."

Georgia was near tears. They left the stage to return to their cars.

When they got outside Clint could see that Georgia had been crying.

"You should be the happiest actress in town, you just got a good part in an Elvis Presley picture, for God's sake. You should be kissing my ass. Shame on you... You're crying. Where have I gone wrong?" Clint threw his hands into the air.

"Clint, I can't tell you now. I'm sorry."

"Georgia, it's one of those situations. "No ticky, no washy." Georgia nodded her head as she got in her car. She looked up at Clint with tear-rimmed eyes.

"I'm sorry, Clint. I can't do it." She started her car and drove toward the gate.

Clint stood in disbelief as she drove away.

Georgia walked in the bar of the "Garden of Allah" at ten after nine that night. She wore a black silk sheath dress with spaghetti straps. It fitted tightly to her curved body. She had her long blonde hair pulled back behind her ear. A large red flower had been pinned behind her left ear. A simple strand of small pearls adorned her neck.

She saw Luis sitting in a corner booth along the bar. He got up to greet her. In her high heels she was taller than he. He kissed her on both cheeks and she sat down. She glanced around the bar and saw how crowded it was. Renè Touzet stood on stage playing the new dance craze, the cha cha cha. The dance floor was packed.

Georgia wanted to tell Luis all about the "Garden of Allah", what a great Hollywood past it had, that Erroll had lived there once, how it had been built by a famous twenties silent screen star, Alla Nazimova, and how Scott Fitzgerald, Humphrey Bogart, Robert Benchely, Dorothy Parker, and Sheila Graham, to name a few, had partied, got drunk and lived it up there. She had heard this information from Marty, who knew all about Hollywood history, but she couldn't tell Luis now, because of all the noise.

The music got them up to dance. By their first few steps they moved ideally on the dance floor. Before they realized it, the other dancers had stopped to watch them dance, as if they had been dancing for years. Georgia had learned to dance to the Latin beat from her past lover. They had danced in the clubs around East Los Angeles before she called it quits. She thought she loved the Mexican, but she found out he had too many girlfriends. She wondered if Luis would be like that. How was she to know? It was a Latin male trait, she thought. She and Luis moved their bodies around the floor the entire evening. Georgia couldn't remember when she had danced better and felt better in a man's arms. She was falling in love with Luis and falling hard.

They left the "Garden of Allah" and walked back to Georgia's apartment.

"What about doing the picture? I hope it's yes," he said.

"I have to work out a few personal things before I can give you a definite answer. I'm hopeful."

"You have made me happy. Everything is going to change in my country. We can get married at my father's *finca*. You will like my family and they will adore you. *O, mi amor*, I love you." He reached over to kiss her and she responded to him.

Their lovemaking brought them together in unity as they explored their bodies and their souls throughout the night and by morning they had cemented a relationship that would last for a lifetime.

TEN

Clint's bright red 140 Jaguar roadster swung into Thorton North's curved driveway and parked under an expansive portico. As he buzzed the front door, a bright light flashed on and a tiny television camera focused on him.

A cheery black maid opened the door.

"Hello, Mister Clint. Mr. North is in his office."

"Thanks Maisie. Is Marge home?"

"No, she's out shopping". Maisie left for the kitchen.

Clint went behind the bar and fixed himself vodka. He peered out to the expansive view of Los Angeles and Beverly Hills below as Thorton entered and sat at a tool at the bar.

"Hello, Thorton, what will you have?"

"Fix me a double." Clint thought Thorton looked sober so he fixed him a weak scotch. He watched Thorton pick up the drink and gulp it down.

"What kind of calf piss is this?" asked Thorton as he pushed the glass back for more.

"Thorton, are you racing in Havana?"

"Yes, we're getting the Ferrari ready. I've been on the phone with Havana. I got a couple of suites at The Nacional. We can watch the race from our balcony. Don't have to go near the damn track".

"I'm going too. My client, Marty Fallon, has a club date at Meyer Lansky's Riviera, and Fangio's racing. That I gotta see".

"Make me another double." Thorton pushed his empty glass toward Clint. "A little girl Jimmy introduced me to has been calling. I told her to come up."

"Do you think that's wise with Marge here?"

83

"Hell, she'll never know."

"I wouldn't be so sure about Marge"

They heard the door latch open and Marshall, Thorton's business manager, walked in. His open shirt revealed lots of gold around his neck; a chunky gold watch hung from his wrist and a heavy linked gold bracelet on the other.

Gifts from Marge, thought Clint.

"Marshall, I'm glad you're here. Thorton is about to call one of his whores. Talk him out of it. You can't fool Marge."

"Clint's right. Wait till we get to Cuba. I'll get you all the whores you want down there," said Marshall.

"Hell, I woke up this morning with this big throbbing hard on. It won't go away. I even put on the air-conditioner," said Thorton as he got up and left the room.

"We're in for it," said Clint.

"I'm leaving," said Marshall.

"No, you're not. It could be fun," said Clint.

When the doorbell rang, Clint yelled out, "I'll get it, Maisie. It's for me." Clint made his way to the front door. He checked the monitor and saw a young girl and let her in.

"Hi, I'm Shirley," said the blonde as she extended her hand. She was sexy, about twenty with big breasts and a cinched small waist. She wore a black and white large polka dot dress, open in the front. A young Mae West, thought Clint. "I'm Clint," he said. Thorton is in his room. Follow me."

He opened the door to Thorton's bedroom. Thorton sat on the large bed in a pair of long boxer shorts looking like he had just gotten out of a concentration camp. His stick legs were crossed as he peered into a glass of scotch. Clint knew the white plastic dish placed by his feet was used for spit and vomit.

"Hello Mr. North," the girl said. "I'm Shirley, remember?"

"Why sure, honey. Sit down next to me. I want to tell you a story." he said. Shirley sat down.

"Thorton, why don't you and Shirley go to the office? SOMEBODY will be here soon. Have you forgotten?"

"Now that's a pregnant thought. Why didn't I think of it?" said Thorton as he pushed himself to his feet while Shirley steadied him.

Clint called into the bar. "Marshall, go to the kitchen and keep Maisie busy. I don't want her to see Shirley." Marshall went off to the kitchen.

"Thorton, you lead the way," said Clint.

"Clint, you're such a good friend," he said as he moved slowly toward the rear of the house.

Shirley stayed back and pulled Clint aside. "Is he okay? He's a no-go to me."

"You're in for a big surprise," said Clint.

"What's that mean?" she asked.

"You be the judge."

Shirley was puzzled and caught up with Thorton and followed him into the office.

"Honey", said Thorton. "Did I tell you, you're the best looking piece of poontang I ever did see?"

Shirley closed the door behind them.

Clint went back to the bar and poured himself a big drink. Marshall came in from the kitchen.

"The last hooker he had here he wouldn't pay. So she cleaned the steaks out of the deep freeze before she left," said Marshall.

"You mean he does this all the time?"

"Yeah, but never with Marge in the house."

The sound of a latchkey in the front door was heard followed by Marge's entrance. She was dressed in a light green silk Pucci top with bright fuchsia slacks. Her white blonde hair was done up in a smart do.

"Why Clint, I didn't know you'd be here. Will you stay for dinner? I picked up some divine lobsters at Jurgensen's. Where's Thorton?" she asked, as she glanced into the living room for him.

"He's around, isn't he, Marshall?" asked Clint uncomfortably.

"Look!" She put her hand forward to show off a large diamond ring. "Thorton bought me this for my birthday. The girls at Saks just died when they saw it."

"I don't blame them, its a queen's ransom," said Clint.

"I wanted to go on this cruise to New Zealand, but Thorton thought it was too expensive; I'm sure this ring cost a lot more. Anyway, we're going to Havana, have you heard?"

"I'm going too," said Clint.

"How divine! We'll have so much fun. Fix me a drink. I'll tell

Maisie you'll be staying for dinner," said Marge as she left the bar and went into Thorton's room on her way to the kitchen.

Clint poured himself another strong drink.

A few minutes later Marge was back. She picked up her drink. She stared at Clint and then Marshall suspiciously.

"I went by the office. The door is locked. I smell whore!"

Clint and Marshall exchanged looks.

"I've got to go." Marshall said getting up to leave.

"You're staying right here," said Marge. "Thorton has a whore here, doesn't he?"

Clint and Marshall said nothing.

"I knew it. That dirty old man has brought a whore into my house. That horrible creature." She moved fast and left the room for the office.

Clint and Marshall could hear her pounding on the door with her fists.

Clint worried she might hurt herself or have a heart attack.

"I know you're in there you dirty old man," she yelled. "Let me tell you. You're going to stay there. I'm going to sit in front of this door. I don't care how long it takes. I'll stay here all night if I have to. There's no bathroom in there and no windows. You're going to start stinking soon. How's that going to go over with your whore, you old bastard?" Marge came away from the door exhausted. She went to the terrace and picked up a chair and brought it to the door and planted it. Clint joined her. Marshall had disappeared.

"The years I have put up with that old sonofabitch. All the horrible things he's done to me. I saved his life many a time. I spent years watching out for him. Saw to it that he had proper care when he'd go on a drunk. I kept him alive through it all. I'm so mad I could spit." She sat in the wrought-iron chair.

Clint handed her a fresh drink. "Marge, this incident could work out for you".

"What the hell does that mean?"

"You've never had Thorton in a more compromising position."

"Yes," she said interested.

"You can take that cruise to New Zealand. See your sea-captain friend. Who knows, you might just stay."

"What would I do for money? Thorton had me sign a quitclaim

deed on all his property. I'm screwed."

"Here's your opportunity. Get a blank check. Write it for a hundred thousand dollars, paid to you. Push it under the door for his signature. If he signs, you'll let him out."

"Why didn't I think of that?" She asked excitedly.

"You're too upset."

"Do you think he'll do it?"

"Does he have a choice?"

Marge went into the house and returned with a check and a pen. She wrote out the amount and pushed the check under the door.

"Thorton, you dirty old man, the only way you and your whore are getting out is to sign that check. This will teach you, you old bastard, to honor my home." Marge started to settle down with her fresh drink.

"You know, I was the best-looking girl in town. Used to walk around with a walking stick. Every one thought I was eccentric. Thorton was the richest boy in town and was crazy about me. We used to have a lot of fun, did a lot of drinking though; you could say we still do. I was nineteen when I married him. He was twenty. He had this red Buick convertible. Now that I think back, I married him for his car."

"Look, Marge, the check." The check had been pushed back from under the door.

"Is it signed?" she asked. Clint picked it up.

"Yep," he said. Marge got up from her chair and went to the door.

"Thorton you old fool. I'm going in and get ready for dinner. You get that whore out of here, or this time I really am leaving for good." Clint and Marge left for the main house. Marge stormed to her bedroom and Clint went to the phone to call a cab for Shirley.

A cab drove under the portico. Clint was outside waiting. Marge went to the kitchen checking on dinner when Shirley ran by the window. Marge saw her and raced to the front door to accost her. Snarling she said, "Does your mother know you're a whore? How could you do it with... with... that dirty old man?" Suddenly Marge became aware of Thorton who stood at the front door looking ridiculous in his baggy shorts.

"What do you say to yourself when you look in the mirror?" asked Marge of the girl.

"Have you looked in the mirror yourself lately, lady?" said Shirley as she got into the back seat.

The cab and drove off just in time, thought Clint.

Marge walked back to the house and took a swing at Thorton with her fist. "You, you... dirty old man." Thorton took a step backward to miss Marge's fist and fell to the floor. Marge lost her balance and fell in the opposite direction. Clint went to help Marge to her feet. At first he thought she was crying, but realized she was laughing, hysterically. Thorton started to laugh too, and so did Clint.

Maisie walked in and in her cheery voice said, "Dinner is served."

ELEVEN

Dorothy felt it was about time to find a husband. She dated the cream of Hollywood's eligible. Producers, directors, a major star or two, playing the field. At the same time Nathan Wise had become stronger in her life. She leaned on him for strength and his good advice. Nathan's personality had to control, so he introduced her to Morris Marsh, a man he did business with from the east coast.

Morry was attractive, in his late thirties. He wore tailored clothes and worked out in his gym at a newly acquired Beverly Hills house. Morry had gotten divorced from his childhood sweetheart and moved to California to start a new life and to play. He liked the sun and arranged his business meetings around his pool, where he would sit with a silver sun reflector tilted in his face. He fell hard for Dorothy, his first movie star. Her image on his arm around town gave him the look he needed for his ego.

After their first date, he had a white Rolls Royce convertible delivered to her garage. After getting used to driving the new car, Dorothy wondered when she would get the California ownership registration in her name. The document never arrived. She could have fallen for him, but she discovered he was cheap and a bull shitter; the car was leased. She realized why Nathan had introduced her to Morry; it had to be one of his control games he liked to play on her.

Nathan had set up a corporation to build and to buy hotels and casinos in Las Vegas. He brought in Morris Marsh to front for him and his syndicate. The gaming commission checked Morry's past with a sieve. Morry's background was on the fringes. He had done business with members of the underworld, buying some of their interests and turning them into moneymakers.

Nathan arranged for Morry to front the points in the casinos for Meyer Lansky and his group. Lansky could not be listed as a casino owner because the Nevada law stated you could not own points in a casino if you owned one in Havana.

Dorothy, through Nathan, was able to acquire a block of stock in the corporation and a hidden half-point in the casino at a low price.

The corporation had acquired eleven acres on the Strip in Las Vegas. The action had moved out in that direction since the Flamingo started the trend. Nathan and his group started building the El Dorado, the world's largest hotel and casino. The hotel consisted of eight hundred rooms plus fifty high rollers' suites. Never had so many fine restaurants been in one hotel: a steak house, French gourmet, Oriental, and Italian all under one roof. The casino, the world's largest, was to be state of the art with a showroom to seat twelve hundred guests. Danny Kaye had been booked to open the Desert High Room. A French nude revue had been booked to open the lounge. The Paris act had never been seen before in the United States. The publicity hype was extraordinary; everyone looked forward to the opening.

With the success of "The Battered Spouse", Clint had arranged a four-year, million-dollar movie contract for Dorothy with one of the major studios. She would have to make two pictures per year for the studio and could be loaned out to other studios. Dorothy felt secure enough to go house hunting. She found a small, Spanish-style house in the hills overlooking Beverly Hills. She bought it for a hundred thousand. Nathan arranged a large loan with a small interest rate with one of his pension funds. The first thing she did was fill the pantry with canned goods because of her actress insecurities. She had been collecting cookbooks and had a huge collection from every master chef around the world. She could sit and talk recipes with any expert with authority, but she couldn't cook. But, with her ego she thought she was a gourmet.

After one of her elaborate dinners, attended by nervous guests too polite to say the chicken was raw, only Nathan said, "I can't eat this shit." This brought tears to Dorothy's face and she went to her bedroom to cry. She'd hoped to get an elaborate present from Nathan when he came by again, for her tears.

Dorothy started a new movie at the studio and had finished a scene when she was called to the phone. The assistant told her, her agent was calling. Dorothy picked it up.

"Something has come up. I have to see you."

"Why can't you tell me now?"

"I'd rather not."

"Come to dinner tonight. You haven't seen my new house."

"What time?"

"About 8:00. I'll prepare a dish you'll die for."

"I hope not," he laughed. "See you at 8:00."

Clint stopped by David Jones, the florist, on the way and picked up some flowers. He stood at her front door at eight sharp. Dorothy's maid let him in. Dorothy's decorating was dark and heavy, he thought. Oak paneling, no feeling of individuality, no pictures of herself, which was odd to him. Her English furniture was covered in dark fabrics. The light outside shined bright, but it didn't find its way into the house. It looked like a man's house instead of a glamorous movie star's, but he knew Dorothy must have a reason. Dorothy came into the room. "How's the Million Dollar Baby?" he said giving her a kiss on the cheek. She wore a black turtleneck sweater and black slacks. Clint thought back to when he had seen her in the same outfit. The night she turned him into a burglar, but he thought better than to bring it up.

"I love your expression, the Million Dollar Baby. Money has become important to me now. It must be that I know what I can buy with it. What are you drinking?"

"Scotch and soda."

She poured him a drink. She poured herself some soda water.

"What's so important you have to see me in person?"

"You got troubles. Confidential Magazine has dug up your time in jail. They're going to publish it in their next issue."

"I knew this would happen. It's public record."

"You seem calm about it."

"Well, what do you suggest I do? The timing couldn't be worse. Could it? Confidential is a piece of shit."

"True, but everyone reads it."

"Nathan will handle it. He has juice on those sleaze bags. There seems to be nobody, even Washington, who will stand up to him, which makes him exciting. Wouldn't you say?" Clint nodded.

"I'm seeing him tomorrow. He'll fix it, he always does. He's paranoid about everybody, even me. I think it's time for you to meet him. He could be a big help to you. He finances movies. You could become a producer with him behind you."

"Thanks. You're always thinking of me."

"Why not? Hollywood's an animal's world. We need to stick together to survive. I hear you're going to Havana."

"Yeah, Marty's got a club date at Meyer Lansky's Rivera and the Havana Grand Prix is on, and one of my young actresses, Georgia Evans, is making a movie there, which is a mistake."

"You're her agent, why are you letting he do it?"

"I've been overruled. She's seeing Marty, and sees the trip as some kind of vacation. She'll find out what a location is like in the jungles of Cuba with that drunk Erroll Flynn and some guerrilla leader named Fidel Castro."

"Nathan has asked me to go Havana. He's having some meetings with Meyer Lanksy. I've been having second thoughts about going. But with you there we can play. Come let's have dinner."

Dorothy led Clint into the dining room. A large brass English chandelier hung in the middle over the large oak planked table. Dorothy lit the candles, which warmed the room with a soft light. The table was set with old English ironstone china and the silver was heavy King's Pattern sterling.

Clint's thoughts were on the opportunity she was giving him. Dorothy's taking care of Clint again. He liked that.

The maid brought in oxtail soup. Dorothy served it from a soup tureen and passed it to him.

Clint noticed it was not clear in color. "It's wonderful," he said as he tasted it.

"It better be. It took all afternoon." They finished the soup and the maid brought in medallions of veal. Dorothy served them. When Clint tasted them he could tell they were overcooked. "It tastes great." Dorothy was pleased. The sauce was separated and she had added too much tarragon.

"Clint, I've given you a career and you've become successful. I keep promoting you, I guess it's because I trust you. Or do I still have a thing for you? I could bring you down if you fucked with me."

"What do you want me to say? That I've always known you're my angel? Our relationship, let's say, it's different."

Dorothy smiled. "I have a stock for you. Marsh International Gaming. It's listed on the Exchange. I recommend you buy big. It's selling for forty dollars. In six months it will be one hundred and fifty."

"How do you know?"

"Let's say, I know someone on the inside." "Can I pass it on to my friends?"

"Why not? The more that buy in, the more the stock goes up. You'll be a hero."

When the dessert came Clint was so excited, he thought, if it were horseshit, he would have eaten it. Dorothy dished up the omelet Norwegian and served it.

"It's delicious," he said as he took a large bite, and it was.

After dinner they adjourned to Dorothy's bedroom to watch television. To Clint this room looked the most lived in. It had a large fireplace, a fire was burning. Overstuffed down chairs sat in front of a low marquetry table. Dorothy's bed was king-size and a four-poster. Clint thought it was like the kind of room any man would feel comfortable in. He could take off his shoes, put his feet up on the table, take out a cigar, smoke and relax. Everything was masculine, except for the sheets on the bed. They were white fine cotton with tiny lace embroidery around the borders. Large pillows with tiny lace and small pink bows attached lay puffed up on the bed. The sheets were to be the only feminine touch in the room. Clint settled into one of the large comfortable chairs and Dorothy turned on the television and sat on her bed.

"I like the comfort in your bedroom. Can I take off my shoes?"

"Of course, would you like to smoke a joint?" she asked.

"A joint?"

"Marijuana."

"I've never done it."

"Do you want to try? It's fun. It makes you happy." Clint was skeptical, not sure he wanted to try.

"You sure it won't make me do anything I might regret?"

"Like what?"

"Hell, Dorothy, I don't know. I'm cautious of anything I don't know about."

"I didn't bring you in here to have you to do anything that you don't want to do. Three of your senses will come alive. You'll laugh, you'll feel horny and you'll die for something sweet. Save the horniness for someone else. I'm not interested."

"Why? You always wanted to get it on with me before. Have I become ugly, or have bad breath or something?"

"Sweetheart, you're the same unspoiled handsome cowboy I met at that old bag's house, but times have changed for both of us. We had a good time together, but we can't go back even if it's for a fast orgasm."

"That's a shitty way to look at the past. I'm disappointed. Where's the marijuana?"

Dorothy went into her closet and came out with a rolled marijuana cigarette. She picked up a book of matches by the fireplace and lit it, took a long drag, and handed it to Clint.

Clint examined it and then put it in his mouth and took a drag. Dorothy watched him as he inhaled. His eyes started to tear as he handed back the joint. Dorothy took a drag. They both settled down. Dorothy on her bed and Clint in the chair.

Clint peered around the room and said. "You know...this has got to be the most comfortable room in town....What would you do if one of these old farts you entertain would have a coronary while he visited. What would you do?"

Dorothy got up from her bed, gave him the joint and went into her closet and came back out wheeling a large cylinder tank of oxygen. "A girl has just GOT to be prepared," she said in a cute way. Clint started to laugh and laugh and couldn't stop. He grabbed his stomach; it hurt. Dorothy watched him and began to laugh too. She fell over on to her bed laughing and couldn't stop. Finally they quieted down.

Clint said. "What have you got that's sweet?"

"How about a big piece of chocolate mousse cake?"

"The thought gives me an orgasm," said Clint.

Dorothy got up and went into the kitchen.

Clint felt horny. He yelled to Dorothy.

"Can I use your phone?"

"Go ahead!" she yelled back from the kitchen.

Clint picked up the phone and dialed. "Hi, it's Clint. What's going on? Are you busy? There was a pause. "Can I stop by? I just did something I've never done before." Pause "I can't tell you over the phone. I'll see you in thirty minutes. Bye." He hung up the phone as Dorothy entered the bedroom with two big slices of cake.

She handed one to Clint who dived into it. "Who was it you called?"

"Tana Williams"

"The black actress?"

"Yes. Do you know her?"

"We've worked on a picture. What is it with you guys? You get horny and the first thing you do is call a black girl. You're not from the south, what makes you think they're a better fuck?"

"I never thought of it that way. You sound like you're pissed off. You asked me who I called."

Dorothy's phone rang. She picked it up.

"Hello. Hi darling. Can you hold for a minute?" She put the phone on hold. "I got to take his call. It's Nathan. Remember what I told you. Let yourself out. I'll see you in Havana."

As Clint drove down the hill, he couldn't help think of what an ego Dorothy had. She's a bitch, he thought. She has changed but not for the better. I wonder if I've changed too?

TWELVE

Georgia gazed out the porthole window of the DC7 airplane as it banked for a landing. She could see the green covered mountains emerging from the fluffy meringue-shaped clouds in the distance. The sun had set in the west over the violet and blue tropical sea as they made their descent into Port-au-Prince, Haiti. Going through Haiti was the only way for them into Cuba because of the tight security there. French was spoken here, but no one in their party spoke a word. When they left the plane they could smell the smoke burning from humid tropical fires amid the exotic fragrant flowers.

Jake, their cameraman, gave the customs man some money under the table for passing the camera equipment.

A man approached Luis when they walked into the small corrugated-metal-roofed air terminal. He was dressed in olive green fatigue pants and shirt with a matching hat. He started speaking Spanish, waving his hands, obviously telling Luis something he wanted to hear.

Luis brought the man over to be introduced. *"Es la Senora Evans, Senores Flynn Y Jake permitar presentar al Senor Alfonso, un fidelista,"* said Luis.

"Mucho gusto," said Alfonso and took some of their luggage.

Erroll peered around. "Where's el bar, old boy?" he said to Alfonso. *"No se Sr. Flynn, no hay tiempo, ahora vamos."*

"The hell with you, old boy. I want a drink and I'm going to have one." Erroll looked inside of the terminal and saw the bar at the end of the building. He walked up to the bartender.

"Dos Remy Martin, Dos," he said and held up two fingers. The bartender took the bottle of Remy Martin and poured him a double.

"Aqui" The bartender was confused. Erroll realized that he didn't speak Spanish, so he motioned him to leave the bottle. Erroll was contented.

Jake approached. "Jake, thank God you speak Spanish, old boy. What's this Alfonso say?"

"We have to leave right away. It will take all night to reach Cuba. There's a boat waiting for us at a private inlet up the coast, fifty miles from here. A two-hour drive." Erroll pulled a wad of U.S. bills out of his pocket and laid them on the bar. He picked up the bottle of Remy Martin and followed Jake out of the terminal. The waiting car was packed with luggage and camera equipment, so Luis arranged for a cab to follow.

After two hours of bad roads, mule-drawn carts, pigs in the streets, old trucks, broken-down cars and bicycles, they pulled onto a deserted beach with palm-frond-covered roofs of shacks along the shore. Dusk shone its last light as they peered at a twenty-five foot fishing boat anchored close to shoreline.

"I hope we're not getting on that tub, " said Erroll as he left the cab. He watched the boat as a black man brought a small dingy to shore. It took two loads to get them aboard. Erroll surveyed the small craft. It had a marine diesel with a center mast with sail. He went below and saw the cabin with four bunks, two on each side and a small table.

"There's no frills, but it's safe," he said when he came back on deck. Georgia was concerned.

"Will we fit on this little boat?" she asked.

"It's going to be tight, but we'll make it. I know a lot about boats. I've owned a few in my time. These old fishing boats are built to take rough seas, most of the time they're safer than a fast cruiser. Don't you worry your pretty little head, darling," he said.

Georgia felt reassured. She glanced at Luis who smiled at her. She held on to him as he helped her into the cabin. The others got aboard and Erroll became captain of the ship as they made their way out to sea.

Erroll knew boats, all right. It was small for comfort, but it would get them there. Erroll could tell the boat operator had a lot of experience, but he spoke French. The sea was calm and the swells were small. Erroll knew this part of the world, for he had sailed these seas in his schooner, the Sirocco, which he kept in Jamaica. They would be traveling on the windward side of Cuba, so when the winds came up it could prove to be rough. The swells could grow to a two-story building.

Georgia started off the trip in the cabin, but came up on deck. "I get seasick down there. I need fresh air," she said.

"It's a wonderful night, darling. Go up front and sit on the cabin roof," said Erroll.

"I hate the ocean, and I hate sailing. I always get seasick, but worst of all I imagine all kinds of black awful creatures down there waiting for me. I'm scared to death. I could be in Hawaii with Elvis, living in a four-star hotel having a driver pick me up and take me to the set. Look where love has put me. I'm sorry, Erroll, I don't want to sound spoiled, but I'm frightened."

"I understand, dearheart, when we get to Cuba, everything will be fine. I hope," said Erroll.

Georgia called down to the cabin. "Luis, Luis come on deck. Come, hold me."

Luis had been checking the camera equipment with Jake. He came up on deck. Georgia moved to hold on to the mast. When he got to her she was crying. He lay down next to her and held her.

"Luis, Oh, Luis, I'm frightened. Hold me."

"My darling, please don't cry, mi amor." He kissed her on the forehead and the cheeks.

She peered up at the black sky, with its millions of bright flashing beams, as the soft tropical wind dried her tears. She felt this overwhelming urge to have him.

Erroll watched from the stern of the boat as he kept on course. Georgia rolled over on the top of Luis. Erroll motioned to the boatman to take the wheel. The wind had come up and filled the sails. He called down in the cabin. "Hey Jake, can you give me a hand with the sail?"

"I'll be right up." Jake climbed out of the cabin and untied the rope that wrapped around the sail. He pulled on the halyard that hoisted the spinnaker and secured it. A soft wind filled the billowing sail and the boat moved ahead on course.

Erroll went below. He opened his handbag and brought out a hypodermic. He pulled up his pants leg and injected himself in the leg. By the expression on his face, he got instant gratification.

They sailed all night. A freighter crossed their path in the early morning. It came close enough to throw them around in its wake. Georgia, who had gotten used to the motion of the waves, had gone below to sleep on one of the bunk beds. The freighter's wake threw her from her bunk against the mast, bruising her leg and arm. Luis, who was on watch, rushed down to the cabin, reassured her and explained what had happened. She glanced at Erroll who slept in the bunk across from her, still in a deep sleep undisturbed by the incident.

Their boat sailed into a small fishing village east of Santiago de Cuba. It was an arid part of Cuba, because of the high mountains. Cactus grew instead of tropical plants. The village was deserted when they docked. Most of the villagers were working up in the hills where they raised sugar cane, Alfonso told Luis.

Alfonso went ashore to make contact with the rebels for the journey into the mountains.

The wardrobe for the movie was simple: olive green fatigues. Georgia tried on the fatigue hat to hide her long blonde hair. Being a blonde in this part of Cuba would be like carrying an American flag.

Alfonso returned to the boat. He escorted three mules with burlap bags on their backs. He opened the bag, which contained peasant clothes: straw hats, white shirts, denim pants, leather belts and crude leather sandals. He spoke to Luis in Spanish giving him instructions. "Get into these clothes to make the trip. The army is very close." Luis picked up an outfit and gave it to Georgia. He also gave one to Erroll, who was reluctant. Georgia went below to change. Jake wrapped the camera and film in burlap sacks. They were ready for their journey into the mountains.

With their new wardrobes, they assumed the role of peasants who had come in from the sugarcane fields. They helped each other off the boat. Jake, with Alfonso's help, loaded camera and film into the mule packs. They covered the equipment with the raw sugarcane and started to leave the village in a caravan. Georgia adjusted her straw hat.

"How do I look?" she asked Erroll.

"Like a Cuban doll, my love."

Georgia laughed. "Erroll, you always know what to say. Have you heard how long we are going to be with these mules?"

"I understand we will be picked up by a vehicle as soon as we get out of this village. These outfits are supposed to camouflage us for the time being. Christ it's hot. I'll be glad when we get up in the mountains where it's cooler," he said.

As they proceeded up a narrow dirt road outside the village, they were approached by a platoon of Cuban soldiers. Georgia started to panic at the sight of them.

"Keep your head down. Stay behind the mules," said Erroll.

The troops passed without incident. They were tired and beat. A few soldiers walking in the rear of the platoon were wounded. Georgia's heart beat fast. She felt like she might faint. She held onto the mule for support. Luis saw her condition and walked up beside her and took her hand. With his reassurance, everything came back in focus.

They started up a steep forested canyon. From the top of the canyon, sentries of the fidelistas gazed down, their guns sighted on the procession.

"How far are we from Castro headquarters?" yelled Erroll. Jake, Luis and a tall gaunt-looking man approached him.

"This is Captain Guzman, of the fidelistas," said Jake.

"*Mucho gusto, Sr. Flynn. Soy ran aficionado et VD.*"

"What's he say?" asked Erroll.

"He told me that we are about five miles down river from Castro's headquarters. The bad news is, we're going to have to continue by mule. The road is bombed out," said Jake.

Erroll looked for Georgia and yelled. "Get me the brandy. I put it in the pack on one of those mules." He asked Jake. "Did he say how the war was going?"

"They're winning. More and more of Batista's army are surrendering every day."

Georgia returned with the bottle of brandy. Erroll took it, drinking big gulps.

"Better get going. I can't believe that I have to ride one of those beasts, but it's better than walking."

With the help of one of the rebels Erroll got on the back of the mule. Georgia was helped onto the other.

Captain Guzman and his troops led the way through the dense tropical forest. Overhead, the sound of airplanes could be heard. They stopped and waited. The forest was so thick that they could hear the planes but not see them.

"Don't fret. They can't see us either," said Erroll.

"Erroll, I know why I'm here, I fell in love with Luis. But you? Why? " said Georgia.

Erroll nursed the bottle of brandy. "It goes back a long time to the civil war in Spain. I had gone there and gave my support to the Fascist cause. Ernest Hemingway was there, also, writing articles on the war. He wrote some disparaging stories about me, and I have never forgot them."

"What does that have to do with your being here chasing after Castro?"

"Hemingway lives in Cuba, but he's ignored Castro. He's stupid. He doesn't see what a great hero Castro is. He's in his backyard and can't see the forest for the trees. The Hearst papers are to publish my stories on Castro, and the world will see what a great man he is. A true champion of his people, fighting for their revolution, and for a better Cuba. Old Ernest will look bad for kissing Batista's ass, and I will have my revenge." Georgia smiled to herself, Erroll's ego has taken us here, she thought.

They approached the village of Palma Soriana, on a plateau in the foothills. Captain Guzman told Luis that they had almost driven the Batista Army from Orient Providence.

"A great feat, Senor, when you think we only had a small force of about three hundred men and Batista's Army had ten thousand troops with air power and artillery," he said.

Erroll, Georgia, and Luis and party entered the village. They rode to an abandoned sugar mill. They were told it was Castro's new head-quarters. Castro, Celia, his mistress, and some of his commanders came out to greet them. Luis rushed to greet him. They hugged and kissed each other's cheeks.

Castro and his group stood dressed in olive green fatigues and fatigue hats. Castro, a tall gaunt man with a full beard, made an impression on Georgia. It was his intense manner. She studied Celia, a small woman with passionate, dark, intelligent eyes. She wore no makeup, and her blouse pockets were stuffed with papers. Celia came to Georgia and helped her off her mule. Communication became a problem; neither spoke the same language, so they stared at each other and smiled.

Luis introduced Erroll and Jake to Castro who introduced everyone to his commanders.

Castro escorted Erroll, Luis and Jake into his headquarters and Celia took Georgia to a tent that would be her home for the stay.

The sugar mill was cavernous. Guns that had been captured from the Cuban army stood stacked in large quantities along the walls. They sat down at the far end of the room and Erroll explained, through Luis, what he came for: about the articles for the Hearst newspapers and the movie that he wanted to shoot. He told Castro that he would like to start shooting in the morning and that he needed some girls from his army to cast in his picture.

Castro was agreeable to all of this, but he wanted to read the script that evening with the help of Luis to see if there could be something in its contents that would offend his cause. Erroll agreed.

Luis stayed with Castro. Erroll went to the tent he was assigned. He had gotten hold of a bottle of rum. He wasn't heard from until the next morning.

When Luis had finished his meeting with Castro, he joined Georgia in their tent. Georgia had taken off her peasant costume and was in panties and bra trying to cool off when Luis entered. He took her in his arms and kissed her, whispering in her ear. She fell back on the cot with Luis on top of her. Their bodies ran with perspiration as they clung to each other. She opened her legs as he entered her, moving fast within her body. She grabbed his shoulder and pulled him down, pulling him deeper inside her. It was like an explosion when he came. She yelled his name as she climaxed. They lay together not wanting to part. Their minds came back to their surrounding as the light dimmed around them.

Luis sat up and said. "Mi corrosion, Fidel, he want me to fly to Venezuela for him."

"When?"

"In the morning."

"You're going to leave me here? I'm going with you."

"No, my darling, you no go. It's too dangerous. Even for me. I am going to bring back money, arms and supplies for Fidel so he can finish the war."

"Why can't he send someone else? Why you? He must have others he can trust." Georgia started to cry. "I don't know what I will do if you leave. I can't depend on Erroll. He's drunk or out of it. Please, Luis, don't leave me here," she started sobbing and held on to him.

He pushed her back and gazed in her eyes. "I am sorry, mi amor, but you have to understand. People like me and Fidel, we have a cause. The cause comes first above anything. Loved ones... our family... our life is always second to the cause. I am the only one Fidel has now who can do this mission. I know the contact personally in Venezuela. This trip is crucial for the cause. It could end the war. Do you understand?" he pleaded.

Georgia said nothing. She continued to sob into her pillow.

Erroll operated better in the early morning before he got drunk. He already had a line of Cuban girls in front of his tent, casting. The girls giggled and laughed among themselves. Erroll did what he learned in Hollywood, getting the girls out of their clothes so he could see their bodies. For this picture their figures were not important. Erroll knew, but the girls didn't, so he was having fun.

Luis had left Georgia's cot while she still slept. He went to Erroll's tent.

"Fidel is sending me on a mission this morning. I don't know when I will return," said Luis.

"You can't do that to me," Erroll protested. "You're the director, old boy. You can't abandon me. It's not kosher. It's just not done. I'll put the word out on you. You won't be able to get a job in a gunpowder factory. I'm a big deal in Hollywood. Hell, I'm a big deal all over the world. Everybody has heard of Erroll Flynn. This is not Al Zugsmith you're dealing with."

"I am sorry, Erroll. Fidel needs me to do this mission. Fidel is my comrade".

"What's this comrade shit? Are you a Commie? For Christ's sake. I hate Commies." Erroll's face went red with rage. He wiped the sweat with a scarf. Then they heard the sound of a helicopter approaching as they left the tent. The chopper hovered low and made a landing in the clearing.

Castro and Celia came out of the sugar mill. Luis ran to them. Together they walked toward the helicopter.

Georgia left her tent and ran to Luis. "Luis, Luis, wait for me," she yelled crying. Luis stopped and she ran into his arms. Tears ran down her checks. "Oh, Luis I love you so." She kept kissing him and holding on to him. "Say you love me. Please say it."

"I love you, mi amor. I will be back soon. I promise," he said gazing into her teary, red-rimmed eyes. Luis left her side and hugged Fidel and Celia and climbed into the chopper. It took off low over the trees and disappeared.

Erroll went into a funk. Everything was distasteful. The food, the water, the location, the film, the ugly women. Nothing pleased him. He proceeded to get drunk and stayed drunk.

Castro sent for him, but he was too drunk to respond. Jake tried to keep everything together, but it was impossible. Castro wasn't happy about the script. Some of the scenes bothered him and he wanted them changed, but Erroll remained too drunk to discuss them. Not one foot of film had been shot.

In the meantime the war kept going on around them. Rebel troops came in and out of the camp. The makeshift hospital was filled with casualties. A temporary prisoners' compound had been set up to take care of the Cuban Army troops that had been surrendering. The local farmers brought in food supplies to take care of the logistics of the large population.

Georgia had come down with depression the moment Luis left. Besides feeling sorry for herself, she saw the film going nowhere. She stopped by the camp hospital and volunteered to help. After seeing all that needed to be done, she forgot her problems, and threw her energy into caring for the wounded.

A few days after Luis had left the camp, with no word from him, Celia and Jake entered the tent hospital. Celia asked one of the nurses who passed them in the entrance where Georgia was and she pointed to the operating room in the back of the tent. When they peered in they found her assisting the doctor, working over a young man on the operating table. Blood was everywhere. The boy had a deep shrapnel wound that had torn open his chest and side. It was gruesome, but Georgia stood next to the doctor, handing him clamps and bandages as if she were a professional nurse. Jake was amazed by her performance. She looked up and saw them standing in the doorway and acknowledged their presence. She continued to assist the doctor in removing the shrapnel and cleaning and closing up the wound. Then she cleaned up and came outside to join them. She noticed the expression in their eyes. "It's Luis, isn't it? Something has gone wrong."

"We got word. His helicopter was shot down into the sea somewhere near Guantanamo," said Jake.

Celia moved close to comfort her. Georgia said nothing. Celia tried to get her to sit down, but Georgia refused. She gazed at them steadily.

"He's alive. I know it."

"Georgia, they said no survivors," said Jake.

Georgia went to her tent. She remained through dinner. Jake brought a tray of food, but she didn't touch it. Normally when she would lie down after her day at the hospital she'd fall into a deep sleep, but that night she could hear the many noises of the camp: dogs barking, soldiers marching, motor vehicles coming and going, women's laugher coming from their quarters, music blaring out from the tents as the smell of pungent smoke from the camp fires drifted into her tent. She wondered how she ever slept before. She turned and turned in her cot, her thoughts on Luis. She could see his image smiling at her.

When she went back to the hospital in the morning, it was like Luis was with her as she went about helping the casualties. It was a difficult task, taking care of the wounded. She changed their bandages and assisted in the operating room. The time passed quickly, and it kept her from dwelling on Luis.

Erroll was impossible. He remained drunk, but he and Castro finally had their meeting about the script. Castro objected to a major sequence. He wanted it changed and Erroll refused. Luis wasn't around to negotiate, so Erroll and Jake were not permitted to film. They would have to do the filming in Jamaica.

Castro wanted Erroll out of the camp. He couldn't tolerate his behavior, but he was very attentive to Georgia. He marveled at her strength. He told his commanders she was a great example to them and their revolution. Castro couldn't believe that Georgia could be an American. They weren't supposed to be like that. Erroll, he called a *"yanqui"*, but Georgia was *"Matama Rubia."*

United Press correspondent Roger Ganz had arrived at the camp to interview Castro and report to the world on the progress of the war.

There were stories in the newspapers in the United States that Castro was a Communist and Che Guerrva, one of his top commanders who had joined Castro from Bolivia, was a known Marxist.

Castro told Gans that the Eisenhower administration had been covertly arming the Batista army for resistance. He wanted world pressure to be put on this administration. He said that Mexico and other Latin countries were going to protest over the U.S. intervention.

Roger Ganz and his photographer, Philip, stayed for two days. Jake talked Roger into taking Georgia with them when they left for Guantanamo. It was a small chopper and it could only carry three people with the pilot. Erroll and Jake had to stay until other arrangements could be made for them.

Early the next morning after the United Press crew had arrived, a lone airplane strafed the camp. Erroll had been hit by a bullet that ricocheted off an old jeep parked by his tent. He was taken to the hospital where they discovered it was just a skin wound and he was patched up and sent back to his tent. It could not have been a better opportunity for him with the press there. They shot pictures of his wound for the world. He wanted to let his fans know not only was he a hero in the movies, but in real life.

Georgia had changed. She wasn't the same woman as she was before she came to Cuba with Luis. She had found strength in herself though her experiences. She thought it had be a fast lesson in growing up. She felt she would hear again from Luis, even though all the reports she had gotten were of his demise.

Roger Ganz told her that she could leave with them in the morning for Guantanamo. Georgia was worried. She was in her sixth week without her period and she felt she had to be pregnant. She had nausea in the morning, and all the symptoms. The thought of having an abortion was out of the question. Her religious background would never allow for that. Thinking over her options, she had a plan and she was ready to put it to work.

THIRTEEN

Clint arrived in Havana and saw and felt danger everywhere he went. He was told that Castro and his rebels were in the hills in eastern Cuba, but the people who sympathized with him were underground throughout the island, especially Havana, where sporadic gunfire could be heard.

Thorton and Marge North with their party checked in at the Nacional, Havana's old world hotel and casino. It stood ten stories on a rocky cliff overlooking the bay and the Spanish fort, Morro Castle, which guarded the entrance to Havana harbor. The hotel was built in the twenties and resembled the Breakers Hotel in Palm Beach. It had been recently refurbished, a casino and a showroom added. The hotel was on a wide boulevard called the Malecon that ran along the sea wall, where the car race would be staged.

Clint took a walk down the Malecon, in front of his hotel, the Riviera. The streets were alive with activity. The city was preparing for the race. Grandstands had been put up at the turns in front of the American Embassy, next to the Nacional. He watched as hay bales were assembled in the corners to protect the drivers if they were forced off the course. Flags of the countries whose cars and drivers were race entries hung along the course and in front of the buildings around the city. The Cuban military stood everywhere, their rifles and machine guns strapped to their sides in anticipation of rebel activity.

The Norths moved into two suites of rooms on the top floor of the hotel. They could open the high French doors and get a magnificent view of the harbor and the Malecon below. They had stopped first in Miami at the new Fountainbleau Hotel where Thorton had gotten drunk. Marge had Marshall send for Jimmy, Thorton's nurse, so she wouldn't have to worry about him. She knew he would be in no condition to go anywhere. This part of traveling Marge hated. Almost always when she joined Thorton on his racing circuit she would end up staying with him in the room. He would get drunk and order room service and never go anywhere. She could have stayed at home and had a better time. She always complained, but nothing much changed.

Moe Dalitz, the old bootlegger and gaming operator from Ohio, and a group had taken over the casino at the Nacional from Meyer Lansky when Meyer built his new Havana Riviera, a four-hundred forty-room hotel and casino, down the street from the Nacional. "The Marty Fallon Revue" was up in lights on the marquee. Moe was out of town when the Norths arrived, but left one of his top boys, Aaron Jacobs, to look after them with instructions to give them or find them anything they wanted. There was no limit on Thorton's credit.

Aaron, a handsome man in his middle forties, was in charge of the credit at the casino. He had respect from the Cuban employees because he would take no abuse from Presidente Batista's army buddies or his officials. He refused them credit if he had to. Many times they would try to take advantage of their position with Batista and not pay their gambling debts. Rumors linked President Batista as the silent partner of Meyer Lansky, but no one knew for sure. The Presidente would seldom show at the Riviera or be seen in the company of Meyer Lansky, but if Meyer needed any help or had any problem in Havana, it was handled immediately.

In the North suite, the hotel waiters had brought in liqueur, champagne, ice, and set-ups for the bar. The waiters were leaving the suite when Aaron Jacobs arrived at the door.

"Hello. May I come in?" he asked as he peered in the half- closed door. Thorton sat on the sofa talking to Marshall. The French windows stood open, and war sounds came up from the street below. Sirens and gunshots could be heard from over the balcony. Marshall glanced up and saw Aaron in the doorway.

"Come in. We're talking about the qualifying of our racecar tomorrow. Do you like racing?" asked Marshall

"I'm looking forward to it," said Aaron. "It's been a big headache this year. Castro is out to sabotage the race. He wants President Batista to look bad to the media. Who knows what Castro might be planning, but we're ready for him. I came to tell you there'd be armed military in the hallways for security purposes. They don't speak English, but they're for your protection."

Marge entered the room and heard Aaron. "Oh my God, are we to be murdered in our beds?" she asked.

"Nothing is going to happen, Mrs. North. We have the best security," said Aaron, reassuring Marge.

"You always make everything worse than it is, Marge. Quit the dramatics, for Christ sake," said Thorton.

"Listen, Thorton, if I had known guards would be outside my door, I never would have come to Havana. It could ruin everything. I came here to have a good time. Wear some of my gorgeous clothes. Are we going out for dinner?" she asked.

"We're going to see Superman, right Marshall?"

Superman was a black man who did a sex show. He had a large penis and performed an act on the stage for an audience. He was famous in Havana to the Americans. To Castro and his sympathizers, he epitomized what happened to Cuba through corruption and vice of the Batista regime.

"Thorton, I'm not getting dressed to see some dirty show. Why is your mind always in the gutter? You're pure trash." The phone rang and Marge picked it up.

"Hello? Oh, hello, Clint. Let me ask Thorton. I'd love to. "Marty Fallon wants us to come over to the Riviera tomorrow night for his dinner show as his guests. We'll go, won't we? We can have some fun."

"Let's do it," said Marshall, and Thorton nodded his head.

"We'd love to, Oh, there'll be six of us. About ten. Good bye."

"I saw the show opening night. A great show. Marty is funny. He killed me," said Aaron.

"I saw him in Vegas. He made me pee my pants," said Thorton.

"It wasn't Marty, it was the booze you drank. I'm getting dressed. They wear fancy clothes here, and I'm going to show off some of mine. Did you hear that, Papie? You're going to have to put on a black tie."

"Oh, cat piss. Marshall, will I have to get in that monkey suit? You're going have to help me with that friggin bow tie," said Thorton.

Over at Marty Fallon's suite at the Riviera, Marty paced the room as Clint watched.

"I'm already into this joint for twenty G's. Don't you tell me these tables aren't crooked. These guys are stealing the food from my table. I know when I'm being cheated."

"Marty, since Batista put Meyer Lansky in charge of gaming, they've cleaned up their act."

"Bullshit! I know these guys. I worked for them before. They're going to make sure that Marty Fallon leaves the money they're paying me... here. I'll have to borrow from you to get out of this toilet." Marty buried his head in his hands.

"Oh, why did I let Georgia talk me into coming here? My little baby out in that jungle, with that drunk Erroll Flynn. Not one word from her. She could be dead! You hear gunfire out there? And we're in Havana. Can you imagine what it must be like in the jungle with those animals? She's nuts. And so am I to be waiting for her to show. I'd leave tonight if it wasn't for Georgia. You couldn't get me to stay if they paid me a million dollars. I want out of this miserable country."

Sounds of gunfire, sirens, racket and commotion arose from the street. Clint, followed by Marty, went to the glass doors that opened onto a balcony. Military jeeps, wagons and troops moved in the streets below. Sirens wailed, and a roadblock had been put up on the Malecon.

"What the hell is going on down there?" asked Marty. It looks as if we've been invaded. What else could it be?"

Clint went back into the room and turned on the television. A picture of Juan Manuel Fangio appeared on the tube. The announcer reeled off in Spanish.

"What the hell is he saying?" asked Marty.

"It's something about the rebels kidnapping Fangio. He says more bombings and a general strike called. Castro wants to stop the race."

"They'll kidnap me next. I'm a celebrity. Get me body guards, now!"

"You're an American. They wouldn't dare!" said Clint.

"Bullshit! They don't care who you are. I hear this Castro is Communist. I hate commies. Get on the phone. Call security before it's too late. I could be next... You know... I could be the next on the list...to be kidnapped." said Marty.

Jimmy and Tana arrived in Havana early that night. After they left the airport they had a rough time getting through the streets of Havana to the hotel. Roadblocks everywhere. Soldiers stopped them and asked for identification numerous times. Neither spoke Spanish. Finally they arrived at the Nacional in a cab. As they came through the lobby, they saw Roman Lebe, Thorton's new driver, walking toward the elevator surrounded by Cuban military. They ran to him.

"Are you in trouble, Roman?" asked Jimmy, concerned.

"Hell no. Haven't you heard? The rebels kidnapped Fangio. These guys are my bodyguards. All the drivers have them now." Roman stepped into the elevator with his entourage.

Tana and Jimmy looked at each other. "Let's get out of this lobby," said Tana. I hate all these guns around. Thorton will have to give me hazard pay for coming here," said Tana as she and Jimmy moved to the front desk.

FOURTEEN

Castro praised Georgia for helping the wounded and the example she gave to his troops. He consoled her on the death of his comrade, Luis Verano. He said he'd never forget Luis and what he meant to both of them. He let it be known he wanted Erroll out of the camp and called him a drunk and a Fascist. Castro warned him if he made the film, it would never be seen in Cuba.

Erroll thrived on the attention he received in Spain and being with Castro at his moment of triumph would add to his legacy. He was smart about star maintenance. He knew how to stay in the newspapers. Good or bad.

The helicopter flew from Castro's headquarters with Georgia aboard. She felt guilty about leaving Erroll and Jake behind, but they convinced her to get out while she had the chance.

When Georgia arrived at Guantanamo a short time later, she was able to hitch a ride to Havana on a U.S. C47 cargo plane. When the plane got into the air for the trip across Cuba, it hit. Her pent-up emotions poured out in tears. She sat on an uncomfortable metal seat and peered out at the rain clouds covering the green mountain scenery. The roar of the powerful engines drowned out her sobs. When she arrived in Havana she felt the need of a modern bathroom, feminine clothes and Marty.

She hired a cab at the airport, but she had no money. She had given what she had to the patients at the hospital. She convinced the cab driver she would pay when she arrived at the Havana Riviera. She still wore her rebel uniform, which made it difficult because the Havanans thought she was one.

At her arrival at the hotel, she told the doorman she was Marty Fallon's girlfriend, but he didn't believe her. She could tell he was paranoid about rebels. He called security and three uniformed men came out of the lobby and grabbed her. The guards cuffed her hands behind her and tried to haul her away. She yelled and kicked. In the tussle her long blonde hair fell out from under her fatigue cap.

"Take your hands off me. I'm Marty Fallon's girl," she screamed. At the exact moment, Dorothy Winters and Nathan Wise drove to the front entrance in a Cadillac limousine and saw the disturbance. "Wait a minute, don't get out yet," said Nathan. "I wanna see what's goin on here." They remained in the back of the car.

Dorothy glanced out the window and saw the blonde hair on a handcuffed girl. "Oh, my God. It's Georgia Evans. For God's sake, Nathan, do something!" she said frantically.

"Are you sure?" asked Nathan.

"Yes. I know it's her... hurry... get out of the car. Help her!" Dorothy opened the door. Nathan got out and Dorothy followed. Dorothy ran to Georgia and put her arms around her.

"Stop! This girl is my friend. She's an American. Her name is Georgia Evans." Georgia was shocked. The confused guards released Georgia while Dorothy consoled her.

"You poor darling! What happened?"

"Dorothy!" she screamed, not believing it was her.

Dorothy helped Georgia into the lobby. "I'm in shock seeing you like this. Clint is staying here. I'll get him down." Dorothy saw a phone by the front desk and went to picked it up and asked for Clint's room. "Clint, it's Dorothy. I'm in the lobby. Get your ass down here. Georgia is here."

"She is? I'll be right down."

Nathan paid Georgia's cab driver and came inside to the front desk to check in. Clint came into the lobby. Nathan acknowledged Clint as he signed the register.

"Georgia. Am I glad to see you," he said, giving her a hug.

"Clint, it was a terrible experience. I can't talk yet. Next time I'll listen to you. I promise," said Georgia.

"Clint, why didn't you tell me what was going on Havana? I would have never come," said Dorothy.

"I thought you knew," said Clint. Dorothy glanced toward Nathan. If looks could kill Nathan would have been a dead man.

Marty's attitude and humor changed with Georgia's reunion. She told him about her ill-fated adventure, leaving out Luis.

"Marty, I think I'm pregnant. I haven't seen a doctor, but I have all the symptoms."

"Talk to Clint. He'll find you someone here in Havana to take care of it."

"I don't believe you said that." Georgia started to cry. "Marty, I'm not having an abortion. I don't believe in them. You know I was brought up in a religious family," she said sobbing.

"What do you want me to do?"

"Marry me."

"I'm still married."

"Get a divorce. You always said you would."

"What can I do, honey? They take time."

"Get a Mexican divorce. Your lawyer can arrange it."

"They're not legal."

"They're legal enough for me. We can get married here in Havana."

"That might not be legal either."

"I don't care. I just want to get married. We can make it legal later. Call your lawyer. Ask him."

"Why do you want to do this now? Can it wait until after a proper divorce? We could have a nice wedding. Your father could marry us."

"The thought of bringing a bastard into the world terrifies me. It's against everything I believe in. I can't face my parents. Please, Marty don't make me have an abortion."

"Okay, we'll get married. I can't stand tears. Get Clint, tell him to make the arrangements."

"Thank you, Marty, darling," she said as she ran to him and hugged and kissed him.

Dorothy and Clint would be the maid of honor and best man. The wedding was to take place that night after the last show.

The race was still scheduled for the next day, but no one had heard from Fangio, who was still in the hands of his kidnapers.

The atmosphere in Havana was hectic. The city felt the drama. It was live and let live, no one knowing if Havana would be the same city in the morning. More people were in the casinos betting. The showrooms did standing room only as everyone drank more and played harder.

Georgia went shopping for a wedding dress. There were shops in the lobby, but the dresses were too gaudy for her taste. She phoned Dorothy to explain her predicament.

"Darling, why don't you come to my room and see. Most of my dresses are low cut, but I am sure we can find you something proper for your wedding," said Dorothy. "I'll be there in a few minutes," Georgia said.

When Dorothy opened the door for Georgia she saw some strange men were in a meeting. Dorothy introduced her to Nathan and Meyer Lansky. They went directly into the bedroom so as not to disturb the gentlemen with their discussions.

Dorothy had laid a number of dresses on her bed for Georgia's inspection.

"Dorothy, they're lovely. You have so many gorgeous dresses." She picked up a white chiffon dress with a long scarf and peered at herself in the mirror holding the dress in front of her.

"This one will work. What do you think? I could wear the scarf as a veil."

"Darling, it's perfect. We're the same size. You'll be a beautiful bride in that dress. It's yours."

"Dorothy, you're so sweet. You came to my rescue twice, hon. How can I possibly repay you?"

"Don't worry, I'll think of something. Why are you getting married here? You surely could wait until you got back to the States."

"I think I'm pregnant... Marty hasn't gotten a divorce... so there are complications. But at least I'll be able to say to my child that we were married when it was born, even if it isn't legal right now."

"I understand. Who's going to perform the ceremony?"

"Clint arranged for a Cuban judge. I have to go. Got so many things to do." She picked up Dorothy's dress. "Clint's put a big table together at ringside. He also invited his racing friends from the National," said Georgia as Dorothy escorted her to the front door. She waved to the men in the room as she left.

Clint had the arrangements made for the wedding, but he couldn't figure out why Georgia wanted to get married in Havana. Maybe she thought that Marty would change his mind.

Clint had invited Meyer Lansky and George Raft. He thought that Nathan would feel more comfortable knowing some of his cronies would be there. Dorothy let it slip that there were some big meetings going on between Nathan and Meyer. It was evident to Clint that time was running out for Meyer and all the boys in Havana. The old era was coming to an end. Castro would be taking over the country. Clint heard that the American imperialist pigs would be gone as soon as he came into power. Meyer must have millions in this place, he thought. There would be no chance of getting it out, even if it was gambling money.

The elaborate, shimmering, sunburst curtain went up on the midnight show at the Havana Riviera. Seated at the front table were Georgia, with her guests: Thorton and Marge North, Dorothy and Nathan, Marshall, Jimmy, Tana Williams, Meyer Lansky, Roman Lebe, George Raft and a girl friend, the Cuban judge and his wife, and Clint Nation. Everyone was in a festive mood. Only Nathan looked glum, but that was to be his nature. Georgia was radiant on her wedding night.

The Cuban chorus line came on stage. The smiling girls in their scanty costumes pranced around on stage to the beat of the Latin music. Topless nude girls dropped down from the ceilings around the full showroom. Everyone waited for Marty's entrance. The announcer said. *"Senores y Senòritas...* The Havana Riviera proudly brings you direct from the United States of America one of its greatest stars: Mr. Marty Fallon."

Marty entered center stage down a long stairway in a costume of baggy pants and shirt, clown shoes, red clown hair and a large hat worn on the side of his head. His front teeth were blacked out. A couple of tall chorus girls passed him, and he did a double take at their bare buns. A big laugh came from the audience. The show continued with Marty doing the hilarious burlesque bits that he was famous for. It lasted for one hour.

Dorothy sat next to Thorton, who was drunk. She flirted with him.

"Pappy, I hear you're Jewish," she said.

"Honey, me Jewish? I got a foreskin that stretches from here to that palm tree," he said pointing with his hand.

Marty came down stage to the center table and made an announcement to the crowd. "Ladies and gentlemen. I want to introduce you to my new wife-to-be, Georgia." Everyone clapped and Georgia got up from the table and took a bow. The curtain came down. A few minutes later Marty came to the table. Meyer, Nathan, and George Raft congratulated him and left. Dorothy stayed on for the marriage ceremony.

The stagehands moved a large horseshoe-like arch covered with an array of colorful and exotic flowers on the stage and put it in place for the ceremony.

Georgia took the scarf from around her shoulders and placed it on her head. Dorothy helped her with it. The wedding party went up onto the stage. Marty dressed in a suit. He and Georgia went under the arch. Dorothy stood behind with Clint.

The Cuban judge took his place to perform the ceremony. It was spoken in Spanish. After he finished he put up his hand and pointed to his ring finger. Clint stuck his hand in his pocket. For a moment he couldn't find the ring. He finally found it and handed the ring to Marty, who placed it on Georgia's finger and kissed her. Clint had bought the ring that afternoon in the gift shop. It wasn't real, but it looked it. Thorton made a speech. "To my friend, Marty, who has just married the best looking piece of poontang." He lifted his glass. "Now I want to take everybody to see Superman."

There was a sheepish laugh that followed from everyone. Marty and Georgia excused themselves and left.

"Who is Superman?" Georgia asked as they left the showroom for the elevator.

"I'll tell you some other time," he said as they got into the elevator.

Thorton was as good as his word. They arrived in two cabs. Dorothy went along. What better time to see something of this nature than with the crowd she was with tonight? It was all a lark anyway, she thought. She had heard about the show and secretly wanted to see it. She wouldn't tell Nathan.

Their cabs pulled into a little side street somewhere in downtown Havana and stopped in front of an unobtrusive building. Marshall paid for everyone's admission. They walked into a cavern-like room that was semi-dark. They had to adjust their eyes to get used to the dim red lights. Thorton stumbled over somebody as they made their way down to the front. The air was thick with smoke and had an unusual sweet smell mixed with it.

They settled into their seats. On stage stood three Roman columns; three shapely nude young women with long hair were chained to them.

Spotlights switched on to illuminate the girls as they moaned and wrenched in their bondage.

Clint peered around the room. As far as he could make out, most of the audience was American. He sat next to Dorothy, who was absorbed in the scene onstage.

The sound of kettledrums rolled as Superman made his entrance. He was tall, slender, of mixed blood. His face was hard, expressionless. He wore a full-length red cape and carried a black whip that he cracked in the air as he walked to center stage.

The chained girls moaned and groaned trying to get free. The sounds of the whip cracked. "Ahiii," they yelled.

The kettledrum rolled as Superman dropped his cape. A low "haaaaaa" came from the girls and the audience. Superman stood center stage in front of the audience, his huge member erect, then turned to provide a side view.

Clint leaned over to Dorothy. "He must have had a blood transfusion to get that thing like that." He looked around in back of them to see the audience's reaction. "Dorothy, there's a man behind you... He's exposing himself..." Dorothy jumped up from her seat, grasping at her hair.

"My, hair. He'll do something awful to my hair?" she screamed and got up and moved down the aisle.

Two muscular young black men dressed in G-strings walked out on stage carrying a white Roman cot and set it down center stage.

Superman danced around flopping his member in the air and rubbing it up against the chained girls.

The two black men unchained one of the girls and brought her downstage for the audience's inspection. She turned and moaned and acted as if she wanted to escape. Superman lay down on the couch with his phallus in the air. The two men brought the girl to the cot and placed her on Superman's member. She screamed, yelling in Spanish as she was forced down on it. This action was for the two other chained girls, who were also crying and weeping.

Thorton left his seat and went down front and hung his chin on the stage to get a better view, which upset Marge.

"Look at that old fool. He is disgusting. He makes me so mad I could spit," she said to Marshall, who said, "I think he's funny."

"You would," said Marge.

After Superman finished up with the last girl he got up from the couch, his penis still erect, and bowed.

The lights went up and dance music started. The three girls went into the audience and brought some men onstage to dance. One of the young women pulled Thorton up on the stage. He shuffled after her, dragging his leg. Superman came down into the audience and took Marge's hand and tried to pull her on stage. Marge was reluctant, but she went along with it. Superman led her to dance. His long penis banged against her beaded dress.

Dorothy came over to Clint and sat down.

"I want to go. This is the most disgusting event I have ever witnessed. These Norths are the sickest and most despicable perverts I've ever met. Are you coming?" she asked. Dorothy got up from the seat and walked out of the theater with Clint following.

She wanted us to come here, Clint thought. Now, she's the Blessed Virgin.

There was a cab waiting in front, and they took it back to the Riviera. Neither of them said a word.

FIFTEEN

After the visit to Superman, the Norths were back in their suite at the Nacional.

"Do you realize what time it is? The race is going to start in a few hours, if there is a race," said Marge as she poured a scotch and water from the bar.

"I wish I had a camera. You should have seen yourself dancing with that big-dicked nigger. You liked that big prick," said Marshall.

"What's a matter, you jealous? Cause you know you got nothing down there," answered Marge as she walked away and sat down next to Tana.

"Sorry, Tana. Marshall has no class. Using nigger like he does."

"I've heard the term before," said Tana.

"Some of my best friends are niggers," said Thorton. Marshall, Jimmy and Tana exchanged looks.

"Get off this nigger crap, for God's sake. Don't you think Georgia's a darling girl?" asked Marge.

"Poor Marty. It will never last," said Marshall.

"What makes you make a crack like that, you shit heel?" said Marge.

Jimmy stood. "What's wrong with all of you? We came here to have fun and go racing. What's getting into everybody? Tana, it's time for bed. Tana joined Jimmy, said goodnight and left.

"What do you suppose is wrong with him?" asked Marshall.

"He doesn't like that kind of talk," said Marge.

"He's right. You shouldn't talk that way. They all got pussies and they all have pricks. They're just like you and me," said Thorton.

"Oh, my God. Isn't Thorton just brilliant," said Marge.

The race was to start at two PM, but Fangio had not been released

123

from his captors, which made for a delay. The time trials had taken place for starting positions. The laps went slow because of the layout of the course and danger of the crowds being close to the road. Roman and his crew were elated with their time; they had been able to get second-row position. Sterling Moss from England in a small Ferrari and Masten Gregory in a big Ferrari placed first row lineup.

The race fans arrived along the Malecon. Grandstands were assembled for five thousand spectators in front of the Nacional and the U.S. Embassy. A section was roped off for President Batista's family and friends.

The Norths asked Dorothy, Clint, Marty and Georgia to watch the race from their suite at the Nacional. Marty and Georgia declined.

Nathan stayed with Meyer Lansky for the day, involved in a business meeting. Dorothy was on her own. She wasn't happy being in Havana, but it could have been worse if Clint and the racing crowd weren't here. She would have been by herself sitting in her room.

Nathan told Dorothy that Meyer was coming through for him in Las Vegas.

Clint said he'd have a late breakfast with the newlyweds. He felt hung-over and tired. He was feeling exhausted lately. Maybe I need a vacation; this place is no vacation, he thought. Or I could take some vitamin pills, they could pick me up. Yesterday had been hectic. Today he wanted to relax, he told himself, and watch the race.

Bodyguards stood in front of Marty's suite when Clint rang the buzzer. They recognized him and let him pass.

Marty let him in.

"I'm so happy. You know what my baby said to me?"

"No?"

"She wants to have a big family. You don't know how happy that makes me. And she told me she's giving up acting."

Georgia came into the living room, dressed in a peach satin dressing gown. She gave Clint a big smile.

"Thanks, Clint, for all you did yesterday. There wouldn't have been a wedding if it wasn't for you." She held up her hand.

"I love my wedding ring. Marty wants to get me a real one, but I like this one. I'll never take it off." She went to Clint and kissed him on the cheek.

"You will when your finger turns green," Clint said with a laugh.

The buzzer in the room sounded. Clint went to the door. The waiter stood in the hallway with their breakfast. One of the guards lifted the silver cover and checked it. He put the cover back and the waiter came into the suite and set up the table. Everyone sat as the waiter served them.

"Did you hear about the Cinerama Theater last night?" asked Marty.

"No," said Clint.

"They threw bombs into the place," said Marty. "I want you to be the first to know, we're leaving in the morning or as soon as Georgia and I can get out of here."

"You have another week on your contract," said Clint.

"Bullshit! You put the makeup on; you do the show," said Marty.

"I'm not Marty Fallon," said Clint.

"Let me ask you something. Do you want a live Marty Fallon or do you want a dead Marty Fallon for a client? Cut the crap. Nobody, I say nobody, is going to blame me for walking out of this place."

"I agree, but first I want to talk to Meyer. Just to be safe. We don't want to piss him off. He carries a lot of weight around the world," said Clint.

"Tell him to go fuck himself."

"I won't do that. These guys pay the best money in show business. I'm not going to let you screw up with them. In fact they're going to open the El Dorado in Las Vegas next year, I've been talking to them about you appearing there, for BIG money," said Clint.

"Listen to Clint, Marty. Now that we're married and we're going to have a family, that costs money. And let's face it, you're not divorced yet. Your wife will stick it to you now when she finds out I'm pregnant," said Georgia.

Clint thought, She's pregnant, I should have known. That explains the fast marriage.

"Why should she have to know? You're not going to be in her company," said Marty.

"There's no secrets in Hollywood, Marty. Our kind of gossip gets around. I won't feel secure until I see our names on a California marriage license."

"I'm trying to please you, honey. Don't give any more problems," said Marty.

"I'm sorry, I'm just thinking ahead," said Georgia.

"What do you think I should do, Clint?"

"The sooner you clear up your marriage with your wife the better. If I were you I'd call your lawyer and have him file the papers." Georgia was pleased.

"Get him on the phone," said Marty. Clint got on the phone.

"Operator, *Ingles, por favor.* Mr. Mike Murphy in Los Angeles, California. His number there is CR 1777. I'll wait. Hello, Mike. Sorry to get you up. It's Clint Nation in Havana. Marty wants to talk to you." Clint handed Marty the phone.

"Mike, put the papers together for my divorce. WHAT!" Marty's face went to a scowl. "Why? I fired the son-of-a-bitch three years ago. What am I going to do? We'll leave here today. Bye." Marty came back to the table.

"What's wrong?" asked Clint.

"The IRS has taken my house, my bank account and tied up all of my assets. I'm broke."

A big explosion rattled the windows of the room. Clint got up and ran to the window. He peered down on the street. A city bus was on fire. Black smoke traveled into the air. The crowd below screamed and ran into the street.

"It's a bomb," said Clint.

"We're leaving today. Call the airport," snapped Marty.

Clint found Meyer Lansky in a meeting in the Lounge. Meyer saw Clint approach. He gave him a sign to wait until he was through. Clint nervously waited for him to finish. After a few minutes the men left. Meyer motioned for him to come and sit.

"Doz guys told me Castro was on the radio dis mornin' telling the people to go on strike and stop the Gran' Premio race. He says the army is coming over to his side. Do you believe that crap? Whatsa matter? Are ya sick?" said Meyer.

"Marty wants to leave today."

"Well, I'd leave too, if I could, but look at dis place. Cost me millions. I havta to stay here, and try to negotiate a deal with Castro. If he says "NO", I crap out. I like your guy Marty. Great talent. The gamblers like the guy too. He's good for business."

"Thanks Meyer. I'll pass it on."

"I checked the books this morning. Didja know his losses are over twenty grand? I'm givin' him fifteen grand a week. As of today he owes me five grand. If he pays the five grand he owes me, I'll cancel the contract. You know I could hold him to it, and I'd collect in the States. The way I sees it, it could cost him the fifteen he owes me for the week and the five grand he owes the house, which comes to twenty grand plus his lawyers. See, I'm being a nice guy, don't ya think?" asked Meyer, smiling.

Clint had been through this before. When you've got a star like Marty who's an irresponsible gambler, they leave their money at the crap tables of the gambling clubs they play. He ends up losing all his salary for the date, plus having to pay the IRS, and owing the casino more dates for nothing, to pay off his debts.

"I'll work it out with you, Meyer."

"By da way. Nathan Wise wanted to know what kinda guy are ya. Vot I think of ya. If he could trust ya. He's thinking about ya handling some deals for him. I told him you vere a OK kind of guy."

"Thanks for the reference. I'll get back to you." Clint got up and gave Meyer a handshake. Meyer's handshake was like a limp rag. How could a man that powerful have a handshake like that, he thought. He doesn't have to impress anybody. That's why! Clint had answered his own question. He left the noisy lounge and went to the house phone to call Dorothy.

"I'm in the lobby. Are you ready? We'd better get started. They'll be closing off the streets soon for the race. I'll be waiting in the lobby. Bye." He then called Marty.

"Meyer is letting you out of the contract. You and Georgia can leave today if you can get out. There's a catch. He figures you owe him twenty thousand dollars." Clint held the phone from his ear. "Calm down... It's the gambling. It's five grand. Don't you call him. You're not going to tell him to go fuck himself. Don't do anything. I'm on my way to your room... I'll explain everything. Bye." Clint put down the phone, and brought a handkerchief from his pocket and wiped his brow. He said to himself. "What a revolting day this is going to be." He went and rang for the elevator.

Dorothy and Clint arrived at the Nacional at one-thirty. They had to go through the back streets because of the crowds. The main boulevards were closed. When they could go no farther by cab, they got out and walked the rest of the way. When they arrived at the Nacional, a mass of people stood in front of the hotel making it almost impossible to enter. The police and the military used a long thick rope to hold back the crowds. They gave them space so they could get in. When they got inside the lobby, it was packed with tourists wanting to leave the city. Their bags were everywhere, making it difficult to maneuver around.

"Where are the fucking elevators?" asked Dorothy, looking around.

"Follow me," said Clint. He led her to the rear of the lobby near the gardens and they saw the elevator. The bronze doors opened and a packed crowd surged forward pushing them backward. Dorothy looked to Clint like she was having an anxiety attack.

"Clint, this place is scary. We could be trapped here," she said as they got into the elevator.

"*Diez,*" said Clint as he held up ten fingers to the frazzled elevator boy.

Some Cuban soldiers got on with them. The old elevator climbed slowly to the tenth floor. The smell of sweat and garlic coming from the soldiers had Dorothy sick by the time they reached the top floor. Dorothy was aghast at seeing all the soldiers in the hallways. Clint knocked on the door of the suite and Marshall opened the door. He had a big smile on his face.

"What's the smile for? I hope what's funny rubs off on me. I've been frightened to death trying to get here," said Dorothy. Thorton sat on the sofa, dressed in his underwear, next to a man who was about fifty, on the heavy side. He had a sun-lined face with deep furrows and a shock of sandy-brown gray hair. When he saw Dorothy come into the room, he took a couple of gulps.

"This is Corky Miller from Texas, he's a wildcatter. He got here early this morning. He and Thorton haven't been to bed yet," said Marshall. Corky tried to get up and then fell back again.

"P-p-pleased to m-meetcha all," said Corky, stuttering. When Marshall said Corky was a oilman, Dorothy took an immediate interest in him.

"You poor darling man. What an experience you must have had," said Dorothy sitting down next to him.

"It w-was k-kinda hairy, ma'am," stuttered Corky.

"What a nice attractive friend you have, Pappy," she said to Thorton.

"He's all right, if you can understand him. I can never understand the old bastard half the time," said Thorton.

"The hell you d-don't. I t-talk to you all the time. Y-you n-never said n-nothing before," said Corky.

"He gets worse when he gets around fancy pussy, dontcha, Corky?" asked Thorton smiling at him. Corky started to blush.

"Hot d-dam, Thorton, you don't have to embarrass me like that you know, huh."

"Pappy, be nice. You're a bad boy. I like this nice man. How many oil wells do you have, Corky?"

"I got ten, m-ma'am."

"Ten! How wonderful," replied Dorothy.

Clint had been on the balcony watching the activities below. He came back into the room.

"Come, quick! Take a look. President Bastista and his family are getting into the stands," he said.

"Fuck him and the ship that brought him over," said Thorton.
There was a knock at the door. Marshall went to open it. It was Jimmy and Tana.

"You sure took your time getting here. Thorton has been up all night. Corky surprised us. They're both drunk. Corky is after Thorton for money to finish the well he's drilling. He's driving Thorton nuts. I got to get down to the pits before the race starts. Thorton is drinking straight scotch. I wanted to give him an IV this morning, but he wouldn't do it. You got your hands full," said Marshall as Jimmy entered the suite. Marshall picked up his gear and went to the door.

"I'll be back after the race. I'm taking the two-way radio with me. I'll keep in touch from the pits with the race details. The other receiver is by the window and it's on. Bye." Marshall left the suite.

Tana walked to the back of the sofa and rubbed Thorton on the top of his head. Thorton grabbed her hand. She wore tight black capri pants, black high heel shoes and a sexy off the shoulder blouse that showed off her sleek figure. Her hair was pulled back tight from her face into a bun, showing off her large, sloe, almond-shaped eyes.

"Did you know, Tana is the first negress they ever let in the Coconut Grove in Los Angeles. Who was that nigger you were with that night, honey?" asked Thorton.

"He's no nigger. His name is Adam Clayton Powell. He's a Negro gentleman and a representative of the United States Congress, if you please. Thorton, you're BAD. Why do I put up with you?" Tana walked to the bar and made herself a drink.

"You like my money, honey. That's why."

Dorothy got up from the sofa and went to the bar and scowled back at Thorton. "Pappy, you're a nasty old man. If I hear one more nigger out of you, I'm leaving and taking these nice people with me. Do you understand?"

Thorton quieted down acting uncomfortable. Dorothy and Tana stood at the bar talking quietly to each other.

"Thanks, dahlin, for sticking up for me. You didn't have too."

"I hate prejudice. I won't put up with it. Anyway, let's try to forget how awful Thorton is. You sure do get around. I understand you know Clint, too. Do you think he's a good fuck?"

Tana broke into a laugh. "You're asking me! He's your boyfriend."

"He's my agent. We don't fuck. I don't mix up my priorities," said Dorothy.

"Clint is a bit kinky," said Tana.

"Oh, how's that?" asked Dorothy.

"He's asked me to bring a man to bed with us."

"Do you think he's gay?" asked Dorothy

"No...but he could be bisexual," said Tana.

"Did you ask him?"

"No."

"I've always been curious about black women, about their sexual anatomy, I heard you have a giant clitoris, almost like a penis. Is that true?"

"If you come to bed with me, dahlin, I'll show you first-hand."

"I'm not that curious. You're a beautiful girl, but I'm not into women."

"I like you and your honesty. I feel I could trust you. There's this friend of mine who'd like you. He's a German industrialist, tons of money and handsome. He comes to California a few times a year. The next time he's in town, I'll introduce you. You'd make a great couple, dahlin," said Tana.

Marshall's voice could be heard calling the suite on the portable radio. "Marshall calling. Are you there?" Jimmy went to pick up the radio.

"Jimmy here. Go ahead."

"We got word. They released Fangio. The race is delayed until he gets here. I'll keep you posted. Over and out."

Marge came out of her room. She was dressed and made up. She looked tired, but glamorous. She wore bright yellow slacks, with a leopard print blouse. Her magnificent jewelry flashed in the light. She went to the bar and fixed herself a bloody mary.

"Christ, between what's going on outside and all this commotion in the suite I was lucky to get my eyes closed." She looked to Thorton.

"Well, Thorton, you're disgusting sitting there in your underwear. Is that your costume for the day?"

"Lay off me, Marge. Can't you see I've got a lot on my mind?"

"Jimmy, call room service and see if you can get some food up here. I'm starved," said Marge.

Jimmy went to the phone and picked it up. He heard it ring repeatedly. "They don't answer," said Jimmy.

Marty and Georgia sat in their suite watching television, trying to make some sense out of what was going on in the city. Numerous bulletins came onto the screen of different areas of Cuba, where they would see fighting. It was in Spanish, so they weren't getting the drift of it. The phone rang. Marty picked it up. It was George Raft.

"Marty, there'll be a car for you in front of the hotel entrance. It'll take you to an airport outside of Havana. A small plane will be waiting for you and take you to Key West. Give the pilot five hundred. Meyer is willing to wait for the five grand. He likes you. He knows you're good for it. Good luck, kid."

"Aren't you leaving, George?"

"I can't, kid. I got to look out for my investment and take my chances and wait to see what happens."

"I understand, George. Good luck to you. George, thanks for everything. You're a great friend." Marty hung up.

"We're leaving, honey. You all packed? Aren't you happy we're getting out of here? Clint fucked up. He should be here. He's missing his chance. That's his problem, not mine."

Georgia had been thinking about Luis. She picked up a small bag, and she and Marty left for the lobby. With Marty's bodyguards leading their way.

Down in the pits the race was about to start. Word had gotten around that Fangio was not going to show. The starting line-up had Gregory of Kansas in a Ferrari, Moss of England in a Ferrari and Shelby of Dallas in a Maserati, followed by Lebe of Los Angeles.

One hundred and fifty thousand spectators assembled around the course. The military had the crowd under control, but they were restless and hot because of the long delay.

The checkered flag dropped. The cars took off in a cloud of dust and smoke with the shrill cry of their powerful engines screaming in the crowd's ears.

Everyone stood on the balcony of Thorton's suite as the checkered flag dropped. They had a spectacular view of the course below. If it weren't for the crazy political atmosphere, Clint thought, this would be an almost perfect day.

Masten Gregory was holding first position with Shelby and Moss right beside him. The crowd leaned forward on the track watching for the cars to appear from down course. Crowd control became hectic keeping the spectators back. Clint thought, what a wonderful sight. All the colors, the cars, their paint glistening in the bright sun, the flags waving in the light tropical breeze off Havana Bay. The sweet smell of Castrol oil traveled upward in the wind. The scream of engines intermingled with the roar of the crowd. He knew they were witnessing the pageant of sport car racing at its best.

Thorton and Corky came in from off the balcony. Corky went to the bar.

"Whacha d-drinking Thorton?"

"Pour me a scotch double, no ice." Corky gave Thorton his drink.

"I gotta to call Texas. Ch-check on my well," said Corky as he picked up the phone.

"H-hello, operator. Get me Midland, Texas. Double-four-two one-six-six. I'll w-wait." Corky looked to Thorton, sitting on the sofa.

"Th-thorton, it's-it's the b-best producing sand in West Texas. I-I'mm dr-drilling in. You got one-th-third of the well for t-wenty f-ive t-hhousand. It's the best d-deal I every put ya in, huh," yelled Corky over the sound of the race cars below.

"Holy shit, Corky, can't you see I'm trying to win a race, for Christ sake. Don't bother me with that horseshit. Jimmy, JIMMY," yelled Thorton toward the balcony. Jimmy came in from outside.

"What position is Roman in?"

"He's running fourth. Masten is still in first. They're getting around slowly. They're having a hard time keeping the crowd back," said Jimmy as he went back onto the balcony to watch the race.

Corky's call got through. "Howdy Dave, Oh, I'm in H-havana. What's happening at the well? Y-you w-what? I'm not hearing y-ya Dave. S-say that again. Holy smokes! I'll c-call ya back." Corky stumbled over to Thorton.

"Thorton, I need twenty-five gggg's fast. You got to g-give to m-me. I'll have to shut down if y-you don't," he pleaded.

"Corky, are you nuts, for Chrissake? Get away from me."

Corky pulled Thorton off the sofa down on the floor and jumped on him. He grabbed Thorton around the neck, choking him. "Get off of me." Thorton's face turned red.

Clint came in the room to get a drink and saw Corky on top of Thorton. He ran to pull him off. Thorton got his breath back and Clint helped him back on to the sofa.

"Corky, what the hell's the matter with you? Are you crazy? You could of killed Thorton."

"Thorton promised he'd give me twenty-five G's to drill the well. He keeps putting m-me off."

A roar and screams were heard from outside. A minute later Dorothy, in a state of collapse, came in from the balcony assisted by Jimmy and followed by Clint. He helped her to the sofa to sit.

"What's going on out there?" asked Thorton in alarm.

"A black Ferrari crashed into the crowd. A lot of people were hurt or killed," said Clint.

"It's awful. The crash brought back all those terrible memories when I saw Geoffrey killed. Oh, I hate this awful sport... all the killing. It should be outlawed. Get me something to drink, Clint."

Clint went to the bar and poured Dorothy a glass of water. She drank it and settled down. "Why did I come to this fucking place?" she said. Tana came to console her. Clint went back out on to the balcony.

Clint saw the driver of the black Ferrari had hit an oil slick and skidded off the course into the crowd directly in front of the Nacional Hotel. It was a mass of spectators lying on the ground in all directions. A yellow flag was up, and the cars on the track moved slowly in a holding position. Ambulances tried to get through the crowds to the causalities. President Batista and his family were escorted out of the grandstand.

Clint came back into the suite and picked up the portable radio. He went back onto the balcony and tried to call Marshall.

"Clint calling Marshall. Come in Marshall."

"Marshall here... looks to be a lot of fatalities. They're stopping the race. The cars went five laps. That qualifies the race as a done event. Tell Thorton our car ran sixth."

"Get back here quick. We want out of this town." Clint waited to hear Marshall's reply. Then he heard a giant explosion. He could see in the far distance smoke and fire rising. He heard guns and aircraft. Canon-fire throughout the city. He could see Havana was under siege.

SIXTEEN

Clint ran in from the balcony and turned on the television. There were pictures of buses stopping in the streets, their drivers leaving their vehicles. Photos of the Havana train station appeared, the trains abandoned. More shots of the airport; no planes were arriving or taking off. Clint went to the phone and picked it up. It was dead. He and Dorothy went to the door of the suite and opened it. The guards pushed them back into the room.

"Are we hostages?" asked Dorothy. Everyone was concerned and frightened.

"There's a possibility. The rebels took American hostages in eastern Cuba. But these guys are Batista's men. It doesn't make sense to me," said Clint.

"We might as well have a drink. There's no food in this damn place. I'm absolutely starved. If they're going to shoot me, I'd sure like a last meal," said Marge.

"You're talking real brave, Marge. Why would anyone want to shoot an old broad the likes of you? The only reason I see is for all those bangles I've bought you through the years," said Thorton.

"They can have my jewels. I only got them to appease your guilt with those whores of yours, you old bastard." Marge spit out at Thorton.

"Naah, come on, Marge. There wasn't a bartender on Sunset Strip you didn't screw," said Thorton.

"Thorton, you're absolutely horrible. Why do you always have to bring up that old crap. You, you, you make me so mad I could spit," Marge, trying to compose herself.

"Come on, you two, this is no time for bickering. We got a serious problem. Let's try to figure some way to get out of here. How much money does everyone have?" asked Clint.

"Thorton?"

"I got about five, maybe six thousand."

"Corky?" Corky reached into his pocket and pulled out some bills. "I got about a g-grand here," he said.

Dorothy took a small diamond and ruby bracelet off her wrist and gave it to Clint.

"Nathan, gave me this. I'm sure he'd mind, but I don't care." said Dorothy.

"Dorothy, we don't need it. It might come in handy later. Thanks anyway," said Clint, giving her back the bracelet.

Tana took off her shoe and took a folded five hundred dollar bill from under the insole and gave it to Clint.

"It's my walkin' around money. It's meant to be used in emergencies," said Tana.

"Thanks, honey," said Clint, giving her a smile. Clint reached in his pocket and pulled out his wallet. Jimmy gave him five hundred.

"Thanks Jimmy, I got about two thousand. Hell, with this kind of money we could buy this place. Here's my plan. We got Marshall on the outside. It's only ninety miles to Key West. We got enough money to bribe the guards and hire a boat. I noticed the stairway comes out by a garden that leads to Jose Marti Park. Marshall can meet us at the park entrance with a car. How does that sound to everybody," he asked?

Dorothy kissed him. "Cowboy, you darling. I knew I could count on you to take care of me. Wait tell I tell Nathan you saved my life," said Dorothy.

"Clint, if y-you g-get m-me out of here I'll g-give y-you a piece of o-of m-my new oil w-well for a sm-small price," said Corky.

"Corky. Darling. What about me? Have you got any of that oil well left for me?" asked Dorothy.

"We have to travel light. Take only the necessities. No high heels, Marge. Jimmy, get Thorton dressed."

"I can't leave my beautiful clothes," said Marge.

"It's your clothes or you, that's your choice," said Clint.

"You're tough," said Marge.

"Someone has to be, with this group," said Clint, as he picked up the radio and called Marshall.

"Marshall, come in Marshall."

Marshall's voice came in over the radio. "Marshall here, go ahead."

"Don't try to come back to the hotel. We're prisoners in the room. Go to the harbor and hire a boat to take us to Key West. Tell the boat owner we will pay him half now, half when we get there. When you get the deal done, come back to Jose Marti Park. Wait for us by the entrance. Good luck!"

There was silence among everyone. Jimmy had been attending to Thorton, who has been quiet. Jimmy approached Clint, not wanting the others to hear.

"Thorton will have trouble staying up with us. He hasn't eaten in two days. All the stairs and the walking will be tough for him. I could give him a shot. It's an upper, but it's bad for his heart. I'd like to give him an IV, which is mostly sugar for energy. He shouldn't be drinking when I do. He's not sick enough to stop drinking, so we'll have problems. Talk to him."

Clint sat down next to Thorton. "Thorton, Jimmy says you'll need an IV. You're going to need some strength for our journey,"

"I don't want an IV. I need a drink," said Thorton.

"No more booze for you. Now get into some clothes. Jimmy, no more booze for Thorton and Corky. Watch them. They'll try to sneak it," said Clint. "Thorton, lay down on the sofa. Act sick. I saw a portable oxygen tank earlier. Where is it?" he asked.

"Here," said Jimmy picking up the tank by the door.

"Bring it here. Thorton, put this oxygen mask on. Tana. help him with it. Act like his nurse. It'll pick up your blood, Thorton. I'll get the guard in charge in here, and tell him Thorton's dying and we have to get him to a hospital. Gather around Thorton, everybody, and look concerned." Clint opened the door. The guards in the hall moved up and stood in his face. Clint, in his bad Spanish said. *"The Guardio, Numero uno, por favor. Emergencia, emergencia, muy importante,"* he said. A fat Cuban guard said. *"Que pasa, señor?"*

"Usted hablas Inglish?" said Clint, standing behind the half open door. *"Poco, señor"*

"Me amigo, corazon, malo, enfermo." Clint pantomimed the heart being sick and at the same time flashed a roll of big bills in front of him.

The guard called another guard who came into the room. Clint escorted the number one guard over to the sofa and the other one stood at the door. Thorton was stretched out on the sofa and looked as if he could die at any minute. Everybody played their part perfectly. The guard was convinced. He called the other guard to have a look. They both agreed the old man was dying.

"Hombres, por favor, nostros vamos el hospital." Clint counted out two thousand dollars for them. The guards' eyes bulged. Clint could tell they had never seen money in that amount being offered to them before.

"Todos." said the guard as he moved his arm to include everybody in the room.

"Si'," said Clint. The guard spoke in Spanish to the other guard. The other one answered him back.

"Okay", he said. It worked. Thorton let go a loud fart. The second guard broke into a roar, and then acted sheepish when the other guard scowled at him. Everyone looked to each other trying to hold back their laughter. The guards left the room.

"Thorton, you could have waited till after they'd gone to do that. It almost ruined everything, but I have to give it to you. You're a good actor," said Marge.

"Hell, Marge, I been acting all my life. How do you think I could have lived with you? Gimme a drink," said Thorton.

"No drinks, Thorton. Not until we get out of here. Jimmy, get some pants on Thorton. He can't stay in his underwear.

"Do you think they will be back?" asked Dorothy. "They will. They're not going to leave two grand behind," said Clint as he held up the money. They heard a rap at the door. Clint went to open it. The two guards were back. He let them into the suite. Jimmy and Tana had gotten Thorton down on the sofa and put the oxygen mask back in place.

"Señor, mil dolares mas," said the Guard.

"He wants another thousand bucks," said Clint.

"OK." He gave them the three thousand, which the number one guard quickly put in his pocket. Clint motioned the guards to come over to the sofa. Thorton had gotten his pants on in time. He showed them how to pick up Thorton and carry him. Jimmy carried the oxygen tank attached to Thorton. Everyone followed Thorton and the guards out the door.

As Clint had guessed, the elevator wasn't working, so they took the stairs. It was ten flights down. Everyone was glad it wasn't ten flights up. As they moved down the stairway, Clint helped Corky with the steps trying to steady him. Clint became curious as to what was happening on the other floors. He went to open the door on the eighth floor, but the guard stopped him.

When they got to the lobby floor stairwell the guards would go no farther. They put Thorton down on the floor and said *"adios"*, walking back up the stairs, yelling obscenities and laughing as they disappeared.

Dorothy said, "Clint, I have to leave you here. I've got to get back to the Riviera. Nathan will be going crazy wondering what happened to me. I'll duck into the back streets. Don't worry, I'll be all right. Goodbye, everybody. You're in good hands with Clint. He'll get you out of this mess. Keep the faith. Bye, Clint, I'll see you in Hollywood." She gave Clint a kiss and put a scarf on over her hair and started to leave the stairwell.

"Dorothy, take my things out of my room with you."

Dorothy nodded as she left.

Clint checked out his group. We're certainly conspicuous looking, he thought. We'd get attention anywhere.

"It could be a long walk ahead. Stick together. Act like Americans. We're above all of this crap. Tana and Jimmy, you hold on to Thorton. I'll walk with Corky and Marge. Okay, let's go."

Clint opened the door as they moved into the lobby. It was filled with people, mostly tourists. Two men who were rebels ran toward them with armed soldiers in pursuit. The crowd opened up to let them past. Shots were fired and the two men fell to the floor in front of them. Screams and commotion followed. Everyone tried to find places to go for cover. The smell of gunpowder and the crack of the bullets moved the air through the mammoth room. Clint could smell the sweat of terror coming from his body. Marge became hysterical, sobbing. The two dead men lay at their feet, blood flowing into a pool on the marble floors. The soldiers ran up inspect them.

"Let's go. Out that door," said Clint as he pointed to a door into the garden. Clint held on to Marge's hand; she was sobbing out of control. He stopped to shake her.

"Marge, get ahold of yourself." He pulled her after him into the garden. The rest followed. After a few minutes they stopped to rest and gain their composure. Thorton and Corky had sobered up from the ordeal. Marge collapsed and lay on the ground.

"Marge, what's wrong with you?" asked Clint.

"I'm so embarrassed, you know what? This is so embarrassing... I peed my pants," said Marge.

"Let's move on. Look for the entrance to the park." Clint studied everyone to see who would need help. Thorton and Corky were holding up. Tana and Jimmy were managing. More sporadic gunfire was heard near them. They froze in a crouched position to avoid the bullets they thought could be coming their way. They got up and moved on. As they approached Jose Marti Park, they found the park empty. The race crowd had dispersed when the gunfire and the explosions started.

"Wait here. I see the park entrance over there," said Clint. They sat under the bronze statue of Jose Marti and were exhausted, keeping quiet, everyone in their own thoughts.

Clint found a fountain and put his head under the water, cooling him off and clearing his head as it cascaded from the top. Marge joined him, throwing water from the fountain on her crotch, soaking her pants and shoes.

"I feel better now," she said. They sat around the fountain as the time passed, with all eyes on the park entrance.

A Volkswagen van pulled up to the entry. Marshall sat in the front seat. He got out and waved to them. They ran to the van to meet him.

"I never thought I would ever be as happy to see you, Marshall, as I am now," said Marge.

"What happened to you?" he asked?

"Don't ask!" said Marge,

"Did you get us a boat?" Clint asked as they climbed into the van.

"It's waiting at the dock. Hurry, get in. Everybody's crazy around here. I saw some Americans pulled from their cab and searched by a gang. They robbed them and left them standing in the street. This is Juan, our driver. He cost us plenty but he helped in getting me the boat. I hope you got lots of cash, Clint. We're going to need it to get out of here," said Marshall. Juan stepped on the gas and they moved off toward the harbor.

"Where is Roman?" asked Thorton?

"He's at the boat waiting. Tony is staying with the car. He wouldn't come. He says they'll have to shoot him before they get the car. I gave him five hundred dollars and told him to go to the American Embassy.

It was all the money I had. I said I'd wire him money there to get the car out of the country. You know how he is," said Marshall.

"Yes, I do. Good ol' Tony," said Thorton.

As they approached the harbor, cars were backed up in traffic. The drivers pushed their horns, yelling at each other and getting out of their cars to see what held everyone up.

"This traffic has happened since I left here. We're not the only ones wanting to get out of here by boat," said Marshall. He opened the door of the van.

"Give Juan five hundred dollars. That's what he charged me to get here," said Marshall. Clint gave the driver five hundred dollars.

"It's best we walk or we will never get there and someone else will try to take our boat," said Clint.

Dorothy pushed through the crowd after she left the Nacional. Most of the people on the street had been at the race and the others were hotel workers who had left their jobs when the explosion went off. She could tell that everyone wanted to get out of this section of the city because this was where all the trouble was centered. She tried to look inconspicuous by holding her head down along the way. When she got to the Riviera, two cars, apparently, abandoned in the driveway blocked the entrance. When she entered the lobby, she could tell the staff had abandoned the place. The management staff was behind the desk trying to deal with all the hotel guests looking for a way out of Havana.

Dorothy went to the house phone; it wasn't working. She walked over to the elevator; it wasn't working. She saw the stairs to the mezzanine and the general offices. Meyer would be there, she thought. When she walked into the foyer, Meyer and Nathan stood at the counter going over papers. They glanced up as she entered.

"I've had everyone looking for you. I thought I was going to have to leave you here. Get your things. We're leaving now," said Nathan.

"I need help with my bags and get Clint's also. How are we getting out of here?"

"We have a plane waiting for us to take us to Miami. Forget Clint's bags. We don't have time," said Nathan.

After walking many blocks the group reached the part of the harbor where Marshall found the boat he had chartered. There were other Americans carrying their bags going from one boat to another asking the owners if they could charter passage to the United States. The boat operators were making a killing. If one party wouldn't pay their price another would. "It's down at the end of this pier. The name of the boat is the *Maria Elena*, said Marshall and they followed him on the water-soaked rickety planks.

"Watch your step," Marshall called back as they made their way toward the boat. The smell of dead fish and brackish water filled their nostrils. The odor made Marge sick. She gagged and stopped to vomit. She felt weak and fell down onto the pier. She tried to stop her fall with the hand she used to carry her bag of jewels. The bag fell into the water and sank.

"Someone help me! My jewels, they're gone! For God's sake, someone get my jewels I dropped them in the water." Marge screamed at Thorton who was helpless.

Clint and Jimmy ran to her. Clint peered into the murky water and saw nothing. He dived into the water. He opened up his eyes and could see nothing around him except old discarded tires and barnacle-encrusted debris in the cloudy water. He came up for air and saw the faces of the anxious onlookers.

"I can't see down there," he said, shaking his head.

In the meantime Marshall had gone to the boat for help and came back with a young albino, who was the Cuban captain's son. He dived in near Clint. Clint swam back to the pier and Jimmy helped him out. Everyone stood waiting for the albino to surface. A few anxious moments later, the albino came up holding Marge's bag out of the water.

Marge yelled at Thorton. "Give that boy a reward, Thorton. He's saved my jewels."

Clint and Marshall helped the boy out of the water and he went to Marge and presented her with the bag. Marge gave him a big hug and a kiss. Clint reached in his pocket and took out the roll of wet bills and gave the boy a hundred-dollar-bill.

"Muchas gracious, Señor," he said, smiling at Clint. He ran off in the direction of their chartered boat. They could see Roman standing on an old fishing boat ahead. As they got closer they could see that the boat was rusted out. There was so much caked rust that you couldn't see the paint except on the wooden pilothouse.

"We're not getting on this horrible thing, are we?" asked Marge.

"It's our only way out of here. In fact I was lucky to find this floating rust heap," said Marshall. The captain, who was a fat, drunken Cuban, came to the side of the boat to help them aboard. His son, the albino, gave a hand to Tana and helped her aboard. Tana's heels had broken off so she walked bare-footed. Clint attempted to go below, but the smell of diesel fuel drove him back up on deck.

After Clint had given the captain half payment of twenty-five hundred dollars, the captain started the engines, and they inched their way into the harbor. The smoke coming from the dilapidated smoke stack blew in their faces. They choked and moved to the front. A salt-water breeze refreshed them as they passed the old fortress of Morro Bay on to open sea. Clint thought, what irony. They had come to Havana first class and left as boat people. He almost laughed.

PART II

Confessions of a Hollywood Agent

146

SEVENTEEN

Back in Hollywood Clint heard that John Fitzgerald Kennedy had announced he would run for President. Clint was pleased and got involved in his campaign organizing a group of actors and actresses to attend numerous functions on Kennedy's behalf.

On the night before the Democratic convention in Los Angeles, a cocktail party for JFK, United States Labor's choice for President, was given by Dave McDonnell, head of the United Steel Workers union at Chasen's restaurant in Beverly Hills.

The guest list was impressive. Mayor Daly of Chicago, Mayor Wagner of New York, George Meany, head of the CIO and the California Democratic leaders.

Clint brought Dorothy Winters, who was gaining worldwide fame for her movie roles. She stood out in the crowd with her long red hair, her full bust and creamy white skin in a Galanos black and white crepe dress, accentuated by some beautiful jewelry.

The old union leaders gave her attention and wondered among themselves what it would cost to keep a woman like Dorothy.

JFK was an hour late and the horde of invited guests were getting loud and restless. When he finally made his entrance you thought you were at an Irish wake.

JFK made his way around the room shaking hands, thanking everybody for their help and asking what he could do for them when he became President. When he got to Clint and Dorothy, he said,

"Kenny O' Donnell tells me you're responsible for bringing new talent into the party. Keep up the good work". He gazed at Dorothy and gave his firm hand. "Dorothy Winters, I've admired your performances. I'm happy to find you're a Democrat. If you're ever in Washington, don't hesitate to call. We'd like to entertain you," he said, smiling, and moved on.

Clint glanced at Dorothy and said, "I think he likes you. I wonder what he meant by we?"

"What do you mean? He's referring to his wife."

"Oh, it's obvious he's more than a fan of yours," Clint said smiling.

"You'd set me up with him, wouldn't you? You horrible pimp."

"Why not? Look what you could do for our country." Mayor Daly passed by.

"Mr. Mayor, I'd like you to meet Dorothy Winters." Mayor Daly gazed at Dorothy, giving her an approving eye.

"I just returned from Chicago, Mayor. Do you know the Blackstone Raiders?" Mayor Daly was taken back by the question.

"How would someone like you know radicals such as...excuse me I have to talk to that fellow over there before he gets away, but I'll be back to ask you how you got acquainted with that group," said the Mayor as he left her side.

Tana Williams spotted Dorothy and took the hand of the man she was with, a middle-aged Germanic-looking man who wore frameless glasses, and pulled him along behind her.

"Dorothy, how beautiful you look. Your dress is lovely. This is the German gentleman I told you about when we were in Cuba, Johannes Diedrich."

Johannes took a small bow and took Dorothy's hand and kissed it. "Good to meet you." he said gazing into Dorothy's eyes. Dorothy was impressed. He had that perverse look she found interesting. She could tell there was mutual interest. She hadn't had that feeling since... Geoffrey.

"Tana, you never told me how attractive he is."

"I wanted to surprise you."

"Can we sit?" Johannes suggested and pointed to a empty table.

"Do you come to California often?" asked Dorothy.

"I bought a home in Beverly Hills."

"We're neighbors. I live there, too."

"It will be easy to see you then." Dorothy liked that comment. "I go to the bar and get champagne for you?" Dorothy and Tana nodded. Johannes left their table.

"Tana, you know my type. He is sexy and he gives me a feeling of danger. Why didn't you tell me who he was? He is wealthy. Are you dating him?"

"We're just friends. He's very generous, but a little kinky."

"Kinky? What do you mean? What does he want you to do?"

"He likes two girls."

"Jeez! What's with these guys today? Can't they get it up for one girl anymore? I told you I wasn't into that. I think I'll pass on him if he wants me to do scenes."

"He'd respect you, maybe. He does give a girl beautiful things." Tana adjusted a pearl and diamond earring she wore.

"I do love jewelry," said Dorothy, looking at Tana, smiling.

Johannes returned to the table with a bottle of Dom Perignon and three glasses and poured their glasses full.

"Can I make a toast?" asked Dorothy.

"Of course," said Johanes.

"To the next President of the United States, John Fitzgerald Kennedy."

The next morning Clint was awakened by the telephone.

"Did you see the man Tana Williams and I were sitting with last night?

"Johannes Diedrich?"

"You know him?"

"By reputation."

"What's his story?"

"He's very rich. By the way, I got it from a good source JFK is seeing Marilyn Monroe on the side. I thought I'd mention it in case you have some ideas yourself." Dorothy kept silent on the line.

"I'll see you tonight at the convention. It's the Sports Arena. Bye." Clint hung up. I wonder what she's up to? he thought. Only time will tell.

EIGHTEEN

Clint bought an option on a book. The novel would be the starting point for his move to producing. Nathan had accepted him and introduced him to the head of MGM Studios. His meetings were productive and they initiated the step process for a future motion picture. He remained at the talent agency and kept his clients happy and working.

Georgia and Marty had their baby. It was a boy. Marty told Clint he felt happier than he had in years, and said Georgia loved being a mother and all she talked about was her child.

Clint spent time in the morning watching the stock market quotes. He and his friends had invested in Marsh International Gaming. A great amount of activity had been going on with the stock. It had risen over twenty points. He picked up the phone and called Dorothy.

"Hello."

"Have you heard? Marsh International Gaming is up over twenty points today. I doubled my money. Should I sell?"

"No, not yet, Nathan just returned from the East Coast. Whenever he goes back there the stock goes up. I think he tells every head waiter between here, New York and Toronto to buy the stock and they pass it on to their customers."

"You think I should stay in, huh?"

"The stock will go up more, " said Dorothy.

"Did I tell how much I love you? You're making me a big deal. I'm being known for my financial wizardry."

"You're welcome, darling."

Minutes later the phone rang. Clint picked it up.

"Clint, it's Thorton North."

"I bet I know why you called", said Clint.

"You do. My broker called me about Marsh International. Should I sell?"

"No. I checked with my source. Hold on. Buy more."

"I'll do that. We got bad news around here. Marge has cancer."

"I'm sorry to hear that. Where?"

"In her lungs." Clint visualized Marge always with a cigarette.

"Is she getting treatment?"

"She's starts radiation next week and if that doesn't work they'll give her chemical therapy." Clint imagined Marge losing her hair.

"I've been sitting around all day wanting to take a drink. Me wanting a drink and not taking one. I won't know what to do if she goes." Clint could hear Thorton choking up on the phone. "I know I have been miserable to her sometimes, but I love her and she loves me in her own way, even if I haven't seen her pussy for twenty years," said Thorton. Clint heard him break up and start to sob.

Clint said, "My other phone's ringing, I got to go, I'll come by." He hung up and tried to figure how old Marge would be.

Marsh International Gaming stock sold rapidly to the public. They had strategic brokers in different parts of the United States and Canada buying and selling the stock between them creating their own market. The stock soared on the exchange. The SEC became suspicious and suspended the stock. Panic broke out among its investors.

Morry, Nathan, and Dorothy, among others were indicted by the SEC for stock manipulation and subpoenaed to appear in Washington D.C. before the Grand Jury.

The Hollywood press picked up the story. Dorothy Winters's name was mentioned as one of the original owners of the Corporation. A few of the Hollywood Ins, knew Dorothy had skeletons in her closet, but so did others in high positions. Dorothy was popular for her dramatic ability and was getting more respect from the industry with every picture she did. Major stardom was on her horizon. Gossip was changing her image to a Virginia Hill portrait, girlfriend of the mob.

Dorothy was dating Johannes Diedrich. Most of the men in Dorothy's life she could control except Nathan and Clint. She had never met a man like Johannes. On their first date, he flew her in his jet to San Francisco for dinner at the Fairmont Hotel. He gave her a diamond and sapphire pin at dinner in remembrance of their first date. He liked to dance, and they danced throughout the evening. When they returned to Beverly Hills, she invited him in. He talked about his life. He told her about his childhood in Germany during the war. He was fifteen when the war was over, about to be drafted into the Germany Army. He had studied engineering and at a early age had invented and patented a valve that was used all over the world. He also developed some large machinery used to rebuild Germany. He had married at an early age to his first girlfriend, a local girl, who hadn't grown with him in life. They were divorced and he later married a French actress to whom he was still married, but separated. She was an alcoholic.

After their intimate evening together, Johannes gave Dorothy a deep kiss as he left and told her he'd like to fly her to Puerto Vallarta for the weekend. As she removed her clothes and took off her makeup she looked in the mirror and examined her face. Dorothy, you've found your husband.

The date for Dorothy to appear in Washington got closer. Nathan called and requested that she come to his office for a conference. They needed to prepare their defense. Morry Marsh had hired a famous Washington D.C. trial lawyer to counsel them on their appearance before the Grand Jury. He was the best money could buy.

Nathan Wise had kept his name in the background. Nobody really knew much about him, but because his name had been mentioned in the indictment, it brought him an association with the mob. Dorothy knew if Nathan wanted a strike at the studio or the racetrack or any other business that had contracts with unions he could nod his head and they'd shut down.

Dorothy arrived at Nathan's office, a nondescript building in Beverly Hills. His name wasn't listed on the building directory. Dorothy took the elevator to the third floor, and rapped on his door. Nathan opened to let her in. Dorothy flashed him one of her famous movie star smiles. She wore a bright chartreuse colored dress that brought out the green flecks in her eyes.

The room was paneled in light beechwood. An oval desk sat in front of windows that looked out on Beverly Hills. A Marc Chagall painting hung over the fireplace. Nathan went around to his desk and picked up a document and gave it to Dorothy to read as she sat down. After some study she handed it back, looking concerned.

"What am I going to do? This is awful. It'll ruin my career. I don't want to answer my phone anymore."

"I got it covered. Don't worry your pretty head. No publicity. The hearing will be closed. They meet in secret. I have been assured," he said.

"You're sure?" she said searching his eyes. Nathan got up from his desk and threw his hands in the air.

"It's that shitheel, Morry. If he hadn't got those bucket shop operators involved, the deal would have gone along smoothly. It's his fucking greed, the son of a bitch. When this is over, I'm going to bury the prick."

"You wanted me to screw him. I'm glad I didn't. I spotted him for a star fucker. You should ask my opinion about some of these guys you get involved with. I could save you a lot of trouble."

"Is that Nazi you see a star fucker?" Nathan had confirmed what she suspected. He was having her followed.

"You know about him? Why do you call him a Nazi?" she asked.

"Because he is. He told a realtor that sold him his house in Beverly Hills that he was Hitler's godson. Does he know you're Jewish?"

"We haven't discussed it. I don't believe you. Why would anyone say such a thing? Especially in Beverly Hills, almost everyone is Jewish. You're making this up. She could tell that Nathan was jealous. It's all right if I screw someone he wants me to screw, but if I find someone on my own, he can't handle it. I've got to get away from him, she thought. Johannes is my only way out. She rose from the chair.

"What do you want me to do?"

"Don't talk to anyone about anything. You got that?"

"I got it. I have to go. There's a luncheon for Premier Khrushcev, who's visiting Twentieth Century Fox, today. I'm going to show him what a real capitalist woman is all about."

"Does that mean you'll suck his cock for a hundred?"

Dorothy peered at Nathan. "It's always sex with you, isn't it?"

"What else? I haven't been by in awhile. Expect me soon," he said as he got up to let her out.

Dorothy thought about her involvement with Nathan as she left his office. I hate the power he has over me. He made me and he could destroy me.

NINETEEN

"Hi, Kid. You called?" asked Marty.

"Howdyado today at the track?" Clint knew the answer. It was always a lie.

"Great, had four winners. One paid twenty-three dollars."

"Raoul Walsh, the director, wants you for a picture in Europe. I read the script. It's a great part. He'll give you one hundred thousand dollars. With eight weeks shooting and two first class tickets. Are you interested?"

"If he pays two hundred thousand I am."

"I'll work on it."

"Do you know someone called Luis Verano?" asked Marty.

"Luis Verano... Luis Verano, yes he's the producer, director, Georgia worked for in Cuba? Wasn't he killed?"

"He's alive! And he's been calling here for Georgia."

Luis was alive and in Los Angles. His helicopter was shot down over the Caribbean Sea by a US Navy plane. The US government kept it a secret. Luis was injured in the crash. The helicopter pilot tied Luis's belt to the copter's pontoon, which kept them afloat. A passing Panamanian freighter picked them up. Luis remained in a coma. When he woke he was on his way to Barcelona, and he was hospitalized in Spain.

Castro came to power in Cuba. Luis had the Cuban Consulate in Barcelona let Castro know he was alive. He remained in Spain until he could travel back to Cuba. When he returned, Castro offered him the job of minister of propaganda.

Luis dived into his new status in Havana as a diligent Castro follower. Within a short time he saw that Castro was a Marxist. Luis

157

was not a Communist; he had been a Socialist and was against Castro's association with the Soviet Union.

His love for Georgia had never faded. She was on his mind constantly. He tried to get in touch with Erroll Flynn to find Georgia's whereabouts, but learned that Erroll had died of his afflictions shortly after he left Cuba.

Luis became disillusioned with his life in Cuba. The revolution had not turned out like he had thought. Castro had become an egomaniac and was beyond reach of his past associates. Luis, an artist and romantic, saw the freedom of the people was more curtailed than during the Batista regime. The motion pictures that Castro wanted Luis to produce became message propaganda movies. Censorship became a problem and Luis hadn't the freedom he needed to be happy. After careful thought he decided he wanted no more of the Cuban dictator, and started to plan his escape to the United States and Georgia.

A conference of motion pictures producers from Latin American countries was held in Mexico City. Luis represented Cuba at the meetings. After a few days in to Mexico City, he disappeared into the crowd and found his way to Tijuana where he crossed the border into the United States illegally. He had a cousin who worked for the Spanish language television station in Los Angeles who put him up until he could find work. Luis found a job delivering flowers and he spent his free time searching for Georgia.

He discovered that Georgia had married Marty Fallon. He located Marty's office and he was able to get Marty's home address from his Latin secretary.

He waited outside the Fallon home watching for Georgia. The first time he saw her, she came out of the house holding on to a small child. It upset him so much that he let her drive off without trying to contact her.

The next day he was back. He had seen Marty leave the same time in the morning so he knew Georgia was home alone except for the maid. Luis sat in the delivery truck on the road across the street from the house when Marty left that morning. He unloaded a box of red roses from the van and went to the front door and rang the bell. Georgia's maid, a Latina, answered it.

"Is Mrs. Fallon in? I have these roses for her. I'm supposed to deliver them to her personally," he said.

"A minute, I'll get her," said the maid. Luis began to sweat. He felt his heart was trying to jump out of his body.

Georgia came to the door in her robe. "Who are these from?" she asked looking at him. "Luis, Oh, Luis!" She flew into his arms holding him tight, then she backed away observing him closely. She took her hand and put it to his face. She ran her finger down a long scar from his temple to his chin.

"Should I leave, or do you want me to stay?" he asked.

"Oh, darling, stay, stay. Don't you ever leave again," she said as tears appeared. She hugged him again. A little boy ran up to her. Luis looked down at him. The boy could be mine, he thought. Georgia pulled Luis inside and closed the door.

The subpoena to appear in Washington weighed on Dorothy. There had been no mention of it in the papers. Nathan had kept his word and kept it quiet. But she knew she had to appear before the Grand Jury and it scared her. At times she thought she should leave Hollywood and marry Johannes. And again she knew she was an actress and had to act. If she couldn't work she felt miserable. She needed accolades from the public to feel good about herself. She asked herself, what do I want? Do I want to go on being a famous actress for the rest of my life or do I want to get married and have children? And from what other actresses she knew had told her it was almost impossible to have both. She wanted the love of a man, but she also wanted the love of her public.

Johannes, she felt, was more sophisticated and attentive than American men, but he hid his feelings and she never knew where she stood. She had always had the upper hand with all her men, except Nathan and Clint. Clint was the only man who knew her for what she was. Johannes was different. He frustrated her. She sought advice from her friends hoping to gain some insight as to how to get him to marry her. Sexually she knew she was superior. She had all the whore tricks to keep her men interested. She was not going to fall into a menage-a-trois. She had gotten advice from a successful courtesan who told her to bring the other girl into the scene. "Don't let the man do it," she said. "That way you control." She thought, if this is the only way she could get Johannes, she would.

TWENTY

Clint had gotten a call from the USO, in Washington. They wanted Marty to come to the Capital to do a benefit and accept an award of merit for his services in the past for entertaining the troops. Clint, through his Washington connections, was able to get the President to ask them to visit the White House while they were in town. Marty was a conservative the likes of John Wayne and Ronald Reagan. Clint knew he'd have a problem convincing Marty to go to the White House even if he told Marty the President was a fan of his. Clint had never been to Washington and knew it would be a good opportunity to take some Hollywood starlets with them. He knew JFK liked attractive, glamorous women and he would make some points with the President. He had given up playing the horses, but going to the track with Marty would be a good place to discuss his invitation to the White House. Marty was always in a good mood at the track.

They arrived at Santa Anita Racetrack, nestled in the foothills near Pasadena. Marty leased a box in the Club House, where gathered the strangest people one could meet. They all suffered from the racing obsession. If you wanted advice about picking a horse, they knew every angle. The Racing Form flew around the box like a kite. Numerous characters dressed in loud coats and ties would approach Marty and whisper in his ear as Marty nodded. An older lady, a regular in Marty's box, told him the voice told her today to bet on the three horse in the second race. Vince Edwards, the actor, came over to compare notes on a horse. Jimmy Durante stopped by to say hello and gave Marty a horse in the third race. Clint was amused for he could remember his poor days at the racetrack sitting in the grandstands where he'd bet to supply his livelihood.

Marty was deep into the Racing Form picking a horse for the next race.

"I got a call from the USO in Washington. They want you to come to Washington to accept an award for your outstanding work for them."

"No kidding."

"We can work it into your schedule on your way to Europe. You wouldn't have to make two trips."

"Sounds good," said Marty, immersed in the Form.

"The President would like you to come to the White House while you're in town," said Clint.

"I'm not going to the White House," said Marty putting the Form down. "I'm a lot of things, but I'm not a hypocrite. Thank the President, but no thanks."

"Marty, the President is a fan of yours, and Jackie has done over the White House. They say she did it with great style and she'll give you a private tour," said Clint trying to convince him.

The announcer voice was heard. "The horses are off."

"Keep quiet. I'm watching the race," said Marty as the horses broke from the starting gate. Marty peered through his binoculars.

Clint tried to keep his mind on the race, but it was impossible. He had to get Marty to the White House. When the race was over, Marty's horse "Weak Moment" ran out of the money. Marty was fuming.

"Look!" He pushed the Form in Clint's face.

"She did a mile and sixteenth three times this meet with better time than today. The sonabitch held her back."

Clint thought, there's always some excuse when he loses. "What if the President personally gives you the USO award at the White House? That wouldn't be hypocritical, would it?"

"You sure want me to go to the White House, don't you?"

"It's an honor for you and good publicity."

"You might be right, but it wouldn't be bad for you either."

"I think the President is a fine man."

"I'll do it, but I want you to know I'm doing it because of you, not the President."

"Marty. One of these years I'll vote for one of your guys."

The rest of the day was devoted to winning a race. Clint learned long ago to stay away from Marty's horses, regardless of what information he had gotten. They both left the track losers.

Driving home from the track, Marty complained.

"I'm getting no sex in my house anymore. Something's going on with Georgia. I think she's seeing someone."

"Nah, she's not the type."

"Bullshit. They're all the type. Remember I been through this before. What about this guy Luis Verano? Did you find anything about him?" asked Marty.

Quietly Dorothy, Nathan Wise and Morry Marsh slipped out of town for their appearance before the Grand Jury in Washington D.C. They stayed in separate hotels in the Washington area to make it difficult for the FBI to bug their rooms.

Dorothy had a meeting in a downtown Washington hotel bar with her lawyer, Matthew Donnelly, to discuss the case. Donnelly was one of the most powerful lawyers in Washington. Dorothy was prepared to get him to like her; she knew he was her only hope of getting out of the mess she was in. Nathan blamed Morry for manipulating the stock. So everyone was at odds with each other. They had to stick together if they were to beat the rap, because if one went down so would the rest. Dorothy's whole life was at stake. Her career would be over. Her involvement with Johannes would be finished. How could he marry a gangster's moll, she thought. She was having a nightmare and it could become a reality to destroy her.

It was five PM when she walked into the dimly lit oak-paneled barroom. She was ushered over to a corner booth where Donnelly sat waiting for her. She observed him closely as he introduced himself. She immediately liked what she saw and she could tell he liked her. She had done her homework on him: he was interested in sports, maybe liked to drink too much, was a Catholic, and had a crazy streak, which he used once in awhile in the courtroom. She also heard he had an eye for beautiful women. She had a plan. She knew that most every man had fantasies. She might risk giving him the idea there could be a chance with her if she thought it would work.

"I hope you don't mind me wanting to meet you without the others, but I wanted to get to know you, because this is so new to me. And frankly, Mr. Donnelly, I'm scared to death. I hope you understand," she said in her sweetest voice.

"The name is Matt. I understand completely. It's difficult to come to Washington like this. It shakes up hardened criminals, so I can imagine what it must be like for an inexperienced young girl," he said in a quiet voice. Dorothy already felt confident.

"My staff and I have been studying the indictment the government sent to us, and frankly I can't quite see where they have a case. They haven't proved the stock was manipulated and that's what the case is about. They're suspicious because of its rapid rise in a short period of time, but that's not proving there was a false market. There's a lot of politics behind this. The President's brother, Bobby, as the attorney general, is out to get organized crime. I think that's why the SEC has opened up this case. It involves Las Vegas and gambling and they have been trying for years to prove that the mob runs the gambling in this country."

This was the first time in months that Dorothy felt relieved. She made a deep sigh. "Matt, you have no idea how what you said makes me feel. I've been under a terrible strain. So what is going to happen? What will I have to do?"

"They'll put you on the stand and ask you questions about your involvement. I can't do anything about that. The Grand Jury meets in secrecy. There'll be no press coverage." He glanced around for a waiter. "Waiter, another double scotch on the rocks. How about you? What will you have?" he asked.

"A Shirley Temple."

"You don't smoke, do you?"

"No, I never have."

"Waiter, would you bring me a cigarette, please," he called to him.

"I have been trying to quit," he said. The waiter brought the drinks and the cigarette. Donnelly fingered the cigarette but he didn't light it.

"Would you like a light for the cigarette?" asked Dorothy.

"No, thank you. I'll play with it for awhile and maybe the urge will go away," he said as he gazed at her.

"You know what Picasso said about smoking?" he asked. "Cigarette smoking was like sex. You never get over the urge. If you had ever smoked you'd know what I'm talking about."

"You're an interesting man. It's easy to see why you're so successful," she said, looking into his eyes.

"And you're a beautiful lady. I'm the man who will get all your troubles to go away," he said.

"You're the man I will be eternally grateful to."

"Thank you for that, said Donnelly. "If I'm out in California, and if I called, would you meet me for a drink?"

"Here's my phone number." She opened her purse and took out a pad and wrote it down and gave it to him. He picked it up and peered at it. "I hear you movie stars change your phone numbers all the time."

"Give it back to me. This is my agent's number. He always knows where I am." She wrote down Clint's number and gave it back to him. She got up to leave.

"I'll see you tomorrow at the Grand Jury. Be there at ten," he said as he put out his hand to take hers. He held it a little too long to be polite. It felt to Dorothy like a seduction.

"Good night," she said giving him the "please call me look". She turned and left the barroom. I like this man, she thought, as she went out the front of the hotel to her waiting car. This is the big lawyer I might be needing soon. I think he fell. God, he's attractive.

Clint and his group flew in on a military plane and landed at Bolling Field across the Potomac from the Pentagon. Clint brought Marty, Tana Williams and Dawn Summers, a new Hollywood starlet, for window dressing. The USO had them booked into the Shoreham Hotel in downtown Washington, D.C.

Clint was excited about being in Washington. He wanted everyone to know that he was on a personal basis with the President. Marty was constantly complaining about everything. He hated Washington. He thought they were all a bunch of phonies. All they wanted was their picture taken with him. They're worse than Hollywood types. A bunch of publicity hounds. Nothing pleased him. He reminded Clint he was here because of him, not the President. Clint was trying to enjoy himself, but Marty gave him a big pain in the ass.

That night Clint, Tana Williams and Dawn Summers went out on the town. They got invited to a party given by Senator Humphrey from Minnesota, in one of the private rooms at their hotel. When they made their entrance they caused a minor incident. Everyone stared as they came into the room. Clint thought, we must look different to these people.

Senator Humphrey came to be introduced. The girls acted giddy over him. And you could tell he liked tall beautiful ladies. He introduced the girls around to all the eager gentlemen he knew. Clint noticed that Washington was much like Hollywood, especially at parties where behind the scenes press agents worked the room getting their clients interviewed and their pictures taken. Jack Anderson, the Washington columnist, stood with Dawn Summers and asked her what she did in Hollywood. She told him she was starring in a new Andy Warhol movie called "The Specimen of Man". Vice President Lyndon Johnson had Tana Williams in a conversation. telling her what he was doing to support civil rights. She was impressed with this powerful man.

The girls had given out their numbers to some important men that night. They had fun being with the VIPs and getting their attention. They couldn't wait to tell their friends in Hollywood who they had met and couldn't wait for there visit to the White House tomorrow.

The limousine waited for them downstairs at the Shoreham the next morning.

Marty had called at 7:00 and told Clint he was canceling his appearance at the White House. Clint talked to him for ten minutes trying to convince him that it was all for his benefit, no one else. As much as he might not like the President he couldn't let down the USO who was giving him the award.

Dorothy called him when he hung up. She was also staying at the Shoreham.

"How's it going?"

"Awful, I hate this place. I can't wait to get out of here. I've been lucky. No one knows I'm here. I go before the Grand Jury at ten. I'm as nervous as a cat and my claws are out. I hate what Nathan has done to me."

"Sometimes that's the cost of fame. When you get it the way you and I have."

"Listen smartass, I can do without the lecture. What have you got planned for this evening? I'd rather be with you than Nathan."

"I'm baby-sitting Marty. He's been a pain in the ass. I want to have some fun. I'll mention to the President that you're in town. Call me at six. By the way, make sure you wear your Virginia Hill hat."

"I don't appreciate that crack, you filcher." She hung up.

They met downstairs at the entrance to the Hotel. Marty had his dark glasses on. Clint knew it was a sure give-away for a terrible mood. As Marty got into the back of the limousine, he said to Clint, "I've been calling the house in LA. She's not home. She couldn't wait to get rid of me so she could go off with her lover."

"You're at it again. Making up some crazy fantasy about Georgia."

"Don't you tell me it's a fantasy. I know when I am being cheated on," said Marty, sitting in the back seat solemnly.

The girls arrived with an attitude they could take on the White House. They were dressed in suits that cinched in their waists and pushed up their boobs. They got into the back of the limousine.

"Marty, you should have come with us to the party. We met Senator Humphrey and Vice President Johnson and all these wonderful people. It was so much fun," said Tana.

"I would have hated it. They're all Democrats. I hate Democrats. The only one I will put up with is my agent. And he's bad enough." Marty looked with displeasure at Clint.

They arrived at the East Gate of the White House. The large black wrought iron gates opened. Clint and the girls were thrilled as they passed under the White House portico and stopped. Everyone remained cool for their entrance, except Marty, who fumed under his breath. The group was escorted into the Cabinet Room, which was taken up by a huge table. The names of the President's cabinet members sat on individual place stands in front of the chairs.

Clint saw one of the President's aides whom he recognized. It was Kenny O'Donnell, the appointment secretary. He waved to him as

Kenny went into the Oval Office adjacent to the Cabinet Room. Someone told the gathering to wait, that the President would be with them shortly, and to please sit down. Everyone looked for a important cabinet member chair to sit in. Clint grabbed MacNamara, Secretary of Defense. Marty sat in Dean Rusk's chair, the Secretary of State. The rest followed suit.

Mr. P.T. Smith, the USO Washington director, entered the room and went to Marty who got up to shake his hand.

"Good to see you again, Mr. Fallon. Thank you for coming to Washington to accept this award. We at the USO are very proud to give you this. Aren't you lucky to have the President himself present it to you?" He let Marty look; Marty's name was engraved on the plaque.

"Thank you sir, I'm grateful to be receiving this from you," said Marty as he sat back down.

The President's aide, Kenny O' Donnell, came out of the Oval Office into the Cabinet Room and announced. "Would you go out into the Rose Garden? The President will be there shortly."

They got up from their chairs and went through the French doors out onto the White House lawn. It was a beautiful day in Washington. It smelled of springtime, the trees and roses were showing their buds. The grass was soft under their feet and the girls had trouble with their high heels sinking into the lawn.

The President came out of the White House. He shook a few people's hands and gave them his good wishes. He looked out over the lawn, saw Marty and came over to him. The photographers followed.

"It's so good to see you again. Thanks for coming to Washington. You know I met you years ago. You wouldn't remember," he said. Marty was puzzled.

"Where was that, Mr. President?" he asked.

"Boston. You were in town for a opening of one of your movies. I happened to be in the hotel where you were staying. I had attended a party on the top floor. I rang for the elevator and when it came, you were on it. You must have been about eighteen. You had a great time going up and down in that elevator. If I remember you had a few that night."

Marty laughed but was upset that the President had something so personal on him. "You can bet I will remember this time. Thanks so much for having me here. It is very kind and considerate of you, Mr. President," said Marty in his most charming manner.

"Next time we meet, call me Jack." The President moved on to Clint and the girls. He shook Clint's hand.

"Clint, thank you for coming and bringing all these lovely young ladies with you. Washington always seems better to me when I see pretty ladies."

"Mr. President, Dorothy Winters is in Washington also, but she couldn't come today," said Clint. The President peered at him with interest and moved on to Tana and Dawn.

"Where are you girls staying in town?" he asked. Tana became speechless. Her high heels sank deeper into the soft grass. She couldn't seem to open her mouth to respond.

Clint came to her rescue.

"The girls are staying at the Shoreham, Mr. President."

Tana got her voice back and said. "Mr. President, I voted for you. It was my first time."

The President smiled and said. "See, your vote got me here."

"Mr. President you're so funny. It was all of our votes. I'm so happy that it's you in this place instead of that other man."

The President smiled and moved on. The girls exchanged looks. They felt they had the same feeling. They had met the Man.

The President went to a podium that had been set up for this occasion. He started to read a prepared speech about the USO. When he got to the end he said, "We are here today to honor a terrific American, a man who has given so much of his free time to make us all laugh. A man who has helped make the USO what it is today, through entertaining and taking care of our service men and women all over the world. Ladies and Gentleman, Mr. Marty Fallon."

The audience clapped and Marty came up to the podium and stood next to the President.

"On behalf of the USO and the American people it is my pleasure to present you with this award, Marty Fallon."

Marty accepted the award and went to the microphone. "Thank you for this wonderful honor today. It will always be remembered as one of the highlights of my life. Thank you, thank you," said Marty as he shook the President's hand and left the podium. He went over to Clint.

"Let's get the fuck out of here. Are you coming?" he asked as he started to walk off.

"Christ, no. Jackie is waiting for us in the West Wing to show us what she has done to the White House. You can't leave now. It would be rude. What's your problem? After what's just happened, you would think you'd be proud of yourself and take a few bows instead of acting like a jerk," said Clint

"I'm not going back to the hotel by myself. You are coming with me. You can come back after you drop me off."

"But I'll miss the tour," said Clint.

"Jackie will wait for you," said Marty.

"In a pig's ass she will," said Clint pouting. He went over to Tana and Dawn.

"Marty insists that I go back to the hotel with him. I'll be back as soon as I can. Tell me everything I've missed." The girls were concerned with Clint leaving. As he was about to catch up to Marty, Kenny O' Donnell, the President aide caught up to him.

"The President would like you, Dorothy Winters and the two girlfriends to come to the White House tonight. We'll have a car for you outside the hotel at 8:30 PM," said Kenny.

"Tell the President we'll be there." Clint ran off to catch up to Marty, who waited in the White House driveway.

Clint had gone back to the White House after he had dropped Marty off. He had straightened out a reservation in Athens, Greece for him. He had the limousine wait for him and was driven back to the White House. He couldn't help but feel important as they drove through the East Gate. Some onlookers stood outside the gate checking on who was going in. Clint felt like he was a statesman VIP as the coach pulled up to the White House door to let him out.

The girls stood at the entrance waiting for him.

"The tour was fabulous. You can't imagine. It's a shame you missed it," said Dawn.

"I'm disappointed, but I couldn't leave Marty. He's just a big kid," said Clint.

"The First Lady is so beautiful and she sure has the best taste. She showed us the Lincoln bedroom. I felt so good in that room. I'd like to get screwed in that bed in appreciation for what he did for my people," said Tana. Everyone laughed.

"Only you could say something like that, Tana. It could just happen. The President has invited us back to the White House tonight for a little party," said Clint. Tana let out a scream as she and Dawn gripped each other.

"Are you putting us on, Clint? asked Dawn?

"Why girls, why would I do that?" said Clint smiling.

"Just to be BAD," said Tana. Clint opened the limousine door and they got in and drove off through the White House gate. Clint waved to the gawkers at the entrance.

"We'll be back," he said, as they drove off down Pennsylvania Avenue.

TWENTY-ONE

At ten o'clock Dorothy, Nathan and Morry gathered outside in the corridor of the Justice building. Dorothy dressed in a conservative suit with very little jewelry. She had gotten mad at Clint when he asked her if she was going to wear her Virginia Hill hat, a tasteless joke, she thought. Nathan and Morry had a battery of lawyers with them, but Matt Donnelly handled the Grand Jury. Morry Marsh was called in first to testify. Nathan and Dorothy sat in the corridor not saying too much to each other. A few people recognized Dorothy when they walked by. Dorothy tried to hide her identity. She had put on large sunglasses to hide her face, but that brought as much attention to her as without them.

"You look as if you shouldn't be here," said Nathan. "I told you not to worry. They've got no case. This will be over in no time. We'll be out of here and never be back," he said as he put his hand on her knee and patted it. "Donnelly said Bobby Kennedy is behind this. When I think of what I did to get his brother elected President and now they turn on us. That's gratitude for ya."

The door opened from the hearing room and Morry walked out.

"They're just fishing. They've got nothing on us. It's just some fucking harassment," said Morry, wiping his brow.

Matt Donnelly approached Nathan. "You're next." Nathan got up and went into the courtroom.

"What kind of questions did they ask you?" asked Dorothy.

"They didn't get any answers," said Morry.

"Why not?"

"Because I took the fifth, that's why. Don't worry. You could be a murderess, and they'd forget who you are in six weeks. Everyone in this country has a short memory," said Morry

173

"But I'm a celebrity. Look what happened to Ingrid Bergman. She had a baby out of wedlock and the public has never forgave her."

"Nah, forget it. That's different."

Morry glanced around. "Where's a phone? I got to find a phone." Dorothy pointed to a phone on the wall in the corridor. "I'll be back," said Morry as he moved to the telephone.

Dorothy sat in deep thought. The only person that knew she was in Washington was Clint. She wanted no one to know, especially the studio and Johannes.

The door from the Grand Jury room opened and Nathan came out acting relieved.

"Did you take the fifth?" she asked.

"Yeah," he said.

"Should I, Mr. Donnelly, I mean Matt? I don't want to."

"Why not?" asked Nathan.

"Because I don't feel right about it. That's why."

"For Christ sake, honey. It's there for your protection," said Nathan annoyed.

"What do you think, Matt?" she asked.

"If you feel you don't have to, don't," he said. "They're waiting for you." Dorothy got up from her chair and Matt Donnelly escorted her to the door of the Grand Jury Room.

"Tell them what you know. They'll believe you," he said as she walked into a walnut-paneled room. An enormous table took up the room behind which sat twenty people, males and females from all walks of life. All were white except for one black woman. Most of them recognized her as Dorothy Winters, the movie star. Some smiled at her, which she felt pleased about. It took the tension away for a moment. She sat in the chair and faced the Grand Jury. A clerk came.

"Would you please state your full name and the address where you reside."

"Dorothy Winters, 1229 Dawn Ridge Drive, Beverly Hills, California."

"Raise your right hand for the oath. Do you Dorothy Winters solemnly swear that you ... according to the best of your understanding. So help you God."

"I do," said Dorothy. A tall, thin young man wearing a dark suit and horn-rimmed glasses got up from a desk in front of the Grand Jury. He came to the witness stand and introduced himself as Larry Simon, a government attorney. He peered at Dorothy closely.

"Miss Winters, you are an officer of Marsh International Gaming?"

"Yes, I am."

"What is your corporate position?"

"I'm the corporate secretary."

"What does that entail?"

"I attend all board meetings. I'm responsible for the corporate minutes."

"What exactly does Marsh International Gaming do?" he asked.

"Marsh International Gaming is a corporation that buys hotels and casinos in Nevada and runs them," she answered.

"Runs them for whom?" he asked.

"For the corporation, the stockholders."

"Whom did Marsh International buy these hotels and casinos from? Was it from known mobsters and professional gamblers?" he asked.

"I never knew from whom the hotels were purchased."

"I'll change the question. Did you know any of the sellers personally?"

"No, I did not."

"How did you, a movie actress, become the secretary of Marsh International? Wasn't that an unusual departure for a screen star to be involved in hotel and gambling casinos?"

"No. They're Hollywood people in business in Las Vegas. Tony Martin was a part owner of the Flamingo. Frank Sinatra has a piece of the Sands and there're others. It's a business deal for me," she answered.

"You didn't answer my question fully. How did you become secretary for Marsh International Gaming?"

"Mr. Morry Marsh, who I was dating, asked me if I would like to be secretary," she said.

"Did he tell you what you had to do to be a secretary?"

"He said I would have to attend board meetings once a month and be responsible for the minutes. That was about it. It didn't seem like much extra work for me."

"Miss Winters, to your knowledge, do you know if the stock of Marsh International Gaming was being manipulated?"

"No, not to my knowledge."

"Did Mr. Marsh or Mr. Wise discuss with you how Marsh International Gaming was being sold?"

"Yes. They told me the stock was being sold through brokers around the country."

"Do you own stock in Marsh International?"

"Yes," she answered.

"How many shares do you have?"

"I have a few shares. How many is my business."

"Okay, then what price did you pay for your stock, Miss Winters?" he asked. There was a long pause.

"I'll tell what price you paid." He held up a piece of paper. "You paid thirty-five dollars per share. The day the stock was suspended it was at one hundred and thirty-five dollars. Now, Miss Winters, don't you think it was highly irregular that you bought the stock at thirty-five dollars and in six months' time it was selling for one hundred and thirty-five dollars? That's one hundred dollars per share in profits. Isn't that right, Miss Winters?"

"I never question a profit, Mr. Simon."

"I see." He lowered his head.

"I have no more questions," said Mr. Simon as he went back to his desk. The jury foreman peered to the other jurors at the table.

"Does anyone else have any questions for Miss Winters?"

A young man dressed in an open shirt asked, "How old are you, Miss Winters?"

Dorothy was surprised by the question and gave him one of her movie star smiles. "On that question I will take the fifth, if you don't mind," she said, smiling at the young man. The rest of the jurors smiled and coughed at her answer. Dorothy knew then she had made a good impression on the jury.

"You are excused, Miss Winters." Dorothy got up from the witness chair and walked out of the courtroom to the corridor where Nathan was waiting.

"How did it go in there?" he asked.

"Grueling."

Matt Donnelly walked into hearing Room and came out a few minutes later.

"I asked for a dismissal. There's no evidence the government produced to back up the indictment. They're voting now. You can leave. I'll call you later with the verdict."

"We'll wait, Matt," said Nathan. They sat down and waited and remained quiet. Finally the door opened and a man emerged.

"Mr. Donnelly, Would you come in?" he asked. Matt Donnelly followed the man back into the room. Dorothy crossed her fingers. She peered at Nathan who remained expressionless. A few tense minutes passed and the door opened again and Donnelly walked out towards them with a smile.

"They voted for a dismissal," he said. Dorothy ran to him and gave him a kiss. She glanced at Nathan who managed a smile.

"Isn't he wonderful? He got us off! Now I can get my life back in order." Dorothy kissed Donnelly again.

TWENTY-TWO

When Clint got back to the hotel there was a message for him to call Gale. Dorothy was using her old name in Washington.

"How did it go? he asked into the phone.

"They dismissed the charges. They couldn't prove a thing. And I'm in love with my lawyer. He's wonderful. So kind and sincere. He gave me the confidence I needed to face everyone."

"What happened at the White House?" she asked.

"We're invited back tonight to be entertained. I mentioned you were in town. I think that's why we were asked."

"Will his wife be there?"

"I doubt it. I think this little party is for us. We can get better acquainted."

"You give me the feeling you're setting me up on a big platter of power."

"I never thought in those terms, but I like the dramatics of you being with the mob in the daytime and seeing the President in the evening. Even Mata Hari couldn't work her charms to get to that echelon."

"What time do I have to be ready?"

"Be down in the lobby at eight-thirty."

Everybody arrived on time. The girls were in the lobby before 8:30. Clint checked their wardrobe. He didn't like Dawn's outfit. She wore black leather with a short mini-skirt and her hair in a thick braid. He sent her back upstairs to change into something less obvious.

Dorothy had on a movie star, figure-clinging green dress, which exposed her cleavage, and some simple jewelry. She wore her hair down around her shoulders. Tana dressed in a slinky black dress and looked exotic.

Clint walked outside and spotted the White House car by its government license, an unmarked Buick. He walked over to the driver and told him to wait for his party. A few minutes later the three girls came out of the hotel and Clint waved them to the car.

As they got in he said," "No one is to talk about tonight. We're a very special group with privileges. If anything gets out about our rendezvous I'll personally take it upon myself to expose that person to whoever I'll have to. I'm sure you understand. Now let's get on to a good time."

They arrived at the White House, not in the manner they had arrived earlier. They were driven around to a back entrance and ushered by an aide into a hall and up some steps to the second floor. They had passed the Secret Service men in doing so. The aide opened a door that led into a large room, which had a blazing fire going. The room was like a combination den and library. The President stood talking to a Latin man dressed elegantly but causally.

The President came to them as they entered. He wore a blue cashmere sweater that covered a white shirt and dark gray slacks. He showed his famous grin as he took Dorothy's hand. He grabbed Tana's hand at the same time and acknowledged Clint. The Latin man walked over to them and the President introduced him as Porfirio Rubirosa. He flashed a big toothy smile and introduced himself to Dawn, who tried to keep from swooning.

Dorothy knew what she was there for. She used a superior poise when she felt uncomfortable. She was meant for the President. A neat little package that Clint had wrapped up for him. She had to admit he was attractive. She asked herself, What's it going to hurt if I screw him? He looks like he wants me. Rubirosa, Porfirio Rubirosa. He's the Latin playboy who marries those rich women. What an odd choice for a friend. The President must be a playboy himself.

"Mr. President," she said.

The President interrupted her. "Call me Jack. I was pleased when I heard you were in Washington and would be here tonight. What brought you to the Capital?" he asked.

"A play. I'm thinking of doing a play here. I wanted to see what the theater felt like before I made a commitment."

"It would be great to have an actress of your caliber working in Washington. You can count on me for opening night. That is, if I'm in town."

"How sweet of you to say that. You're a nice man. I'm thrilled you're in this place. Our country needed a man like you. You make us feel secure and to know there's someone so concerned and real sitting in the White House is a joy to me."

"I hope the American people feel as you do. It's been rough lately. Castro's making my life complicated. It's ironic to think he is only ninety miles off our shores with his kind of government, and the sad part it looks like he's there to stay."

Tana and Dawn were having drinks made by Rubirosa, and getting comfortable. Snacks sat on a table near the bar.

"Do you girls know how to merengue?" asked Rubirosa. "It's a dance in my country. Tana and Dawn glanced at each other and then back at Rubirosa.

"No," said Tana. "Are you going to show us how?" she asked.

"I brought the music." He went to the phonograph and put on a Latin recording. It had an upbeat sound. He took Tana's hand to dance. Tana danced well. She took to his lead as he moved her around the room with the movement of his hips keeping time to the beat of the sound. Clint got Dawn to dance following Rubirosa's movements. It didn't take too long before they were on to the dance, laughing, pushing and swaying their bodies together to the rhythm.

"This is a sexy dance, Porfirio, and you're such a good teacher," said Tana.

"Thank you. The name is Rubi. You're a beautiful dancer yourself," said Rubirosa as they continued to move around the room.

JFK peered at Dorothy with a look in his eye.

"Would you like to dance with me?" asked Dorothy.

"I'd like to, but I've had surgery on my back and I don't think that dance they're doing would help it much." He took her hand and held it. She peered back into his clear blue Irish eyes. He put his hand on her knee. She could feel the heat rising in her body.

"I know this is a big house, but don't you worry your wife might walk in here?" asked Dorothy.

"For your information, there're one hundred and thirty-two rooms in the White House and I've been in but a few of them. As far as my wife is concerned, she went to New York late today. So you can relax. Come! I'm going to take you to see one of those one hundred and thirty two rooms. They got up from their chairs. JFK took Clint aside. "Dorothy and I are going down the hall to one of the bedrooms. Tell Tana to join us there. It's two doors down on the right," he said as he and Dorothy left the room quietly.

Clint nodded. He cut in on Rubi who was still dancing with Tana and they changed partners. Rubi danced with Dawn.

"Are you having a good time?" Clint asked Tana.

"Look at this girl, dahlin. Does she look like she's having a good time? Dahlin, this girl is having a ball." They turned and swirled to the beat of music.

"The President wants you to join him and Dorothy in the other room down the hall."

Tana looked at Clint with a certain amount of surprise. "If he wants that, tell him only if it's in Lincoln's bed."

"I can't do that. You're going have to tell him," said Clint.

"Where did they go?" asked Tana.

"They went out that way two doors down on the right." Clint pointed to the door at the other end of the room.

Tana went to a chair and picked up her bag. She turned and gave Clint a tiny wave and walked toward the door leaving the room with a little sway in her hips.

Three of them were left in the room. Rubi moved Dawn around the room. Dawn laughed and flirted with him as the danced to the beat. They were drinking Remy Martin brandy and were drunk. Rubi was fascinated with Dawn's thick braid. He kept looking at it and touching it. Dawn was annoyed, but said nothing. As they danced by the desk near a window Rubi reached down and picked up a large pair of scissors that was used to open mail. Dawn's back was turned so she didn't see the scissors in his hand. He reached up behind her and grabbed a hold of her braid and cut it off.

Dawn stopped, realizing what he had done.

"YOU BASTARD, What did you do that for?" she yelled into his face. Rubi stood in front of her with a half smile and Dawn's hair in his hand.

"I couldn't help myself," he said.

"You're a sick, spoiled, son-of-a-bitch. Give me back my hair." She grabbed her cut-off braid from him and went to a chair and picked up her purse.

"Clint, do you believe what this asshole did to me? I'm leaving. And you, greaseball, are going to hear from my lawyer." She waved her cut-off braid in Rubirosa's face.

Clint walked up to Rubi and said, "What you did is inexcusable. It's not funny. And you're not cute. Get ahold of me tomorrow at the Shoreham before this incident gets out of hand. Give the President our regrets for leaving. You can tell him what you have to, I'm sure it won't be the truth." He and Dawn left the room.

"Dawn, what a jerk! You're going to be amazed at what kind of money you'll be able to get for that phony piece of hair," said Clint as they went to the waiting car.

TWENTY-THREE

The ringing of the phone in his room awakened Clint.

"Clint Nation?" asked a Latin-accented male voice.

"Yes."

"Porfirio Rubirosa, here. About last night. I displayed bad manners, but I'm willing to pay, if nothing is said. I have a check for ten thousand dollars to cover Miss, Miss, the lady's hair."

"Summers, Dawn Summers. I'll see if she'll accept. Can I get back to you?"

"I'm out all day. I'll call you about four o clock. I trust you'll take care of this delicate matter for me." He hung up.

Clint called Tana Williams's room.

"Hello," Tana answered in a sleepy voice.

"It's Clint. What happened last night?"

"I'm in love. Did you know the poor man sleeps on a board?" said Tana.

"No."

"We wondered what happened to you when we came back?"

"What did Rubirosa say?"

"He said Dawn got sick and you escorted her to the hotel."

"How did Dorothy react when you showed up in the room?"

"She wasn't happy. She didn't want to share Jack, but who would? He's the President, dahlin."

"It's Jack now, huh? I have your tickets for tonight's benefit. Your day is free."

"I'm calling my friend Adam Clayton Powell. Maybe he'll take me to lunch."

"Not a word about last night. No gossip about the President. I'll know where it came from. Have fun."

Clint hung up and dialed Dawn's room. The phone awakened her.

"It's Clint. Your friend called, the Caribbean playboy. He has a check for ten thousand," said Clint.

"Do you think it's enough? " she asked.

"No. He'll pay twenty-five thousand since you and me are splitting fifty-fifty," said Clint.

"I didn't know I had a partner," said Dawn.

"Dawn, I never do anything for nothing. You're lucky to have me negotiate."

"Do you think he'll pay that much?"

"Of course he will. He's rich. He got millions out of the women he married. He's an old whore. I should ask for fifty thousand, but that's greedy. He knows we could turn this incident into a scandal. He won't jeopardize his position with the President. He'll pay cash too. I'll see you later with the money," said Clint and hung up the phone. The phone rang again. It was Marty.

"Where in the fuck were you last night?"

"The girls and I got invited to a party by another Democrat. I was sure you wouldn't go, so I didn't ask."

"I sat all night by myself going crazy. I can't find my wife. She's still not home. I even called her mother and she said she hasn't heard from her, but I don't believe her. I think I heard my kid in the background. They're doing a conspiracy on me. It's driving me nuts. What do you suppose she's up to? I bet she's with that Verano guy. I finally got it out of the maid that she left the house right after I did. She's making my life miserable."

"She'll turn up and have a reasonable explanation."

"You're always saying that. You act like you're protecting her," said Marty.

Clint wanted to get off the subject. "The producer called, he wants you about eight-thirty."

"Where is the benefit?"

"The Armory."

"What are you doing today?"

"I thought I'd go to see the Smithsonian and the Capitol, to watch Congress."

"They're a racetrack in Maryland. You wanna go?"

"I'd rather not. I'd rather catch some culture of DC. Bye."

Clint made a move to get up, but decided to stay in bed. He reached and pick up the phone to call his office in Hollywood. His secretary gave him his messages. Ben Law had called him from Carmel. He remembered Ben. He was a publicist and called him back.

"Hi, Ben. What are you doing in Carmel?"

"I'm on a picture. Whatever this is worth. Marty Fallon's wife's here with a Cuban. He's on assignment for some Latin newspapers covering the film. They were holding hands and kissing in a restaurant I ate at last night."

"Thanks for the tip, Ben. I owe you one. Bye." Clint thought as he hung up, if Marty knew what was going on, he wouldn't go to Europe to make the picture. I better keep this information to myself.

Clint didn't leave his room; he stayed in bed. He got up to meet Porfirio Rubirosa at five o'clock. He negotiated and collected twenty thousand dollars from him. Dawn told him she was going to buy herself a mink coat and a yellow Cadillac convertible with her half.

The benefit went off as scheduled. Marty had them hysterical with his comedy. He was been able to get to a racetrack in Maryland and had won a few races. The winners put him in a good mood that night. All of Washington came to honor the USO.

The next morning everyone got off to their destinations. Marty went on to Europe to do the movie. Clint, Tana, and Dawn left Washington and went back to Los Angeles on the military airplane.

When Clint arrived home there was a message that Marge North had died. Services were to be held that afternoon in Beverly Hills. Clint quickly got himself organized. He called Tana Williams and told her to meet him at the funeral home off Santa Monica Boulevard. When he arrived the services had began. He walked in the chapel and sat with Tana Williams

Marge was laid out in a open bronze casket in the front of the room. Clint thought she looked serene with her hair done up and they had made her up well. After the services were over, Clint walked up to the casket.

Thorton was standing next to the coffin. "I thought you might miss the services," said Thorton.

"I returned last night. I'm sorry about Marge. We'll miss her," he said as he peered down into in her coffin.

Thorton looked on with him. "She looks pretty good laying there doesn't she? To think I ain't had none of that pussy in twenty years."

Clint felt he had never heard anyone speak about the dead like that. He couldn't answer Thorton.

"Come on up to the house for some drinks, and bring Tana," said Thorton, leaving the funeral home.

Clint and Tana followed the caravan up to Thorton's hilltop house. Everyone made a beeline for the bar. It's going be a wet one; I think I'll get drunk, thought Clint. Now that Marge was gone, it wouldn't be the same because Marge had held the place together. When Clint saw Thorton at the funeral he had a feeling that Thorton wouldn't be around much longer.

Marshall sat at the bar. "You look glum, Marshall. You must know that your days are over." Marshall looked at Clint as if to say, "Fuck off." "Nothing to cry about," he said.

"You've never mentioned your wife. Where do you keep her? Locked up somewhere?" said Clint. Marshall walked away from him. Rally Jones sat at the bar. Clint gave him a hello. Rally, who had been drunk since the accident in Palm Springs, peered back at him with a surly look. Clint knew he was going to stay away from him. A big loser, Clint thought.

Tana Williams came up holding a drink in her hand. "I've been talking to the nice black girl over there." She referred to a plain woman who stood talking to a man on the slight side, her same size, wearing thick dark glasses. "That's Thorton's son."

"No. I knew he had one, but I had never met him. What's he like?"

"Oh, he's very nice. Quiet and unassuming, not at all like his mother and father. It's so funny; you know how prejudiced Thorton is? Yet he has a son married to a black woman. Isn't that ironic? I think he knows I've been his father's mistress."

"How do you know?"

"Call it women's intuition. He seems to know a lot about me. Somebody must have told him. I think he likes the idea, myself."

"You're perceptive."

"You know I'm a witch, dahlin." She gave Clint a big smile and left his side.

The room filled up with guests and got progressively louder from drinking. It was an upbeat mood and everyone was having a good time. There was lots of talk about how glamorous Marge had been and how she would be missed.

Rally had been brooding at the bar. He was drunk and talked loudly. He kept looking at Clint. Rally got up from where he was sitting and staggered over to Clint.

"You know. I never liked you. I could never figure why Thorton had you around. It must have been all that pussy you brought here." Clint turned toward him like a cock rooster about to attack.

"You enjoyed it, you overrated Okie plough-jockey."

Rally took a swing, but Clint ducked and grabbed Rally around the neck and ran him through the open door and threw him out onto the terrace. Clint ran back into the house and locked the doors behind him. Rally got up and pounded on the glass trying to get back in. Clint breathed hard but, with great composure, adjusted his clothes.

"I'm not going to defend myself with that loser," said Clint to a heavy-set man who stood next to him.

"I'm an old fried of Marge's. I came a long way to pay my respects to her. Don't you have any regard for her? Fighting in her house, when she isn't cold in her coffin!" he said.

"Are you kidding?" Clint answered. "This is the kind of party she would have enjoyed." Clint left the room.

Thorton's son followed him. "Clint, Clint, can I have a word with you?" He caught up to Clint and put out his hand in a handshake. "I'm Thorton Jr. I want to ask you something. I know you and my father are friends. He told me he told you that I've never had a white piece of tail. Mother told me he told you that too. Do me a favor. You've been to those whorehouses in Tijuana. You know those girls skin is sort of attaché case color. Can you tell father that? Tell him that I screwed those girls. He tells everybody that I never had any white pussy and that's a lie. I know he'll listen to you. Could you do that for me, please?"

Clint couldn't believe what he had heard. It must be a joke, he thought. But it wasn't. Clint could tell by looking at this poor confused young man that he meant every word.

"Sure, Thorton. I'll tell him. I'll take care of it. I'll tell him what he's missed."

"Thank you. You don't know how relieved I am," he said as he turned and went back into the house. Clint watched him go and shook his head. What our parents can do to us, he thought as he got into his car and drove down the hill.

TWENTY-FOUR

While Marty was in Europe, Georgia hired a lawyer and filed for divorce. When he returned he got back on pills and moved into Clint's guesthouse to forget. Clint tried to help him adjust. Emotionally he cried all the time and didn't want to work, and when he did, Clint had to be with him to make sure he was at the studio and able to work. Georgia's attorney asked for the house she and Marty had bought plus an alimony settlement and child support payments. Marty was broke because of gambling and had to keep working.

Clint, through a friend, had found a psychiatrist at UCLA. Marty liked his approach and let the doctor check him into UCLA Medical Center for treatment Marty's addiction had started early in his career. He was overworked going from one major picture to another. Sometimes he'd be filming two movies at the same time. He had hurt his back and neck in a skiing accident so he lived with pain in addition to the overwork. He took pain pills along with sleeping pills to get relief and gradually got addicted. His doctors kept giving him the pills. The quantities he would take would put a normal person into a coma, but Marty built up a tolerance and kept taking more. He would sleep for days and just get up to eat. He wasn't his feisty self; instead he became mush-mouthed when he talked and acted like a child that needed care. The doctors who gave him the pills no longer wanted to treat him because of his hounding them to satisfy his addiction. He had no trouble getting new doctors to prescribe Seconal and Nembutal because of who he was and the con job he would give them. The only way that Marty would get off the pills was to check into a hospital for the cold-turkey treatment. Most good hospitals looked down on the treatment of drug addicts so it was difficult to find proper care.

When Clint asked Marty's doctor about pill addiction, he said, "It's the worst of all addictions and almost impossible to cure."

Luis moved in with Georgia and her child and pushed her to get a divorce. Marty didn't want a divorce and was determined to get Georgia back. She had no grounds except for mental cruelty, which had to be proven in court.

Castro wanted Luis back in Cuba to stand trial for deserting the revolution and to make an example of him to his followers. The Cuban government, through informants, told the CIA that Luis was an agent of the Cuban government and planned a reprisal in the U.S. against the Cubans who helped in the United States abortive attempt at the Bay of Pigs. The FBI had visited Luis's cousin in Los Angeles looking for him. His cousin told them he didn't know where Luis was, but got this information to Luis. Luis knew if he was caught he would be deported to Cuba. He'd rather die than let that happen, and became a fugitive and desperate man.

Georgia knew nothing of his plight. Luis became insecure and wouldn't let Georgia out of his sight. He became jealous and listened in on her phone calls.

Clint called Georgia. "Don't hang up. You've got to hear me out. I'm not your enemy. I'm trying to help you. Would you see Marty at the hospital? If you two talk without your lawyers you'll be able to clear up this mess. The way things are now he's going to fight you in court and have you declared an unfit mother. He's had a detective on you, and he's got a good case. Talk to him. Work something out."

When the phone rang, Luis had picked it up and listened.

"I'll call him." She hung up as Luis came running into the room.

"I heard what you said. You will not see Marty."

"I have to. You've heard he has detectives on me. He's had us followed. He'll try to take the child. I can't let that happen. I have to talk to him," she said as Luis started to brood.

"If you see him he will talk you into coming back to him. I feel it. You will leave me. I will die first," he said in a monotone voice.

"Luis, you're crazy. I love you. I'm not going to leave you, but I do have to talk to Marty. He's not taking my child."

"That boy is mine. Does he know?"

"He's never said a word. Marty is too proud to say anything. His ego wouldn't let him."

"If you love me you will do this for me."

"Do what?"

"When you see Marty you wear a wire hidden on you. He'll never know about it. Please," he pleaded. "I have to know what he says to you, my darling. It means so much to me."

Georgia could see the seriousness of Luis' insecurities. The poor man. He's scared to death that I'm going to leave him. I'm worried about my baby and he's worried that I will go back to Marty. What a mess, she thought. I have got to work something out; something that works for all of us. She dialed UCLA.

"Mr. Marty Fallon, please. Tell him it's his wife calling." She waited for a moment and Marty came on the line.

"Hi, honey, whatcha doing?" he said sheepishly.

"Marty, can I see you about four today?"

"Sure, honey. I'm not going anywhere."

"Bye." She hung up.

"You never answered me about the wire. You wear it? I have used it before in Cuba. No one will know you are wearing it." He peered at her with a pleading look in his eyes.

"If it means so much to you. You have nothing to worry about. I'm not going back to him, I promise." Luis was relieved.

"I go now to get the wire. I think I know where I can get one. *Adios*." He held her tight looking into her clear blue eyes. Georgia felt warmth in her body while he held her. He kissed her and left the room.

Georgia had sent her boy to her mother's for the night. She gave the maid and governess the day and night off and was alone in the house when Luis returned with the wire and a tape recorder. They enjoyed each other without anyone in the house and made love in the early afternoon out by the swimming pool. Georgia worried about her meeting with Marty, but didn't let on. When Luis brought it up she would change the subject. Before they left for the medical center Luis fitted Georgia with the wire. He pinned the microphone on her brassiere and put the antenna in the back of her skirt at her waist and she covered it with a loose blouse. There was no way to detect the wire. He showed her how to turn it on and off.

They drove to UCLA, neither of them saying anything. Georgia thought about what she would say to Marty. When they got to the hospital Luis drove into the parking lot and let Georgia out, telling her he would remain in the car and wait for her to return. He told her to turn on the wire before she went into Marty's room. Georgia hated wearing it. She thought Luis was childish and she did it to appease him.

As Georgia walked down the corridor toward Marty's room she turned on the wire. She put on a pair of sunglasses so Marty couldn't see the emotions that would show on her face. When she walked in, Marty was lying in bed with the television on. His face was strained and he acted fidgety. She could see he was in withdrawal from the pills. She came to his bedside.

"Honey, I can't tell you how nice it is to see you. How's our son? Has he asked about me?"

"He's growing and he asked about you."

"Pick up that chair and bring it over here and sit by me so I can look at you." Georgia brought a chair over to the bed and sat down.

"Oh, honey I missed you so. Why are we doing this to each other? I love you. I have this terrible time in my mind about you wanting a divorce."

"I didn't come here to talk to you about not getting a divorce. I'm getting a divorce, Marty."

"But, honey what have I done? I try to give you everything. I break my ass working to make the money we need."

"Marty, it's the gambling and the pills. I can't take it anymore. It's destroyed our marriage. It's a sickness you have and it drives me crazy."

"Honey, what's a few dollars at the track?"

"You see. 'What's a few dollars at the track'", she repeated sarcastically. "You just don't get it. A few dollars became thousands of dollars. That's where our money goes. There'll be no money to send the kid to school."

"Honey, you know I make a lot of money when I work and I work all the time. Just because I'm laid up in this hospital doesn't mean it's over for me. When I get out of here, Clint has me booked into next year. Why are you always worrying about money? Don't I give you everything you want? You got a beautiful house, a Cadillac, maids, a nanny and a man who loves you. So I'm a little screwed up, who isn't? If it's money that bothers you, you're going to have more money with me than your Cuban communist. He doesn't believe in money. I can see you living in Cuba on what HE makes. I'm willing to forget about your Cuban. And on my baby's head I swear I'll stay away from the track and quit gambling. Look at me! I'm here having to go through hell trying to get off pills. I'm doing this for you! I don't want to lose you, sweetheart." Marty started to sob. "Honey, I love you so. You don't know what I have been through agonizing over your leaving me. That's why I'm here to show you I can get off pills and be a husband and lover to you again. Can't we forget the past and start over again? I'll change for you. You can bet your ass I will." He sobbed and tried reaching for her hand.

"I would like to believe you, but you've told me this before and gone back to your same bad habits. You're such a good actor, you make me believe you, but you'll say anything to get your way." Marty peered hard at her and his tear-filled eyes narrowed. "I was trying not to bring this up, but I've had you followed for months. I got it all, and that means photos. I'll fight you for my kid. If the judge sees what I have on you, there's no way in hell you're gonna get away with my kid. You'll be declared an unfit mother. Think about it, will ya?"

Georgia started to cry. The tears rolled down her face. "OK, Marty what do you want from me?" she asked. taking, a corner of the sheet on Marty's bed to wipe her eyes.

"Stop seeing your Cuban and I'm to come home to you after I get out of here," he said.

Luis was listening and recording their conversation in the car. He became crazy with rage. His face contorted. Sweat appeared on his upper lip. Then the tape recorder went dead. He pushed all the buttons but nothing happened. "She's turned it off," he screamed. He pulled the wire out of the machine and threw the recorder on the floorboard. He stared straight ahead, his face crimson with rage.

"No. No, She can't leave me." His words trailed off into sobs.

Georgia had gone into the bathroom to turn off the microphone because she didn't want Luis to hear her anymore. Georgia was confused and trapped. There was no solution but to go back to Marty. She could see he loved her very much and she would have her child. That was more important to her than Luis. Life with Luis would be difficult. But how she was going to tell him? she wondered.

Georgia came out of the hospital about twenty minutes later. When she approached the car she saw Luis waiting for her standing against the car fender. She could tell he was suffering by the way he looked at her.

"You're going back to him? I won't let you. I will kill myself first," he said out of control.

"I had to tell him that to get away from him. He's so clever. Before you know it, he has me believing it's all my fault."

Luis watched her like he wanted to believe her. He got back into the car and Georgia got in next to him and they drove back to the house. Luis remained quiet and listless.

Georgia went on to the bedroom when they arrived home. Luis went to the den and pulled open the desk drawer where a .38 caliber revolver lay. He picked it up and checked it for bullets. The pistol was loaded. He put the gun in his pocket and walked down the hallway to the bedroom where Georgia had gone. She was not in the bedroom. He locked the bedroom door behind him and went into the bathroom.

Georgia peered at him as he came through the door. "Are you all right? You look pale."

"I'm OK," he said as he walked to her. He took her in his arms and stared into her face. Georgia didn't know what to make of how he acted. He reached down into his pocket and pulled out the .38. He put the cold barrel up to her jaw and pulled the trigger. The bullet entered her, passing through her mouth and into her brain. She collapsed in his arms and died instantly. He let her fall onto the marble floor. He then put the gun barrel into his mouth and pulled the trigger. His body fell on top of her, the gun still in his hand.

TWENTY-FIVE

Nobody was the same to Clint after Georgia's death. Georgia's mother took her boy. He was too young to know what had happened to his mother. Clint kept Marty working as he adjusted his life. Murder is a hard reality to face, thought Clint, and he blamed himself thinking he could have done more to help Georgia, but he didn't know the seriousness of Georgia's problems and she wouldn't have listened to him anyway. `Love is blind' could not be expressed in better words.

When Dorothy came back from Washington she went into a picture at Paramount. Her studio loaned her out for the part. It was a big-budget picture with name stars in the cast. Dorothy's part was the mistress of a New York racketeer.

Nathan was true to his word. There was no mention of their appearance in Washington. No more indictments, so Marsh International traded again on the stock exchange.

Dorothy's relationship with Nathan had cooled. Washington had caused the rift. Through the years Dorothy had given Nathan sex and the privilege to be able to tell his cronies how much money she cost him. She was his girl and expensive. What better way for Nathan to show off his money than through an expensive mistress. She had heard that he had a new mistress, some new starlet that could use his help. She'd miss his presents, but happily she didn't have to see him again in her bed. He had made it happen for her. She wished him luck and happiness.

Dorothy was spinning the marriage web. She made every effort to get Johannes to marry her. She had learned through observation that men don't marry women, women marry men, and Johannes was a formidable task. He gave her no idea that he would marry her, so she plotted constantly to get him. He divorced his French wife which was one

197

of the major obstacles to marrying him. He gave her expensive gifts: a diamond watch, three strings of twelve millimeter pearls, an emerald ring; but he hadn't told her he loved her or spoken of the future. Teasing her with beautiful presents, but no talk of marriage, had her frustrated. When she finished her part in the picture, Johannes asked her to fly to Aspen, Colorado in his plane for a skiing vacation. They checked into a suite at the Jerome Hotel in downtown Aspen.

Aspen was a quaint little village built at the foot of a mountain and in its early days silver was mined. Most of the homes were Victorian. Gary Cooper and his family spent time there in the winter skiing and brought attention to the place. Now it had become a major ski resort that rivaled Sun Valley. Skiing had become a major sport in the United States and attracted a large group of enthusiasts. Stein Ericson, the Olympic gold medal winner from Norway, ran the ski school and taught a new technique of skiing that everyone tried to learn.

Dorothy saw how good she looked in Bogner ski pants and bought them in all colors with sweaters to match.

Johannes had been skiing since his youth. Dorothy was new to the sport and took private lessons from Stein while Johannes skied on the upper mountain. They would meet for lunch at a restaurant at the bottom of Little Nel, a ski run near the town. She enjoyed the sport and was getting on to its technique, according to her instructor, Stein. She and Johannes acted like kids in the snow.

The beauty of Aspen relaxed her. She couldn't remember the last time she felt so comfortable. All the pressures of Hollywood had disappeared, until she tried to ski by herself practicing what she had learned. A tall man skied up beside her and said. "Nathan sends his regards," and skied off.

The remark upset her. Will I ever get away from him? she thought.

Sex with Johannes was like a dream. No more acting out phony climaxes, not with Johannes. What he did with her in bed made the real Dorothy, not the actress, cry out in the night. Johannes had changed. He wasn't as cagey. He spoke to her with feelings and emotions. She could tell they were falling in love.

He asked her to join him for lunch on the top of the hill and after lunch they would ski together down to the bottom. Dorothy was nervous. She didn't think she was ready, but was willing to give it a try. She took the lift to the top. She marveled at the beauty of the snow-covered mountains in the distance and the serenity and quietness of the upper mountain. In the silent surroundings she could almost hear her heart beat. As she approached the top of the lift she knew she was going to fall when she got off, and she did. She was glad Johannes wasn't there to see her make a fool of herself. There was no shortage of young men to assist her in getting up from the snow. She thanked them and proceeded cautiously over to the snow hut that served as the restaurant.

When she took off her skis and entered, she saw Johannes sitting at a table that looked out over the Rocky Mountain range. She felt exhilarated with the view, the height, and how she felt about him. The wind had made her skin feel hot. She checked herself in a mirror when she walked by it and saw the rosiness of her cheeks and the clearness of her eyes. Johannes got up when she came to the table. She gazed into his eyes and could see her reflected beauty in his face.

"I'm so embarrassed. I fell when I got off the lift," she said smiling at him.

"Ja, happens to all of us," he said as she sat at his table.

"I love Aspen. Do you think we could come back next year?"

"We will. I was skiing with this man, and he told me he would like to sell his house. It's over on Red Mountain right above the town. I told him we'd come over later and have a look."

Dorothy smiled. He said we. I love that word we, she thought.

"Are you thinking of buying a home?"

"Why not? I like it here. They say the summers are better than the winters. How about you, would you like to live in Aspen?"

"You bet your handsome face I would. I'd move tomorrow if I could."

"Why couldn't you?"

"I work, darling, I've got a contract at the studio." She peered at him closely but he said nothing more.

After they had finished their leisurely lunch they went to put on their skis. Johannes helped her get hers on. He led the way as they started down the slope. Johannes took off slowly turning around keeping an eye on her as they skied down the mountainside. He gave her some tips on how to handle her skis, which improved her skiing immediately. He yelled out. "You're doing well. Keep it up. Keep those skis together. *Wunderbar, machen*," he said.

Dorothy felt she was doing better with every turn. She had fallen twice coming down that long hill. Johannes was always there to help her back on her skis. He was so handsome in his ski clothes, she thought. It was the best time she had ever had with him. When they got to the bottom of the hill, they went back to the Jerome Hotel and sat in the bar telling each other stories of what a great day it had been.

Johannes checked his watch. "Let's see that house." They left and drove up to Red Mountain. They came up to a large log and stone house sitting at the end of the road that peered out over Aspen Valley. They rang the bell and a man greeted them and welcomed them in. They walked into a massive living room constructed of logs with a stone fireplace where a fire burned and crackled at the end of the room. The floors were large wooden planks. Bright red Navajo rugs were scattered around. The furniture was covered in old Indian rug fabrics. An impressive collection of Indian baskets sat on a shelf in the corner. "How many bedrooms?" asked Johannes.

"Four, a master and three others. Come, I'll show you." They followed the man through the house. Dorothy imagined how she would decorate it.

"How much did you say you wanted?" he asked the man.

"Two hundred thousand," he answered.

"If you throw in the furniture, we'll take it," he said.

The man thought for a minute and said. "You got a deal." He shook Johannes' hand.

"Would you excuse us for a minute?" Johannes opened the door for Dorothy and they walked out onto the broad deck.

"Do you like it?" he asked.

"Like it? I love it! I could be very happy here with you."

"Will you marry me?" he asked.

She gazed at him with wonderment. "Yes, yes I'll marry you." She moved into his arms.

A cold wind came up as they peered into the sky. They could tell a storm was on its way and returned to the house. Dorothy felt she had never been happier.

Johannes talked over the details of the sale and said he would have his lawyer get in touch in the morning and they left for the Jerome Hotel. Dorothy held on to him, not wanting to let him go. When they came into the hotel lobby and got to the desk to pick up the key, the desk clerk handed Dorothy a message.

"It's from my agent. I'll call him from the pay phone." She pointed to a phone booth in the lobby.

Johannes left and took the key and walked up an old staircase off the lobby.

Dorothy got on the phone to Clint.

"I'm getting married. Johannes has just proposed to me. We're buying a house here and moving," she said excitedly, rushing her words.

"That's the most stupid thing you've every said to me. What about your career? What about me?"

"I'm quitting the business to become a housewife."

"Ha! You're making it sound worse. You a housewife. Get a hold of yourself. If I were there I'd shake you to bring you to your senses."

"Why are you so nasty? Don't you want me to be happy?"

"You're happy when you're working in front of a camera."

"I need security in my life, and Johannes can offer me that."

"What happens when you get bored with him? And you will. The social life you think you want won't be there. Remember your past, darling. There are more holes in it than a cheesecloth. It wouldn't take much work for a private detective to put a thick file together on you, and it won't be redeeming to a future husband. Some people shouldn't get married, and you're one of them. I never heard you discuss having a baby. Isn't that what marriage is about?"

"I can't believe you are saying these awful things to me. You sound like you don't want me to be happy. Johannes tells me he loves me. That's all I care about. You're just unhappy because you can't find anyone. That's why you're being so mean."

"Meanness has nothing to do with it. I always thought that maybe, you and me could find a good reason to be together. We're better suited for each other. Remember you put me where I'm at, and I helped it happen for you"

"Ah, that's it. You're jealous. What are you calling me about?"

"They need you back at the studio for retakes. You'll have to come back tomorrow, because one of the leads is to be in Paris for another commitment. Can you get out of Aspen by tomorrow?"

"I'll try."

"It sure would make everything a lot easier if you do. Call me back with your schedule. I'll meet you at the airport and take you to the studio. I love you, and I'm not going to say congratulations." Clint hung up.

When Dorothy left the phone she was confused. Maybe he's right, she thought. She peered outside and saw a snowstorm on its way. The wind was blowing the snow into small drifts. She checked the barometer by the front desk and saw it falling as well as the temperature.

The desk clerk watched her. "That blizzard is finally getting here. It'll be no fun out tonight," he said.

Dorothy looked out again and then went to the stairway and up to the suite. When she got in the room, Johannes had already changed for dinner.

"I have to go back to Hollywood tomorrow for some retakes. I hate to cut our wonderful vacation short," she said.

Johannes was concerned. "There's a blizzard. I hope we can get off in the morning. I'll call Tim, my co-pilot, and have him get the weather for tomorrow," said Johannes as he went to the phone.

Dorothy went into the bathroom and drew a hot bath. She poured strawberry Jell-o into the tub and removed her ski clothes and got into the steamy tub. The smell of strawberry came up around her neck as she lay back and stretched out in the large old-fashioned claw-foot tub. As the cold chill of the day disappeared from her muscle-sore body, she started to think back on the day she'd had, and imagined what their life would be like together. She'd have to spend time in Europe with him, which she looked forward to. It would be wonderful to have Johannes show it to her the way he knew it. Hollywood had served its purpose. She felt she wasn't going to miss it. What better way to leave the business than on the top? She started thinking about what Clint had said. Clint had his nerve to bring up my past, she thought. Should she tell Johannes about her time in jail? No. That he'd never understand.

She got out of the tub and dried herself with a large bath towel. She gazed at her reflection in the long mirror in the room and examined her body. It was no different to her than it did when she met Clint. Her soft pink nipples still made her look like a girl of twenty. Not bad for not doing exercise. I wonder, she thought, how long all of this is going to last. She put those thoughts out of her head for the time being and began to think about planning her wedding.

She put on a pink sweater and a pair of pink stretch Bogner ski pants. She pulled her hair into a ponytail and tied it with a pink scarf. Her skin glowed from the hot bath. She checked herself in the mirror in the bedroom. She might look twenty, but didn't feel it as a result of the new muscles she never knew were there before she began to ski.

Johannes watched her as she entered the room.

"How long do you think it will take before I can start skiing with you, darling?" she asked.

"About another week of lessons and you'll be going to the top of Aspen mountain every day," he said. She was happy with that bit of information. "If you spend a season here you'd be a great skier."

"It's too bad we have to leave tomorrow. Did you hear from the pilot?"

"Ja, he called while you were in the bath. He said the blizzard was going to last into tomorrow. I don't like this airport. It can be unsafe at times, but we have the instruments to get off and above the storm."

"Honey, let's stay in tonight and have room service. It's our last night together. I want to be with you alone," she said sitting on his lap. He gave her a small pinch and she let out a tiny squeal.

"You're tickling me," she said as he turned her over and they fell onto the floor next to the bright fire. He rolled over on top of her gazing into her face.

"Johannes, you have made me the happiest little girl alive."

"That's good. I like little girls," he said as they embraced. The phone rang. Dorothy said. "Let it ring."

"I'm expecting a call from Europe," he said and got up to answer. "Hello."

A voice said. "Miss Dorothy Winters, please."

"Who's calling her?"

"The White House," said the voice. "She said it was the White House." Dorothy got up and left for the bedroom and said. "I'll take it in here." And closed the door. She picked up the phone and listened for Johannes to hang up.

"Hello."

"Is this Dorothy Winters?"

"Yes."

"Hold for the President." said a female voice.

"Hi, Red. I'm glad I found you. I'm coming to Palm Springs this weekend. I want see you there. I will be staying at Frank Sinatra's house. Kenny O' Donnell will call you when all the plans are formulated. I'm looking forward to seeing you again. You've been on my mind. It will be lovely to renew our friendship. We can lie around the pool and get some sun. It's cold in Washington and I'm looking forward to some California sun."

"Oh, Jack, I can't wait to see you again. I'll be there. I just got a new bikini from Rio. You'll like how it fits me."

"I can't wait. I have another call to take. I'll see you then, Red. Bye." He hung up.

Dorothy felt excited. He likes me, I can tell. I have to think up a special presidential trick for him, she thought.

The room service waiter had come while she was on the phone and set the table. She came back into the room, felt flushed, and acted vague. Clint was right. I'm just an old hooker. I can't seem to figure out my priorities. Johannes tells me he wants to marry me, and I'm all excited about what I'm going to do with the President.

Johannes helped her into her chair and sat down. He picked up the bottle of iced champagne that the waiter had opened and poured Dorothy a glass and then his own.

"Was that Kennedy calling you?"

"Yes. He called about a benefit he wanted me to appear at."

"It must be an important event to call you personally. Doesn't he have a staff that does that?" He lifted up the glass in a toast.

"May our lives be full of happiness and love," he said as he raised his glass and they both drank.

Dorothy put her glass down. "That's a lovely toast. Thank you for making it," she said.

"Now that we're going to the altar, will you want to work after we're married?"

"I've been working since I was six years old. I have never had a childhood. My teen years were all work, too. I'm through forever. I only want to be Mrs. Johannes Dietrich, your *hausfrau*." A smile came to Johannes and he picked up his glass to make another toast.

"To miem schoen hausfrau." Dorothy clicked her glass against his and they both laughed.

"There's something I have to tell you. I haven't mentioned it because I didn't think it was important, but I want to clear everything between us before we get married. I'm Jewish. Does that make a difference to you?" she asked looking into his pale blue eyes.

Johannes facial expression changed. His eyes went icy cold.

"I can see by your expression it does. I'm absolutely amazed. You're prejudiced! I was told you were a Nazi, but I didn't want to believe it. I thought they were jealous, but I see I was wrong. You told someone you were Hitler's godson. Is that true? I think I need an explanation."

Johannes got up and went to the window and peered out. "It's true. I am, but by decree. During the war Hitler wanted more children born to fight in the war. To get the people to do this he issued a decree, that the seventh son would automatically become his godson. It worked, the German people started having more children, I was a seventh son and to all in Germany a very special person."

Dorothy stared at him with disbelief. "You could never marry me, I'm a Jew. How could I ever explain you to my Jewish friends, if I married you? This is awful. Don't just stand there. Say something!"

"What can I say? Let me think."

"Think about what? That I'm a Jew. You got a lot to learn, Buster. This is America. We're civilized here. The people in this country came here to get away from prejudice."

"You're overreacting," said Johannes.

"Maybe I am, but I'm glad I got this out in the open. I could have made the biggest mistake of my life. If you will excuse me, I'm going to the bedroom for the evening and I'll be ready to leave early in the morning. You'll be sleeping here on the sofa tonight." She got up and walked into the bedroom and slammed the door. Nathan was right. He is a Nazi, she thought. She started to cry as she fell on the bed. She heard a knock at the bedroom door.

"Dorothy, I want to talk to you. Let me explain," he said through the door.

"Go away. You've said enough already. You hate Jews. You don't have to say anything more," she said. Dorothy couldn't believe what had just happened. The love light went out like that. She had been in love five minutes ago. What had happened, she wondered. She obviously was never in love with him. It was his money she was in love with. That was her only explanation, or maybe that phone call. She was proud of herself for telling him to fuck off. She might not be a temple-going Jew, but she was a Jew and she was proud of it. Clint's right. Stay single. You're an actress. The man in your life has to be the right man. He's the man who can put up with me.

That night she slept badly. She tossed and turned. She kept looking at the clock at her bed. It was as if dawn would never come. She could hear the wind blowing outside and she peered out and saw a solid mass of blowing snow reflecting off the lights of a car going by on the road below. I hope I can get out of here in the morning. I'll die if I have to stay another day with this Nazi, she said to herself as she got back into bed and waited for the sun to come up.

Johannes had already left the room when she got up to dress. She felt tired. I'm going to put all that behind me now and get on with my life, she thought. She put her clothes into two bags. She called Clint in Los Angeles but got his answering service. She left him a message that she would go to the studio directly from the plane. She went down to the front desk. She wore a long Russian lynx coat and a lynx hat. It was like she had stepped out of a Tolstoy novel.

"I'm checking out. Are there any messages?" she asked.

"Yes, Miss Winters, Mr. Diedrich has gone to the airport. He said he'd meet you there," said the desk clerk.

"Thank you. Staying here was heaven," she said to the desk clerk. It almost was, she thought Oh, well. She went outside. The wind and the blowing snow made it difficult to see. She got into the car that waited for her and they drove on to the airport. The driver had trouble keeping the car on the road because of ice.

When she got to the Aspen airport the waiting room had passengers sitting around waiting for their flights. She checked with the airline and they told her the planes were grounded. She went to find Johannes and Tim. They were in the weather room, conferring with the weatherman. As she approached, Johannes acknowledged her presence but said nothing.

"What do you think, Tim, can we get out of here?" he asked.

"We could give it a try. I don't like those extra fuel tanks on the wings. They're full of fuel. It gives us weight we don't need. Can they be drained before we take off?" he asked.

"This Lear has the power to get up. I have flown many times in Switzerland in bad weather, with mountains, and had no problem getting off. I need to be back in Los Angeles and so does Dorothy. So let's do it," said Johannes. He motioned to Dorothy, who had sat in a chair by the door to come out to the plane.

"Can you help me with my bags?" she said to Tim. The three walked out on the tarmac to the Lear jet. The visibility was almost zero as the cold wind and snow blew around them as they approached the jet. Tim opened the passenger door and Johannes got into the jet first and sat down in the pilot's seat. Dorothy followed. It was freezing inside the cabin and Dorothy could see her breath as it came from her mouth. She got into her seat behind the cockpit and buckled herself in. She was not letting anybody know, but she was scared to death. If it were under different circumstances she would have not gotten on, but she had to get back and she couldn't stand being with Johannes and wanted to be finished with him. Johannes started the engines. They made a high whirling movement and sound. He and Tim checked the instruments as Dorothy peered forward into the cockpit. She glanced out of her porthole window as the jet taxied off the tarmac. The wind and snow had covered the window and she could hardly see the terminal as they passed. When then reached the end of the flight line, the jet stopped. Johannes turned the Lear onto the runway.

"Aspen tower, Lear Jet 2U11 requesting permission for take-off," said Johannes into his headset.

"Lear Jet 2U11. Visibility zero, wind north, three sixty, forty-mile to fifty-mile gusts. Ceiling obscure. Are you sure you want to do this, Lear Jet?" asked the tower. Tim looked to Johannes.

"We're taking off," said Johannes looking straight ahead.

"Permission granted. Good luck," said the male voice over the mike. Johannes brought up the throttles. The jet engines revved up to their maximum horsepower and the plane headed down the runway.

Dorothy panicked and released her seat belt and jumped from her seat into the cockpit.

"Stop! Let me off!" she yelled as the plane picked up speed.

"Are you crazy? Get back in your seat, put your belt on," yelled Johannes.

Dorothy grabbed Johannes' hand that held the throttle and tried to pull it down. "Please, I want off. Please," she sobbed.

Tim tried to push her back into the cabin as Johannes pulled back the throttle and the plane started to slide and came to an abrupt stop at the end of the runway in a cloud of powdered snow.

"Thank you," said Dorothy relieved, taking a deep breath.

"What's your problem? We could have crashed from what you did."

"I'm scared. I can't fly with you. I had a premonition something horrible is going to happen. I want off. Please! Don't go! Please wait for the weather to clear." She cried.

Johannes and Tim looked at each other. Johannes said. "Let her out."

Tim released his safety belt and crawled back through the cabin to the door. Johannes turned the jet around and taxied back to the terminal and stopped. Tim opened the door and took Dorothy's bags from the plane and left them on the ground.

Dorothy turned to Johannes as she exited.

"I beg you don't go."

Johannes kept his head straight ahead his eyes peered into the blowing snow.

Clint had gotten out of the shower and stood shaving. He liked to listen to the Today Show in the morning to get the news and to find out what was going on in the world of entertainment. A bulletin came on the air. He heard the announcer saying, "Motion picture star Dorothy Winters, German industrialist Johannes Dietrich and pilot Tim Farley crashed in a blizzard leaving Aspen Colorado this morning. All are believed to be dead. We will give more information on the crash when it is received. We now return you to your regular programming." Clint froze.

TWENTY-SIX

"Tana?.. it's Clint... I'm in trouble," said Clint, his voice barely audible. Come over to the house... Dorothy's...dead."

"What! I'll be right there, dahlin."

The phone rang and rang. He didn't answer it. He felt weak. He wanted to get up but fell back on the bed. His thoughts were on Dorothy. Why was I so tough on her? Why? Why? I loved her... I really loved her, the fucked life I lead...his thoughts went home to the ranch when he was young... Ma was right, I should have stayed in Montana.

He remembered how he used to break horses. How the neighbors would bring their wild horses they couldn't break to his dad's ranch. They'd say, "Clint's the only kid in these parts that can get on that mare. Give her to Clint, he'll break her," he'd heard them say. His dreams of coming to Hollywood to be somebody. Was he somebody? he asked himself. Some people might think so. But I'm miserable. The town is miserable. Everyone's insecure. Nothing's real and I'm the sham, a facade. I could go back home. I got enough money to buy a ranch, run some cattle. Nah. How could I lived there again after I've lived here... I'm stuck in Hollywood. What will I do without Dorothy?

Tana arrived. It was too early for her. Her eyes were still puffy. She rang and rang the bell, no answer. She walked to the back of the house by the pool and saw a window open. She pulled it ajar so she could get her long legs through and crawled in. She walked through the house checking the rooms. When she got to Clint's bedroom she saw him lying on the bed, his face in the pillow.

"Clint, it's me. I heard the news on the radio."

"I need you, Tana. I feel so alone. I need your sympathy." Tana sat down next to Clint on the bed. She held his hand.

"My life's so fucked. Georgia killed. Now Dorothy. I made her get on the plane. I blame myself. I could have worked something out with the studio, but I insisted she come today."

"Don't be so hard on yourself, sugar. How could you know about the storm? I flew with Johannes. He knows his airplane. He was a good pilot... don't blame yourself. It was an accident."

Tana put her hand on Clint's forehead and pushed his hair back.

"Leave town for awhile. Go home to your family...You never take a vacation...See them. They love you, I'm sure." The phone started to ring. Tana picked it up. "Are you here?" Clint shook his head.

"Hello...Dorothy! You're supposed to be dead!"

Clint jumped from bed and grabbed the phone..."Dorothy? I love you, baby... Tell me again it's you."

"It's me, Clint. I've been trying to call you. I wasn't on the airplane when it went down. I made Johannes let me off. I had this terrible intuition the plane would go down. I tried to warn Johannes, but he wouldn't listen. He thought I was nuts. My name was on the passenger manifest, so everyone thought I was dead too. You were right about Johannes. He wasn't for me. I would have been miserable with him. May he rest in peace."

"The studio and your fans must be having a heart attack. I was about to abandon Hollywood and go back to Montana," said Clint.

"You?"

"Yeah, me," said Clint.

"Can you imagine," said Dorothy. "I was thought to be dead and come back to life all in one day. My picture is all over the papers and on television. I'm more famous for my death than I ever was for my work. I've become a household name. You'll be able to get me a higher price for my next picture."

"I know for sure I'm talking to you, Dorothy. It's the buck you're always thinking about."

"You got that right, cowboy. I'll be in Los Angeles tonight."

When Dorothy returned from Aspen, a message to call Kenny O'
Donnell, at the White House, was on her answering service.

She called O'Donnell back and he told her the rendezvous with the
President had changed. She found out later that Bobby Kennedy didn't
like the idea that JFK should stay at Sinatra's house, because of his
association with the mob. He made him change houses. She was to go
to Bing Crosby's house instead and be there between eleven-thirty and
twelve AM.

Dorothy thought, if the FBI checked my background I wouldn't
have been asked. She wondered how long she'd be able to keep her
affair with JFK going before they got on to her. She hoped she'd have
some time with him. She loved his sexiness and the power be represented. I bet he'll be amused when he finds out that Dorothy Winters,
the movie star, has been the girlfriend of the mob and spent almost two
years in jail. Only in Hollywood could such a farce happen, she thought
and laughed.

Dorothy left Beverly Hills early Saturday morning. She hadn't told
Clint or anyone where she was going.

She arrived at the address Kenny O'Donnell had given her. The
secret servicemen stood at the front gate. She drove her car into the
driveway and stopped. The guard recognized and greeted her. Another
secret serviceman rolled a device under her car. And another guard
called into the house for clearance.

"What are they putting under my car?" she asked.

"It's a bomb detector," he answered. Word came back from the
house to let her in. The gate opened and they waved her through. The
driveway was full of cars, which made it difficult to park. The house
was a one-story low rambling stucco structure, with a wall surrounding and a white stone roof. She rang the front door and the butler let
her in.

"Hello, Miss Winters. You're expected at the pool. Through those sliding glass doors," he said pointing to the other end of the living room.

Dorothy walked through the living room, and went out to the pool. A party was going on. Kenny O' Donnell came to her and introduced himself.

"Miss Winters, it's a pleasure to meet you. The President will be out shortly," he said. "You can change your clothes in the pool house. Did you bring a bathing suit?" She nodded.

She recognized Porifiro Rubirosa. He was in a bathing suit and had a deep tan. He gave her a big toothy smile. Clint had told her about Dawn Summer's hair, in Washington. She didn't like him and wondered why the President would have a man like him around so much.

"Well, we meet again. How nice," Rubirosa said as he reached for Dorothy's hand and kissed it.

A tall woman who looked to be a New York model came to be introduced. Dorothy said hello and went into the pool house to change. She put on the bikini she had just bought. The clerk in the store told her it was from Rio and made a joke about its brevity that someone refereed to it as the "dental floss bikini." Dorothy gazed in a mirror and turned around to examine herself. Her body was perfect for the suit. Very few women would look good in this, she thought. Only if you're sixteen. When she went back to the pool she got lots of looks and smiles. She noticed as she sat down, pool furniture was in the pool. Someone has been having a good time, she thought.

It was one of those perfect Palm Springs days. Hot and dry. The sun shone directly overhead and the guests sat around in their bathing suits getting California sun on their pale Washington bodies. A Filipino houseboy brought her a tall tropical drink. It tasted delicious. She could feel the alcohol on her first sip. She finished the drink and ordered another. The warm effects of the drinks made her feel happy and a little wicked. She thought, I'm going to have a good time today.

The President came out of the house followed by Peter Lawford. They walked over to her as she lay on a lounge. Both were in bathing suits. Dorothy noticed that Jack had a skin-colored back-brace strapped around his waist. She remembered he wore the brace the night at the White House. He had told her he had a back injury, but she couldn't remember the circumstances. All she knew was his back caused him great pain and he always had to wear it for support and comfort. She remembered it was an obstacle in their lovemaking.

"I'm glad to see you're alive," he said. She heard the comment from everybody. "Have you met my brother-in-law, Peter Lawford?" he asked taking her hand and holding it.

"Yes, Peter and I have met," she said. Peter, she thought, still looks wonderful and handsome. She remembered their little fling; she had turned him on him to grass. She heard he now smoked it constantly. He knows a lot about me, but he's too cool and would never tell Jack of their relationship, she hoped.

"Do you still live at the same place in Los Angeles?" asked Peter. She loved his voice. It was the British accent.

"No, I live in Beverly Hills, now. I'd love to work with you, Peter. Let's see if our agents can find a script for us to do. It would be fun to do a comedy."

"Now wait a minute, you two. Dorothy, you came to see me. I think I better get you away from Peter. I know he has a way with the ladies," said Jack with a smile. He pulled up a lounge and lay next to Dorothy, glancing up to see where the sun was. He removed his sunglasses and fell back on the lounge to let the sun shine on his face.

Peter went to the bar to get a drink. Dorothy felt sexy. The liquor had taken the tension away and she felt relaxed with JFK. They lay quietly letting the sun tan their bodies. JFK turned to Dorothy and took her hand and held it. Dorothy gazed into his clear blue eyes. She wanted him to hold and to make love to her. She could tell, he had gotten her message.

"Let's you and me go in the pool house," he said in a low appealing voice. She nodded and they got up and went inside and closed the door. The guests around the pool glanced at each other with a knowing smile.

"I wonder how she likes getting laid on a board?" said one of the President's aides to another as they lay soaking up the sun.

"Why don't you ask her when she comes out," said the other.

"I'll do that."

"Marilyn never complained. What do you think of this one?"

"She's got a better body, and she looks to me she knows more about a prick than Bulova knows about a wrist watch."

Inside the pool-house Dorothy and JFK lay on a double lounge holding hands.

"Jack, I'm so happy you wanted to see me again. I've been dreaming about you and I being together. You bring out the juiciest in me. I've been thinking since your phone call of what I'm going to do to you. Shall I go on?"

"Please do."

"You're the most attractive man in the United States and also the President, which makes you doubly irresistible. And to find a woman like me as a plaything, and I'm not kidding myself. I am that to you."

"You could be my mistress. A plaything is like a one night stand. That you're not."

"The President's mistress. I like that. I'm glad you said that. You're such a diplomat. Do you think our past presidents had mistresses?"

"I've heard tell. Why not? Terrible pressure goes with the job. A president is like everyone else. He needs a little diversification to relax. What harm is there if the players know their place."

"I couldn't agree more. You'll have no trouble from me. I'm here for your pleasure, my sweet. I thought up a presidential trick for you. I'm giving it to you as a gift," she said in her most seductive voice.

"Cut the suspense. What is it and when?" he asked as he adjusted his legs on the lounge.

"I'll need some props. Call the kitchen, have them brings us some champagne grapes, cherries, bananas, strawberries, whipping cream and a maraschino cherry."

"What are we going to do with all that fruit?"

"I'm going to show you how to make a fruit salad, but this is a very special fruit salad and only for you."

"I believe I'm getting what you're up to. Are you suggesting where I think you're suggesting?" he asked, smiling.

"Oh, Jack, how cute you are. You're going to squigg it in my couzie woozie... and I can hardly wait." JFK laughed and got up from the lounge.

"Where are you going, Jack?"

"To the kitchen. Oh, I don't like maraschino cherries. Is that a problem?"

"Of course not, darling, but...don't be gone too long."

214

TWENTY-SEVEN

The Sea Cloud, a magnificent tall ship sailed into Los Angeles harbor with its owner, a Caribbean playboy, who was also a general and a son of a dictator. The ship was fitted with three large masts and carried a crew of one hundred sailors and thirteen musicians. It caused a sensation when it docked at San Pedro. The newspapers were full of stories about the yacht and the man who owned it. The playboy cut a path around Hollywood, dating some of the major female stars. The press kept a vigil at the dock site checking the coming and goings of his guests.

The night of July 3rd, a party was held on the yacht. Clint had been invited. His reputation for knowing the young starlets in Hollywood got him the invitation. Clint constantly got asked to parties where he never knew the host or hostess, but everybody acted like they were old friends.

When Dorothy heard about the party she wanted to meet the general and invited herself, joining Clint on the long ride to San Pedro.

As they drove down the Harbor Freeway Dorothy said. "What's wrong with you lately? You seem depressed."

"My life. It's not turning out the way I planned."

"I guess I could say that, too. I'm a successful actress, but that's all I am. Sounds awful doesn't it? I'm sure most women would love to trade places with me. The glamorous life they think I have. If they only knew what I had to do to get it. And the assholes I had to screw to make it happen."

"Don't put that in your memoirs. You're still that girl I met in Beverly Hills years ago, Gale Lawrence, who got the cowboy out of me and gave me a fast education. I liked that girl; she was fun and wild."

"Clint, how sweet of you. Sometimes I think I'm a terrible person, and I wonder why I do what I do. I hate my past. I look back and see how my mother lived, and I want to cry. Being a bastard is a hard reality, Clint. I'm constantly haunted by the thought. I've tried to help my mother, but she resents it. I don't blame her for not marrying my father, he's a monster and I haven't spoken to him in years. I try to give her things, but she puts me down. I never seem to get her approval. She never lets me forget how I got what I have, but she forgets my talent and I don't think that's fair."

"We're no different from any of the others we know. Products of our environment, I say. We do what we have to do to survive. You can take it, you're tough. I thought I was, but I'm not. I have a conscience and it bothers me. I've been living a lie," said Clint.

"What do you mean, a lie? We're both pathological liars and you know why? Because we need to feel good about ourselves. That's why we lie. It's our protection. But it's wrong because we believe our own lies and they become reality to us, and that is where the trouble starts."

Clint glanced at Dorothy keeping his eye on the freeway. "Aren't you smart. I've got a confession to make. I've been carrying around this terrible guilt for years. I've felt I was inadequate. I wasn't fulfilled in my life. I wasn't sexually satisfied."

"You're finally going to admit you like boys." Clint glanced at Dorothy sitting in the passenger seat, almost swerving into the other lane.

"You mean you know?"

"Of course, darling. I've always known. That's what I like about you. You're sensitive, but strong. I like that. A fuck is a fuck and God knows I've had my share. We had a few good fucks, but I could tell you were uncomfortable. A girl knows those things. I'm so happy, Clint. You're being honest with yourself." Dorothy moved over in the car seat and kissed Clint on the cheek.

"You mean you don't mind? You don't care? I've been trying to hide the facts about me for years. You know how homophobic Hollywood is. I felt I could never risk letting it get out."

"Sweetheart, darling face, they know, and frankly, I think no one cares what you are, as long as you don't hurt anyone. You've never killed anybody. You've never robbed a bank. You're a good guy, Clint, and we're a good team. So, you pimped me off to a few important men, but that doesn't make you a bad guy."

"I don't like that word. It was an introduction. It's life, and life has to be lived the way you have to live it. Does that make any sense?"

"I like your philosophy. The Golden Rule, said Dorothy that made Clint laugh as they drove off the freeway in the direction of the harbor.

The sign said Pier 10. Two police guards stopped to check their IDs and to see if they were on the party's guest list. As Clint parked his car, he checked out the Sea Cloud and marveled at its appearance. It was long, white and graceful as it sat tied up to the pier. The sounds of Caribbean music coming from the yacht put them in a party mood.

A throng of faces stood behind a fence and gawked at the arrivals. It reminded Clint of a Hollywood premiere. The crowd squealed when they recognized Dorothy as she got out of the car. She waved and smiled to them as she and Clint walked toward the gangplank.

The word of the party had gotten out to the press because Clint noticed a few of its members, as he and Dorothy were about to go aboard. A reporter Clint recognized from Life magazine called his name.

The man motioned Clint to come to the fence. Clint left Dorothy's side and joined the reporter.

"I know you, you're Clint, a movie agent? Right?" said the reporter.

"Hello, not letting you in, huh?" asked Clint.

"No press allowed. Be a sport, Clint, and help me out. Call me tomorrow and tell me what went on at the party." The reporter handed Clint his card. "This playboy's causing talk in Washington as to why he's here spending money like he is, when his country has gotten millions of dollars in aid from our government to keep it propped up," said the reporter.

"I'll try if I can," said Clint taking his card. The last thing he needed, he thought, was to get mixed up in a Washington scandal.

He joined Dorothy and noticed the dress she wore. The gown flowed to the ground in white and blue chiffon over a sheath with shades of blue disappearing into almost white. A long scarf covered her head and draped around her shoulders. She looked taller and thinner than he had seen her before, almost like a model of high fashion.

"Has anyone told you how beautiful you look tonight? I like your dress," he said.

"It's an Irene. I borrowed it from the studio," she replied with a big smile. They walked up the gangplank.

Two ship's officers waited to greet them, dressed in white uniforms with signets on their hats of their country and epaulets on their shoulders. They bowed and tipped their hats as Clint and Dorothy boarded, giving Dorothy an approving look.

Clint knew Dorothy had to be the most beautiful girl at the party tonight and it was the first time he felt really comfortable with her, no more games. Why hadn't he told her before, he wondered. My demons, they needed protection, he answered himself.

The orchestra performed on the fantail. More than a dozen musicians played Latin music, dressed in their country's white navy uniforms. The waiters, dressed in bow ties, carried trays of food and drinks around offering them to the guests. Clint thought the party had a feeling of an old movie he had seen. He recognized a few of the guests, but one he wished he hadn't was Porfirio Rubirosa on the dance floor dancing the merengue with a tall model. Dorothy saw him, too and said. "Do you see who I see? I hate that man. I'm sure he'll tell everyone here I'm sleeping with the President. That island Casanova seems to be everywhere. Come, Clint, let's get out of here."

Rubirosa spotted Clint and Dorothy at the same time. Clint grabbed two glasses of champagne from the waiter's tray and went on to tour the ship. They walked into the main salon. The walls and ceiling were paneled in dark mahogany with carved tables and matching chairs covered in dark green fabric. The maroon carpeting felt thick under their feet. A fire blazed in a fireplace at the end of the room.

"Look who's here? Do you remember him?" asked Clint. A tall Latin-looking man dressed in a dark suit, his hair slicked back, stood in the room as they came in. "He was at Billie Rodgers house the night we met. He's famous now. Not as a gigolo, but as a painter. His oils are the rage. He paints poppies that look like vaginas to me," said Clint, laughing.

Clint and Manuel would meet from time to time at parties and would laugh about how they had met. He remembered what Manuel had said to him once. "You show me a mirror and fifty bucks, and I can get it up for anybody." They kissed each other on each cheek, as was the custom in South America.

"Clint... I have to paint your beautiful lady friend," he said as he gazed at her. Clint winked at Dorothy.

"Dorothy, this is Manuel. You remember him. He used to play the guitar for Billie Rodgers." Dorothy gave him a knowing smile. Clint could tell Manuel didn't like the reference to his past. Manuel smiled and took Dorothy's hand and brought it to his lips and kissed it, something he did very well, thought Clint.

"We've met. I'm Dorothy Winters, the actress."

"Yes, I know, but I can't remember, where was it?"

"That's your problem, darling."

Manuel was confused. "You look prosperous, Manuel. I didn't know you knew the general," said Clint.

"I just met him and he bought three of my paintings. A nice man," said Manuel.

"Three paintings! I hear he's a big fan of pussy. No wonder he likes your painting," said Clint with a laugh. A big smile came over Manuel's face. They looked over and saw the host enter the salon with an actress that Clint and Dorothy knew, Mona Walker. The general was dark, trim and handsome about thirty-five, with a full head of slicked-back black hair, wearing a white double breasted suit and black tie. Mona was in a bright red gown, which showed off her dark hair and white skin.

"There's the general now, let me introduce you, come," said Manuel. They followed Manuel. "General, meet Clint Nation, he's a big Hollywood agent, and this is Dorothy Winters, the movie star."

"Mucho gusto," said Clint showing off his limited Spanish. "Good to see you, Mona," Clint said to Mona. The general took Dorothy's hand and kissed it peering into her eyes. Dorothy smiled back at him causing Mona to frown. "Enjoy yourselves. I have a surprise for you later," he said as he and Mona moved on into the room.

They watched Rubirosa approach the General. Rubirosa had him deep in conversation. The general glanced in Clint and Dorothy's direction with a serious frown on his face. This alarmed Clint. He could have told the general that Clint had blackmailed him. Clint sensed trouble, but didn't want to mention it to Dorothy. They walked back to the fantail and went onto the dance floor and danced to the Caribbean rhythms.

For a moment Clint thought of Georgia and how she would have liked the party and what a good dancer she had been, especially to Latin music. Dorothy danced well, but couldn't dance the way Georgia had. While they were dancing near the starboard, Clint peered over the side and saw an armada of small boats milling around trying to get a peek at what was going on aboard, and calling out obscenities to the guests. Clint became paranoid thinking of what could happen to him.

The yacht started to move. Everyone stopped what they were doing and went to the port side of the ship and saw the gangplank had been brought up. The ship moved away from the pier into the harbor.

"How strange. I think we're moving," said Clint.

"We're being kidnapped. How exciting," said Dorothy.

"This must be the surprise the general talked about," said Clint. None of the guests had been told about leaving the harbor. It increased the party mood. The band played louder and the guests danced faster and drank more, making it a night to remember. Clint realized what Dorothy had said was true. The general had in effect kidnapped them and there was no way they could get off the ship. When they got out into the harbor the crew pulled up the sails on the three giant masts. What a glorious sight, but there was little wind to pick up the sails. The word got out that they were sailing to Catalina Island, for a 4th of July party.

Clint spotted Manuel coming his way, acting concerned.

"If I were you I'd find a way to get off," he said.

"Why?"

"The general told me you blackmailed Rubirosa and he's pissed off about it. An accident could happen to you. We're in a foreign country on this ship. You're on their territory and anything could happen.

"I'll have to jump. Make sure that nothing happens to Dorothy. Take her home. And thanks, Manuel, you're a friend."

Clint said nothing to Dorothy. She was too busy watching the activities for him to be missed. Clint made his way along the railing of the ship. He knew he had to make his move soon, before the yacht got too far out to sea.

The crew was readying the big guns on the port side preparing to fire them.

Two of the ship's crew was following Clint as he passed one of the cannon stations. Clint stopped to pick up a life preserver he saw on the deck. As he bent down to pick up the life jacket, the two men came from behind. One hit Clint with an iron pipe on the head and the other pushed him over the side. Clint fell into the water as one hundred canons fired, one after another in a salute.

TWENTY-EIGHT

Dorothy walked around the ship to find Clint and found Manuel.

"Have you seen Clint? He's disappeared."

"He jumped overboard."

"He what? What do you mean, in the water?"

"He didn't want to alarm you. Rubirosa was going to have an accident happen to him. I found out and told him. I saw a small boat pick him out of the water, don't worry, he's OK."

"Rubirosa. What a dick."

"They say that about me too," said Manuel with a whimsical smile. "We're just a couple of old whores."

"You make me laugh, Manuel. Dorothy noticed Rubirosa on the dance floor. "Look! The asshole is on the dance floor again. I'll fix him for Clint." Dorothy left Manuel's side and walked onto the crowded floor where Rubirosa was moving his date around. She pulled his arm away from his partner. He stopped and turned toward her. "Rubi, this is from Clint," she snapped, and slapped his face.

The Latin put his hand to his chin and hissed. *"Puta."*

"Me? Look, who's calling who a whore...you asshole."

Rubi gave Dorothy a cold smile and led his date away. Dorothy's scene didn't seem to make much difference to the other guests; they continued to dance away as if nothing had happen.

The party went on and the music never stopped. Dorothy felt better after her encounter with Porfirio. She was amazed how these Latins could party, and the drinking they could do. One of the general's aides ran around the dance floor with a scissors, cutting the ties off the men who weren't in tuxedos. It was as if none of them cared they were being made fools of and kept on dancing. She went below and found an empty stateroom and locked herself in. She worried about Clint, and hoped he made it to shore. She heard a few couples outside the door pounding to get in and screw, but she refused to give up her refuge and remained until the yacht docked at San Pedro the next day.

Manuel offered to take her home, but she took Clint's car back to his house. She saw that he hadn't come home and got on the phone to the police and the hospitals in the harbor area. A nurse at Long Beach Medical Center told her about a man that answered Clint's description who was brought in last night. He had no identification and was unconscious in the emergency room. She left for Long Beach and the hospital.

She entered the intensive care unit. A man who was a doctor stopped her.

"Are you Dorothy Winters?" he asked.

"Yes, I'm told a friend of mine could be here. He's about thirty, sorta tall. He jumped off a yacht last night in the harbor."

"I'm Doctor Lucas. Your friend is here, but I have bad news for you. He's been injured in the fall. He must have hit something when he jumped into the water. There's a large contusion on the right side of his head. He has a concussion. I think there's brain damage. It's a little too early to tell how bad, but as far as I can tell his right side is paralyzed."

"Where is he? I must see him."

The doctor escorted Dorothy to a bed at the end of the room. Clint lay with his head wrapped in a bandage and was unconscious, strapped to a monitoring device with a tube down his throat and an IV in his arm. Dorothy was shocked when she saw him. She bent down and gazed into his face and took his hand that lay on his chest.

"Clint, it's me. Can you hear me, darling? It's Dorothy, Clint. Clint, it's Dorothy." She looked to the doctor.

"He won't die, will he?"

"No. But he'll need constant care."

"Does he have family?" asked the doctor.

"His parents live in Montana, but I'll take care of him. He'll stay with me."

"He might have to learn to walk and talk again. It could be a long recovery. He could be a hardship on you."

"I don't care. I'll be there for him. No matter what."

224

"He'll need physical therapy."

"He'll have it."

"He's a lucky man to have someone like you in his life."

"Doctor, I always felt like I was the lucky one," said Dorothy looking into Doctor Lucas's eyes as her tears appeared.

After Clint was able to leave the hospital Dorothy moved him into her house in a bedroom down the hall from her. The room had French doors that opened up to a view of Los Angeles below. She hired a pleasant and pretty nurse to help her with his daily care.

Clint's damage was severe. The muscle on the right side of his face had fallen, causing his right eye to drop, which gave it a stare. He favored his right hand and it lay to his side and always remained in the same position and was useless to him. He was losing the muscles in the right leg and he dragged it to move. The therapist Dorothy hired came every other day and helped him with the exercises he had to do to improve his condition. He talked out the left side of his mouth, making his words slow and deliberate and difficult to understand.

For months he sat and said nothing and was in a constant state of depression. He would see no one. If any of his old friends would call, his nurse Trudy would let him know they called, but he didn't call them back. He remained a recluse. Clint's only activity was watching television. He watched by the hour. Some days he'd feel like he could get up and walk away and others he wished he'd die.

Dorothy was offered a prestige picture in England starring with Lawrence Olivier. She turned it down. She'd have to leave Clint. She didn't tell him because she knew he would insist she do the film.

Clint kept telling Dorothy he didn't want to be a burden to her that his mother could and would take care of him if he wanted to go home to Montana. Dorothy would have none of it and told him if the accident had happened to her, he would do the same for her. He'd had to agree.

When President Kennedy was killed in Dallas, Dorothy and Clint went into a depression. They stared for three days at the television, watching history they felt they were involved in take place before their eyes. The tragedy was so personal to Dorothy she felt she'd never get over the loss of JFK.

Dorothy noticed Clint had travel information sent to the house, and gazed longingly at brochures of different parts of the world.

One evening when she sat down to dinner a pamphlet of the Mayan Temples of Yucatan was by her plate. She picked it up to examine. Clint peered at her from across the table and asked.

"Is...there...possibility...that...you'd...take...me to Mexico...to see...Chichen Itza?"

"Chichen Itza! What a wonderful idea. What ever made you want to go there?"

"I...always...wanted...to...go...Before...I...had...no...time...Now I...have...too...much."

"Why of course we can go. When?"

"Next... week...And...Tana...go.. with...us. She...can...help...you with...me. I...read...the terrain...is...flat..easy...to...wheel...me."

Dorothy thought Clint was considerate to have Tana Williams travel with them. She could use her help.

"I'll call the travel agency tomorrow, darling," she said smiling. Clint lifted his wine glass to her.

On Sunday they left Los Angeles for Yucatan. The travel agency made arrangements for them to stay at the Mayaland Hotel, a Mexican colonial compound a short distance from the ruins, with acres of tropical gardens. Flowers of every description grew on the walls and paths and in and around the courtyard. The sounds and sight of bright-plumaged birds made their presence felt everywhere. Tame parrots visited them as they sat in the patio of their three-bedroom cottage. The daily rain made the air warm and damp.

After a light lunch the girls wheeled Clint over to the site a short distance from the hotel. The majesty and the enormity of the place was overwhelming. Only the pyramids of Egypt rivaled the architectural splendor. Dorothy hired an English-speaking Mexican guide who filled them in on Mayan history.

"Not much is known because when the missionaries came with the Spanish armies, they were so intent on converting the Mayans to Christianity they burned most of the records of the past. Only three books remain. But we do know they were a violent war-like people who used human sacrifices in their religion."

Dorothy and Tana rolled Clint under a shade tree and peered up at the great pyramid before them.

"Come, Tana, Clint wants us to climb to the top and report to him what it is like."

"Look at those steps. There's hundreds of them and so steep, God, I hope I have the strength in this heat," replied Tana.

Clint smiled and said in his slow speech, "Three...hundred...and sixty...five...the Maya...calendar."

"How did you know that bit of information?" asked Dorothy. He showed her the brochure.

"Built... one... thousand... years... before.... Christ."

Dorothy and Tana left Clint to start their ascent. They moved slowly. Dorothy felt the strain in her leg muscles. She glanced to her side and saw a tiny older woman in tennis shoes passed her moving rather fast up the pyramid. Dorothy wondered how she did it. Tana climbed behind her, stopping every so often to get her breath. Dorothy thought, Tana is really out of shape. Too many late nights. Their climb brought them to the temple's summit. Dorothy felt a little dizzy. She stopped and peered out over the miles and miles of flat Yucatan green jungle and marveled at the spectacle that had been erected so many thousand years ago.

"I hate ruins," said Tana. "Give me a modern skyscraper with a fast elevator." Tana sat on a stone ledge and wiped her face with a large handkerchief. "I can't see why everyone's so gaga over these falling-down stone relics and why Clint wanted us to come here?"

"Maybe he's improving your mind."

"Is that a crack?" asked Tana giving Dorothy a scowl.

"Come on. Let's get off of here. I'm swimming in sweat," said Dorothy as she climbed into a small passage that went into an inside passageway. Tana followed. Dorothy had to duck her head because of the size of the tunnel. They followed a line of people moving slowly down inside the stone structure.

Dorothy glanced back at Tana, sweating and said. "My God, these Mayans must have been midgets to get through these passageways." The terrible heat was getting to her as she put her hand up on the stone ceiling to take a break. She looked back at Tana, then let out a scream and fell to the stone steps in shock. Tana and the older woman that had passed her on the way up came to her rescue.

"What happened? Are you all right?" asked Tana in alarm.

"I stuck my finger in that socket." She pointed to an empty light socket on the ceiling. "It shocked the pee right out of me." Tana and the lady helped to her feet. The lady recognized her and said. "What's a nice Jewish girl like you doing in a place like this?"

Tana and Dorothy broke into laughter as they made their descent to the bottom.

They joined Clint and told him of their experience. He laughed as Dorothy wheeled him following their guide. After they had seen most of the ruins they moved on to a small road that led to a long path where a sign said, *"Cenote"*, "Sacred Pool."

Dorothy felt an eerie feeling when they came upon it, and when the guide told them the Mayans would throw young virgins into the pool for sacrifice to their gods, it made her want to leave. She walked to the edge of the pool and peered down and saw the steep honeycomb walls fall straight to the dark murky water, fifty feet below. The guide continued with his speech. "Years back, when the site was found, a professor from Boston College had it dredged and they found human bones, gold artifacts, jade statues and other valuables that had been there for hundreds of years."

Clint made a motion for Dorothy to bend down to hear him.

"Do you like this place?" she asked. Clint nodded.

"Move... me... closer...so.. I...can...have ..a.. better.. look."
Dorothy moved the wheelchair within a few feet of the edge.

"That's close enough, Clint, there's no guard rail."

The guide came up and pointed and said, "There's a Coca Cola stand under that palapa, would you like a cold drink?"

"What a brilliant idea. I'd love one." Dorothy asked Clint. "How about you, darling, would you like a Coke?" Clint nodded.

"I need one too, I'll come with you." said Tana. "We can sit in the shade for a moment."

Dorothy said to Clint. "Will you be all right, Clint? We won't be but a minute." Clint nodded.

Dorothy, Tana and the guide walked a short distant to the palapa stand and ordered four Cokes from the attendant. The sound of a loud splash came from down in the pool. The expression on their faces was shock. They looked to where they had left Clint. He was gone.

The End